UNDERTOW

ANTHONY J. QUINN

HEAD
ZEUS

First published in the UK in 2017 by Head of Zeus Ltd
This paperback edition published in 2018 by Head of Zeus Ltd

975312468

A catalogue record for this book is available from the British Library

ISBN (PB): 9781786696045
ISBN (E): 9781786696014

Typeset by Adrian McLaughlin

Printed and bound by CPI Group (UK) Ltd, Croydon, CR0 4YY

Head of Zeus Ltd
First Floor East
5–8 Hardwick Street
London ECIR 4RG

WWW.HEADOFZEUS.COM

*To my grandfathers John Daly and Patrick Quinn,
and my granduncle Thomas Peter Daly, men of faith who
consecrated their lives to their families and their craft*

UNDERTOW

PROLOGUE

Andalusia, Spain

At first, he did not believe it. The white letter peeking out from beneath the cotton curtains that hung, hot and shivering, in the heat of the morning. He watched the shadow play of insects dancing across the floor, flickering upon the envelope, which was crisp and sombre-looking, unlike anything else in the room. He almost detected a bluish tinge to the whiteness, reminiscent of the colder climate it had been dispatched from, a northern country of treacherous skies and loughs brimming with fathomless gloom.

In spite of the heat, a cold spasm travelled down his spine. For months now, he had been waiting without knowing who or what he was waiting for. When his fear had turned into waiting for fear, a terrible sense of estrangement had descended. He wondered how his story would unravel, this net of betrayal and bitter secrets that had nothing to do with the pursuit of justice or the truth. His adventure as a spy had ended with the ringing of lies in his ears, and the realization that he was running on his own, supported by nothing but shadows.

He noticed the letter on his return from shutting the back door, which he had kept open all night, facing south into the grove of olive trees. He had hoped that the cool night air would add to his chances of sleep. Several times he had drifted off, imagining that he lay tucked under a wizened old olive branch in the valley of terraces below, listening to a secret family of nightingales singing their notes, precise and tender, and the gushing of meltwater from the high sierra flowing along the valley's myriad irrigation channels.

It was mid-morning, and he had carefully barricaded the finca against the Andalusian sun whose drenching heat was a gift he had been unable to accept. And now this letter lay before him. The first addressed to him since he had arrived in Spain. He saw from the postmark that it had been sent from Ireland. The handwriting on the envelope looked familiar, which was why he had not opened it immediately. His name, Tommy Higgins, spelt for all the world to see. For the past year, he had used a PO box in Malaga, stayed off the internet and avoided mobile phones, but she had found him anyway. Beads of sweat formed on his forehead. There was not a whisper of air in the room, yet the curtains wafted in the heat, fluttering upon the dusty floor. He sat by the window and smoked a cigarette. The rays of sunlight seemed suspended, falling upon the letter and the handwriting that had been fashioned fifty years ago in a single-room school on a bleak mountainside. His mother's careful hand. He had not had any contact with her since leaving Ireland, and the sight of his name printed so clearly by her troubled him. What news lay inside? And why the dread in his stomach? Was it his fear of home, the pull of the past, the womb still searching for him? A letter was too fragile a form of contact to channel the depth of injured feelings that existed between them.

It was another hour before he settled himself down and opened the letter. Her hand was steady, the words almost printed, as though she were communicating to a child or a person with poor eyesight. She unravelled his story, walking him backwards in time to his painful past. He read it several times. Each reading altered it slightly. What secret was his mother hinting at? Was it the possibility of redemption or revenge that he saw forming between the lines?

The first section of the letter held little meaning for him. Their relatives and neighbours were strangers to him now, and her gossip about their stifled lives lacked value even as entertainment or diversion. She included a few biographical details in brackets after each name, in case he had forgotten who they were. Then the tone of the letter changed. She wrote about his disappearance, the rumours of his suicide, and the sightings of him reported by neighbours while holidaying in far-flung places. She had heard reports that he had changed his identity and appearance. She recounted the stories matter-of-factly, even the chilling ones hinting at his torture and death. However, she had discounted them all. 'A mother always knows,' she wrote. No one had come close to finding him, not even the cleverest of his enemies.

A mother always knows. He could feel her at his shoulder when he read those words. In that airless room, he brooded upon the past. He read on, beginning to see how her gossip and his misfortune had a connection. His mother had always had her own way of saying things. How many times, growing up, had he kept his mouth shut, letting her talk as long as she wanted, waiting for the important message to emerge?

She said that after he had fled the village, her first thought had been to sell up and move to the opposite end of the country. However, she soon realized that leaving Dreesh would have been an admission of defeat. She had always thought it a good place to live. She wrote about the local criminal gangs, the men he had informed upon, without mentioning their names, one of whom was the devil incarnate.

Time slowed as he read on. The air thickened and the letter transformed itself. For several long paragraphs, she berated the justice system, and the carelessness of police officers like the local sergeant and his cronies who ignored the criminal forces now running the village. She had heard the rumours of suspicious payments, bribed villagers, unsavoury business deals, and secret bank accounts.

'I have been patient...' she wrote.

I have walked the long road. I have waited at the narrow door.
I have watched your enemy grow powerful in your absence.
He has penetrated the daily life of our community. He has
exploited it pitilessly and at the same time showered it with
illegally earned money. Any questions or doubts about him
are stifled by fear and the desire to keep the money rolling in.

He was drawn to the certainty in her words, her determination to right the wrongs of the past. She said she was no

longer shocked by her neighbours' complicity, or their claims that they did not know what was going on. They were content to lead their lives in the least critical way, to ignore what was going on under their very noses.

As the shafts of light advanced across the floor, he retreated deeper into the shadows. He almost dropped one of the pages, there were so many of them. He read the letter again, holding the pages with concentration, his back stiffening with the effort.

Detective Brian Carey had called to her door one day, she wrote. He had come to apologize for the way the intelligence handlers had treated her son, dangling the promise of a new life, an escape from the madness of an informer's life, before cruelly casting him aside.

They added to the wrongs done to you. They were eager to erase you from their memory, to pretend that your life counted for nothing. But every secret has its time, and if you are prepared to wait all those stories that were left incomplete or utterly blackened by lies will be told in their entirety.

Her words were a greater comfort than he expected. They presented new possibilities. Detective Carey had told her he wanted to reopen the investigation. He was keen to make contact with her son again and had booked a flight to Spain. He had all the details arranged, ready for Tommy to set off along the path towards justice and the truth. It was time for him to bear witness, she wrote, even though he would be a marked man for life.

When he folded away the letter, the room had grown hot and claustrophobic. Surveying the dim outline of the furniture and the shuttered window, he felt a degree of contentment. For the first time in over a year, his life had meaning. Now that he had a plan, he felt transfigured. It was a dark plan of revenge that breathed and whispered to him, persuading him that his mother was correct. It was time to go back home. He parted the curtains and walked out on to the terrace.

Immediately, the Andalusian light hit him: the jolt of blue sky, the shining whiteness radiating from the walls, and the red and white geranium flowers blazing with life. It was enough to step into the sun's presence for his dark fears to be swept aside. He stretched out his arms, the heat dripping from the vines overhead, the light seeking him out like a gushing torch of raw petrol, feeding the anger inside him and the love that welled up for his mother, the woman who had delivered him into the world and was now going to deliver him again, from the nightmare of a fugitive's exile.

He looked into the searing sky, the sun bleaching everything, giving the terrace, the whitewashed walls, and the groves of olive trees in the valley below a ghost-like cast, while memories of the past rained down upon him darkly.

CHAPTER ONE

Lough Neagh, Northern Ireland

Fog, dragging across the shoreline, hung over the heaving expanse of the lough.

The view at the jetty had no depth; nothing to see or touch but a cold stagnancy pressing upon everything, no stealthy shapes or shadows and no sign of the drowned corpse. The vast mass of the lough and its secret, washed ashore overnight, had slid into oblivion.

A disorientated Inspector Celcius Daly stepped from his car and listened for the telltale sounds, the churn of the waves, the wash of shifting currents, the web of birdcalls bubbling up from tree-lined coves, but heard nothing. It was early in the morning, too early for most. He had worked all night, and had been looking forward to clearing his head with the exhilarating air of the lough, and a glimpse of its wind-slapped waves, their rainy glitter and gloom thrusting towards him. Since his father's death, this great wild space had been his only respite from the two habits that governed his existence: work and insomnia; the only place he could breathe freely and figure out his thoughts by himself.

Daly groped in the direction of the water, trying to get his bearings, but almost immediately the fog enclosed him in walls of whiteness, and all he could see were floating fragments, dark rocks, thorn trees, and an abandoned fishing boat with rotten timbers. No sounds, no sense of direction, no signs of his colleagues or police tape, no sad clues as to what had happened overnight, only these white suffocating corridors to roam.

Where was everybody? Lough Neagh might be the largest lake in Western Europe, but it was small in the parochial sense. Bad news travelled quickly along its shores, and Daly had expected to encounter a few press photographers and gawping members of the public fringing the scene, but the shrouded cove was completely devoid of life. Perhaps he had made a mistake and parked up at the wrong place. A solitary swell broke, heaving and sucking along the invisible shore. He wheeled around and changed direction.

He was supposed to know this terrain by heart, but this morning the very presence of the lough seemed unimaginable. He clambered along a muddy bank, shuffling slowly, playing blind man's buff with the shoreline.

To his relief, the fog had other occupants. The profile of a young man floated into view, a police officer minding the crime scene, his face becalmed by the fog.

Daly flicked open his ID. 'Which direction?'

The officer pointed the way. A colleague drifted close by,

another ghost, and then the world whitened again. Daly slithered down an embankment of rocks, treacherously greasy with algae, hearing waves splash nearby. Gobbets of water soaked his trousers and dribbled down his legs. Thin air one moment, deep dark water the next; he'd better mind himself. He reached out a hand to steady himself against a post, the strangeness of the invisible shore made stranger by the fact that each footstep was one he had taken countless times before, loping and clambering over the uneven terrain as a boy, but somehow the fog had swept those memories aside. Wary of jumping from one rock to another, he plodded on, slipping down the sides, getting his feet soaking wet.

A thorn tree in blossom appeared and then disappeared, recoiling into the fog, otherworldly. Again that disorientating sense that the lough was suddenly far away, that it had fled with the crime scene under cover of the fog, its waves breaking on a distant shore.

He shouted: 'Hello, police,' hoping to call his way out of the murk. His words came out more querulously than he intended, half strangled and hoarse. Annoyed at having to draw attention to himself in this way, he shouted louder, and then listened. The lough lay cushioned in silence. Then it came, a murmuring response further along the shore. Followed by another gurgling call, further away, repeating the first. Was it just his muffled echo? Or were there other detectives out there, searching for corpses, trying to yell their way out of this mist-shrouded labyrinth?

For a moment, the fog dissolved and Daly was rewarded with a view of the shore lined with the debris of winter gales. The Lough Neagh landscape was a deserted, inhospitable place, prone to sudden flooding that impregnated the surrounding fields and cottages with mud and slime. Apart from a few bird sanctuaries, it did not attract many visitors. Across Ireland, developers had built wherever they wanted, erecting expensive shiny apartments and holiday homes right on the banks of lakes and rivers. The planners' sleight of hand that allowed builders to ruin the country's waterways did not apply here. The lough and its shore was one of the country's last true natural spaces, a marshy landscape Daly kept returning to for reflection, to help shape his thoughts and memories, but this morning all that was wiped away.

Stirring amid the breaking mist were the white figures of scene-of-crime officers, moving like maggots across a little beach. A shore full of strangers to announce the arrival of the mud-smeared corpse that had washed up during the night. Ignoring the other officers, Daly slipped down the stones to where the body lay sprawled on its back, feet still in the water, face turned to one side, bloated by the long immersion, its lifeless eyes and patchy beard several inches long covered in slimy liquid.

'Typical Irish suicide,' murmured Detective Derek Irwin as he came up beside him.

Daly turned to the grey face of his colleague. 'There've been no reports of a missing person.'

'That's why forensics are still here.' Irwin gave a bored sigh. 'The body of a middle-aged overweight male consigned to a dismal lough. Sounds like a suicide to me.'

There was indeed something sad and shameful-looking about the corpse, his bedraggled beard and the water rippling over his bare feet, and the lough was a notorious location for suicides. Daly's former commander, Ian Donaldson, had chosen a similar stage for his final dreadful act over three years previously. Daly examined the dead man's face, wondering what bitter curses or desperate words had spluttered on to that Rasputin-like beard in his dying moments. Yes, perhaps a typical Irish suicide and nothing more. A spur of the moment decision with no witnesses, no one to appeal to the poor sod's saner side. The most solitary and mysterious act imaginable for a detective to investigate. Even a ruthless murderer might be encouraged one day to break his silence and make the excuse that he was out of his mind with rage, and that he regretted his terrible act for the rest of his life. Suicides could never explain themselves, or be held to account, or deceive detectives with lies and innocent looks.

As Daly watched, bubbles gurgled from the dead man's tongue, as though he were trying to speak for all the drowned bodies of the lough.

'Not the nicest start to your working day, eh?' said Irwin.

Daly felt a vein throb in his temple. 'You're wrong. I'm on my way home. I've been on duty since yesterday evening.'

'Still doing overtime?'

'Yes.' His work schedule had been the same for six months now, and he felt exhausted to the core. 'Who reported the body?'

Irwin nodded in the direction of a ragged-looking fisherman, who stood apart from everyone else, drifting in and out of the scene like an uninvited ghost.

Daly beckoned to him. The fishing folk were a superstitious breed and they tended to get nervous around a corpse. This one appeared keen to be on his way.

'Am I supposed to wait here all morning?' the fisherman complained, clambering over the rocks. Daly thought he looked a little shaky on his feet.

'No, just as long as it takes to ask you a few questions.'

The man avoided Daly's eyes, his face contorting with a frown. His cheeks were puffy and there was a nasty cut to his forehead.

'What happened to your head?'

The frown knotted itself into a scowl. 'I hit a rock.'

'When?'

'The moment I realized I'd found a body.' His eyes bulged at the memory and slowly focused on Daly. They were as dark and murky as the lough itself.

Daly smelled the stale whiff of alcohol. He thought he knew the fisherman's type well. These days the lough's fishing community was a motley crew of restless men without families, part-time alcoholics, sulky teenagers who had dropped out of school; a buoyant gang of society's dregs, jostling together like stray flotsam. They knew the secret currents of the lough, and every strategy and subterfuge to avoid the fishing wardens and police patrols.

'Were you sober?'

'No. I'd had a few tins of Guinness, but not enough to make me drunk. I fish this bay most nights. I know it like the back of my hand.'

He had probably been dredging the mud for eels to sell to upmarket restaurants. Daly doubted it was the season for fishing eels or that he even had a licence.

'How did you find the body?'

'It knocked against my boat. At first I thought it was a

dead animal.' His eyes stared at Daly. 'It took me a while to realize my mistake,' he said apologetically, as though the delay mattered.

The old man made a move to return to his boat, but Daly needed more information, and the fisherman seemed the person best qualified to give it.

'Tell me about the currents in the bay,' he asked. The lough might be a void to the detective, but he understood enough to know there was nothing arbitrary about the corpse's arrival on the beach. Hidden currents, the influx of rivers and the prevailing winds would have influenced the dead man's last voyage in different ways.

'The eels gather along the currents here. They're handy for fishing with the old-fashioned nets.'

'I don't want to know about fishing. Where would the currents have carried the body from?'

'Your man would have drifted in the same way I did. From the south, just below Coney Island. Neither of us had a sail or compass to bear us here. I'd say he went in somewhere close to the River Blackwater at Maghery. Everything that floats down the river is driven on to this beach.'

'And what if he'd fallen in beyond Coney Island?'

'He'd have spun into the centre of the lough and made landfall on the east coast. Depending on the wind he might have got as far as Crumlin.'

The fisherman began shuffling over the rocks to his boat, but Daly stayed on his heels. 'Come across anything on your fishing trip? Again, I'm not talking about fish.'

'I saw nothing.'

'No sign of strange boats or figures along the shore?'

'Nothing.'

'What about your nets? Snag anything unusual?'

The old man turned away and grumbled to himself.

'A piece of rubbish maybe, something that you threw back in?'

They had reached the point where his wooden boat was wedged in the rocks, the water lapping against its low sides. Daly recognized its flat-bottomed design: a cot boat, one of the most primitive forms of water navigation on the lough, but also its stealthiest, the poacher's boat of choice, capable of creeping into shallow coves beyond the reach of the high-powered fishery boats. Inside it were floats, lines, a bucket, and a small tiller. So far nothing to pique Daly's interest. He lifted the row of floats and found a sodden-looking canvas bag full of wet clothes. They were neatly folded and expensive-looking. A quick rummage, and between them he found a plastic folder with the boarding pass from a flight to Spain, in the name of Brian Carey and a departure date, 22 May, two days previously. 'Where did you find this?' he asked sharply, hauling the bag on to the rocks.

'It caught on one of my nets just before I found the body.'

The rising sun peeked through the mist, casting an eerie glow across the scene. The fisherman shifted anxiously from foot to foot, staring at Daly's frowning face, waiting for the detective's response, and then he froze. 'Wait a minute,' he said. 'I know you. You're Celcius Daly. Do you know me?' He thrust his face closer to Daly, eager to be recognized, but all Daly saw was old age and decay.

'I don't know who you are.'

'I wasn't sure but now I'm certain.' The fisherman flashed

a gummy leer, the canvas bag now quite forgotten. 'You look different. But you're still the same old Celcius Daly, I bet.' He grabbed Daly by the sleeve and held him closer. 'Don't you know who I am? We share a secret, don't you remember?'

'I doubt that very much,' said Daly, wondering how this sodden old drunk could have the nerve to grab him like this. Perhaps he was one of his father's friends.

He looked at Daly with a sudden, angry stare and let go of his arm. 'You might have changed but I know the real Celcius Daly,' he said in a boastful voice. 'I know you too well. What a surprise to see you here, acting the big detective, asking questions, sniffing for clues.'

Daly backed away but the fisherman pitched forward, his boots splashing through the water, his coat flapping open, revealing a half-drunk bottle of whiskey tucked into an inner pocket. The secret knowledge he held over Daly had made him sprightly, like a young bull bounding up to a fence.

'What a cheek you have, acting the detective with me, asking was I drunk, cross-examining me, looking right through me as though I was a guilty stranger.'

Daly turned away, blinking at the swirling mist, the grey absence of the lough, forgetting what he was going to say or do next. Everything went quiet in his mind, as though the fog had seeped in there, too. He groped for the right response, a memory from the mental vacancy, anything that might make him warm to this foul-breathed stranger.

'What an unexpected stroke of luck,' said the fisherman. 'To think that a moment ago I was worried you might arrest me for breaking some arsehole fishing law and haul me down to the police station. I hadn't counted on being so lucky.'

He jumped on to some rocks, surveying Daly from this new vantage point, his body breaking in and out of the mist.

But it was Daly who needed the vantage point. He felt as though he were in the company of something overwhelming and precarious – the past. The fisherman's presence loomed in his senses, magnified by the watery air and the murk of dark rocks and skeletal branches. Somehow, he had been transformed from a prickly but harmless witness to something more hostile, a cause of concern, perhaps even a threat to the investigation.

'You've asked me questions, now let me ask you one,' said the fisherman. 'Do you ever think about what you did to my brother?' He spoke with an air of moral superiority, and clearly relished it, glaring at Daly, willing him to make a confession.

Daly teetered as if brought to a dangerous brink. Surely he had never known him – with his leering face reeking of the past's decay – or his brother. Daly belonged to the side of law and order, regular jobs and a working routine, not out on the buffers with this old fool, who was now pulling his half-rotten boat into the water.

'Forgetting me and my brother, avoiding looking at me, don't think that will get you off the hook, Daly.'

'What do you mean?'

'Your career won't make things right. What you did to my brother can't be wiped away just because you stand there in smart clothes asking questions about a drowned man.'

The aggrieved face staring at the detective carried a threat, but no matter how much Daly racked his brains, he could not recall any wrongdoing for which he might bear responsibility. He returned the fisherman's gaze with a look of incomprehension. The old man must be harbouring some grudge from the past, a piece of scandal or dirt that he believed was damaging to Daly's reputation. Surely it couldn't have been that terrible if he had forgotten it. His conscience was unstained. Assuming the old man was being truthful, Daly must have learned to live with the alleged misdeed and get on with his life. Did that suggest he had committed the deed in the belief that it had no consequences, or that no one knew or would find out? Was this why he had been able to put it beyond his consciousness?

The fisherman pushed off with one of his oars, the boat scraping against some rocks and then floating clear.

'I know the truth about you, Celcius Daly,' the fisherman shouted. 'I'll remember it when the wind has scattered your ashes and every bloody thing you did as a policeman.'

The scene-of-crime officers stopped what they were doing and looked over at the pair. Daly no longer wished to be detained by the past. Ever since discovering the truth about his mother's murder during the Troubles, and the role played by former police officers in the ensuing cover-up, he had spent all his time staying out of that dangerous territory. That was how he was able to draw a comb through his hair and shave every morning. He did not think about the past any more. He drove to work, kept himself busy, all the while devising new ways of staying out of the past.

Above, the sky was shifting from mist to early-morning sun, light blazing across the lough. The gap between Daly and the fisherman widened. 'Wait,' he called. He shouldn't let the old man leave like this. 'Stop,' he shouted. 'You haven't told me who you are or where you live.'

'Don't worry, Daly, I'm not going to disappear. My family have lived on this shore for generations. I'll be paying you a visit very soon.'

When he was gone from sight, Daly returned to the drowned man and squatted down to compose himself. He stared into the lifeless eyes of the corpse and said nothing. He stayed like that for a while. Then he rose and said, 'Let's get the body out of here.'

His fellow officers watched him with interest. Irwin shrugged. 'We're waiting for the ambulance. They take their time these days.'

When the ambulance finally arrived, Daly clambered back along the shore to his car. It turned out to be a fine morning to drive home but he was deep in thought, his mind trying to fill in the blanks of his conversation with the fisherman. Shafts of sunlight illuminated the dying spirals of mist on the road. He forced the car at speed along the narrow byways as if he were steering through a sinuous line of ghosts, the long, grey floating backwash of the past. That was the problem with coming back to live in the place you were born and reared. Going home meant that the past never really left you. It watched over you and appeared in the form of wild old men who took relish in dredging up events buried deep in your memory.

CHAPTER TWO

Dreesh, Republic of Ireland

'No one leaves until I've checked all the delivery documents.'

Tom Morgan's voice cut through the heavy air, which was a smuggler's feast of diesel fumes and engine noise, shadows and urgent voices, all enveloped in the hum of pipes feeding laundered fuel into underground tankers. It was a sight to see how the faces of the lorry drivers went deathly white just hearing the growl in his voice. He was their fearsome boss, the smuggling king of Monaghan, known as Red Tom or just Red to his few friends and many enemies. He had assembled the men at his illegal fuel depot in the village of Dreesh, just south of the Irish border.

It was early in the morning, and his sheds were full of vehicles carrying red diesel laundered at anonymous sites deeper in the Monaghan countryside. In an hour, another convoy of lorries would take the fuel to suppliers in the North, less than scrupulous filling-station owners and criminal gangs including Loyalist paramilitaries. However, these were deals for later, this morning he had another, more pressing problem to contend with.

'Anything you want to get off your chests?' he asked the group of men, who mutely shook their heads in reply.

The youngest lorry driver, a dirty cap pulled low over his head, had stepped down from his cab later than the others. The delay was only a few moments, but Morgan had to fight to keep his anger in check.

'Take off your cap so I can see you properly,' he told him.

The youth removed the cap and shifted about while Morgan examined his papers. When he looked up, the young man had returned to his lorry, sitting in the driver's seat with the door hanging open, waiting for permission to leave. He looked insolent and out of place sitting at the wheel, as if he were the one in charge of the smuggling operation. By contrast the older lorry drivers had not moved, casting nervous glances at each other, uncertain as to whether they would be allowed to drive away with their vehicles.

'Why would any of you betray me?' asked Morgan, picking up a hurley stick from the shadows. 'Why would anyone do something like that?' He held the stick in the air, letting the lorry drivers see the edges of hardened ash wood, the smooth planes catching the fluorescent light from the sheds.

As a child, his grandmother used to send him to the open sewer at the bottom of the family farm, telling him to sit beside it with a stick in his hands and whack to smithereens every rat that came creeping out. Rats had yellow teeth just like his grandmother, and whiskers, too. She had told him tales of rat kings, how the creatures would breed if left unchecked, swarming together in the rotten depths of the farm, tails knotting together, bodies coiling into a rodent empire on the move. He remembered beating the rats to death as they came scurrying out of the darkness, sniffing with their whiskers, slashing their long tails in the mud and slime.

Was that a smile on the young man's face or a sign of nerves? Morgan stared at him. The youth looked away and began drumming a tune against the door of the lorry. The idling throb of the vehicles and the pumping of diesel drowned out all other sounds. He seemed oblivious to the wary glances of his older colleagues. More stupidity, thought Morgan. Blind, greedy stupidity. He had no idea of the ordeal that awaited him.

Morgan beckoned to the youth. 'Come back here, I've some questions for you.'

'What do you want to know?'

'Did you stop on the way here?'

'Only in Monaghan town.'

'Monaghan?'

'Yes. To get some cigarettes. At a filling station.' The youth's eyes were evasive, glazed.

'Oh, that explains it.'

'Explains what?'

'Some bastard must have siphoned off five hundred litres of diesel while you were in the shop.' Morgan was leaning towards him, his eyes glaring. 'Either that or you're lying to me.'

'I'm not lying. What the tank has now is what I started with. Not a drop more or less.' The youth turned to the other drivers for support but their faces were grim. A shudder passed through them that had nothing to do with the cold air gusting through the yard.

As betrayals went it seemed banal compared to what Morgan had endured as a young IRA recruit, this furtive double-cross involving a few hundred litres of diesel siphoned off on some back lane, but he was the kind of person who had a rigid sense of values, who demanded loyalty from his employees, and he hated to be reminded of their shortcomings.

'Check it again,' said the youth. 'I swear I'm not lying.'

'I've checked through the ledger and the records tally up. Except for four entries in the past month. All of them on your run.' Morgan flipped through the pages and shoved them in his face. Then he turned to the other drivers and asked had anyone else been in possession of the ledger.

They grunted no, looking ready to dissolve into the darkness.

He turned back to the youth. 'Have you any other explanation for the difference?'

The young man hesitated and then shook his head. In the old days, Morgan would have used a pair of pliers and wired the little bastard to an electricity generator. He had refined his methods of interrogation since those chaotic times when every second IRA man was suspected of being a tout and the country was scrambling towards a ceasefire. The day the IRA finally ended their campaign of violence had been the worst of Morgan's life, more savage than anything the British Army had thrown at him. It had felt humiliating to watch the soldiers mount their patrols along the border without fear or restriction when for years it had been too dangerous for them to travel anywhere other than by helicopter. Betrayed and sickened he had slunk away from the negotiating table, from the new era of politics and peace, and turned to his diesel-laundering and smuggling business for consolation.

'I want you to be honest, son. How long have you been cheating me?'

'I've no idea what you're talking about.'

'You think you're sly, so sly.' He ran his hand up the youth's inner leg, feeling for a sign that he had wet himself.

'Fuck off, you bent bastard.'

'No one talks to me like that,' he growled, but the youth stared back at him with empty eyes. He saw the void in the young man where fear and respect for authority should be. It was clear to Morgan that the lack of respect was total and would infect every order and summons he made. He grabbed the youth by his hair and dragged him closer. He wanted to fill that vacant space with terror, but the youth's eyes stared back, black and cold, agitating Morgan further.

Ten years previously, the IRA had officially retired Morgan from their ranks, while secretly encouraging him to develop his special talents. Along the border, he could move in shadow and secrecy, fight his corner if necessary, resist any form of authority, even that of his former IRA comrades. The ceasefire had been the making of him and his criminal empire. In the intervening decade, he had grown very wealthy, but also wary and paranoid. His greatest fear was that he would lose the protection of the IRA. The ceasefire had made conditions dangerously variable. Prominent figures were dying of old age, or slipping into senility; influences waned and political leaders changed. Without the IRA's support, he would be walking through a dangerous darkness, full of trapdoors opening and closing on all sides. Republicans who disturbed

23

the political harmony found that their circumstances deteriorated very quickly. They were immediately isolated and their reputations undermined.

'Which road do you want the police to close tonight?' asked Morgan.

'What do you mean?'

'Where would you like me to dump your fucking body? North or South, it's your choice.'

He pawed the youth's leg again. This time he felt what he had been searching for: the damp trickle of urine. He knew the smell of fear, its odour and excretions from the body, and it gratified him to see that the youth was beginning to unravel. 'I see you're getting worried now, son.' He grinned. 'But don't panic just yet. We're going to do this by the old rules. You have one last chance to do this honourably. Tell me everything while you're still fit to.'

'What are you talking about?'

Morgan grabbed the hurley stick and delivered a blow to the youth's stomach, enough to hurt but not incapacitate completely. 'That was a mistake, son. You don't ask questions. I ask questions.'

The youth flattened his body and tried to slide across the concrete.

'Who put you up to this?'

'Don't know.'

'Have you been blabbing to anyone?' This time Morgan kicked him in the stomach.

'No.'

'The police? MI5? What about Detective Carey and Sergeant McKenna in the village?'

24

'Can't.' The youth could barely speak. He looked around as though the humming yard was an immense hole he had fallen into, a cave with no hope of escape. His tormentor's silhouette filled his vision.

Morgan paused to get his breath, his eyes enlarged, gloating. 'Are you a fucking spy? An informer?'

The youth shook his head, dazed.

Morgan had never challenged the new direction of the IRA, even though he secretly disagreed with it. He had done what was asked of him by the organization's ruling council. He carried out punishment beatings, smuggled, and paid his dues. He invested their money in complicated property empires, laundered cash in currency-exchange outlets, all the time inflating their secret bank accounts. As an extra precaution, he had corrupted a few local detectives. No one could harm him now. He was a servant of the IRA, and he had their protection. In a twisted way, he had become the servant of the new political peace process, too, its shadowy henchman. After all, a bloody legacy had to be tidied up in the background.

The youth whimpered as Morgan swung the hurley stick again. Once the violence began, there seemed no good reason to hold back. Not that he had thought the punishment through clearly, standing in the clutter of the yard with the youth on his knees. He looked around. At least there was a hose and tap nearby, which would help clear away the blood. He delivered several more blows to the youth's body.

Every now and again Morgan's masters would chide him, urging him to tone down the criminality and violence, but what else could he do? His life was on a tether and tied to this one spot, a border village and his adjoining farm. How

25

else was he to make a living from a run-down fuel depot and his fields full of marsh and thorn thickets?

Every swing of the hurley stick restored his sense of pride. Tom Morgan, former IRA man, farmer and parish hurling captain, a smuggling king grafted by hundreds of secrets to the border and its terrain of fear and blood. He felt a lifting movement in his heart, his thoughts racing through the blind tunnel of his anger. His victim's body altered underfoot into a squat sack that pleasingly fitted the weight of his swinging boot, and the hurley stick gripped in his hands felt huge and long, a magnificent instrument of his power.

Pausing for breath, he removed a set of key fobs from his pocket. He pressed one and the shutter doors of a nearby shed rolled upward, revealing within its capacious interior a dirt-encrusted bin lorry. He pressed another key and the rubbish-crusher began to grind into action, its reverberations filling the yard, transforming it into an echoing cone of torture. His hair, bulging in mounds from his skull, was lit up in a halo of light like an angel's, but his body was more like that of a shuffling beast.

The youth made a desperate attempt to crawl across the yard, his face full of terror, his feet skidding on oil stains, his tongue wagging apology after apology. The rotor at the back of the lorry kept turning; lumps of rag-bodied bin bags, their insides ripped open, churned and clung to the teeth of the crusher.

Morgan grabbed the youth by the hair and wrapped his head in a bin liner, which did little to muffle his screaming. He squatted down beside him and whispered into his ear. He wanted what he said to permeate his consciousness, to run like a recorded message in his brain, reciting the same instruction repeatedly. 'Stay away and don't ever come back.'

The boy stopped moaning and listened. Morgan could hear his breath scraping his throat and nasal passages. He was satisfied that his voice was totally inside his head.

'Don't even think of running to the police,' he said. 'I've bought the services of the local detectives. They'll tip me off if you start blabbing. Then I really will fuck you up.'

The young man cowered on the ground, expecting the violence to resume, but the pause stretched.

Morgan stepped back, and the faces of the other drivers sharpened into focus. 'Stupid little bastard,' he said to them.

'Fucking idiot,' one of them agreed.

Morgan pulled the bin liner from his head. The young man's face was dull as wax, his nose and mouth covered in blood, his eyes half-closed and swelling already as he looked around forlornly.

'Take yourself off to England or Spain and get yourself a proper job. Don't ever come back. Not even for a funeral. Stay away. For your own fucking sake and your family's.'

The youth coughed up some blood and exhaled a ragged breath. 'Can I go now?'

'Fucking sure you can.'

Afterwards, Morgan marched up and down his yard, watching his lorries leave, their tanks filled to the brim with illegal fuel. He was sure of himself now, in control of his benighted empire. He had practised for this type of interrogation, like an athlete, and it was a delight to revel in his mastery. He felt an urge to laugh. What a relief to turn his back on the new world of political wheeling and dealing and laundered investments. He no longer felt nervous or cowed by his former commanders in the IRA, those preposterous, earnest monsters of violence who had laboured up out of the mire to take their seats in the highest political circles. The country had secured a lasting peace, but many had suffered and died on its long and crooked road.

He would not perish or be subdued like the others. He walked tall out of his yard and up the street to the village of Dreesh. The aching in his feet and arms produced by the binge of violence was a small price to pay for this sense of relief and power.

A silhouette stepped out of the shadows, a man in a Garda uniform, coming forward as though he had been waiting for Morgan. He touched his police officer's cap as a form of greeting.

'Hello, Tom,' said the figure. His cap was cocked at a sterner-looking angle than the one Morgan was used to.

'Is that you, young McKenna?' replied Morgan, even though the Garda, Sergeant Peter McKenna, was fast approaching retirement age. He smiled cheerfully, astute enough to notice that the sergeant's casual manner was not entirely effortless. McKenna was a man of the law, after all, a servant of the state, and despite all that had happened in Dreesh over the years there was a flicker of concern in his face, a shadow on an otherwise placid countenance. Years ago, he had been a tall, imposing fellow, but age and the grind of being stationed in Dreesh had taken their toll.

They stood in the early-morning light, neither of them moving, facing each other with caution.

'Are you all right, Peter?' asked Morgan.

'Yes, fine.' The sergeant looked down at the fuel depot, which was still busy, the figures of Morgan's men moving about the yard, tidying away the snaking fuel hoses. 'I haven't spent four decades in this village without learning a few things about how you operate. That's three nights in a row your lorries have been churning up and down the roads.'

Morgan decided to ignore the sergeant's accusing tone. 'We're working through the night because business is brisk,' he said, grinning. 'Someone has to keep the economy going.'

McKenna nodded. 'I've been watching your vehicles coming and going, thinking about things. I'm nearly sixty now, you know.'

'Anything on your mind?'

'I've been thinking how did I end up here? Stuck in this village with you, Tom Morgan. The two of us at opposite ends of the same street, but somehow inseparable.'

'You make it sound like we're prisoners chained together,' said Morgan. What was the sergeant hinting at after all these years hiding in that station of his, wrapped up in his gloomy silence like Tutankhamen's mummy? What was he looking for, sympathy? Gratitude?

'I was thinking all the time... and then I heard a scream. It came from your yard.'

'Are you sure?'

'Yes. I heard it several times.' He turned to look at Morgan. 'It bothered me.'

'Must have been a rat caught by one of the dogs. The place is crawling with vermin.'

'Maybe.'

'Even if it wasn't a rat why would it bother you?'

'I'm a police officer. It's my job to be bothered when I hear screaming like that.'

The sergeant had never deigned to remind Morgan of that fact before. Why now, after all these years? Had McKenna forgotten his part in the village's economic survival? If he was troubled by what was going on at the depot then he must be troubled by himself and his colleagues, troubled by every resident in Dreesh.

'A police officer?' said Morgan. 'When was the last time you played that part here?'

'This isn't about playing parts. This is about maintaining law and order.'

The expression on the sergeant's face, the sudden glint in his eyes, made Morgan's anger flare up.

'Like I told you. I heard screaming. The sound of a young man.'

The silence grew as Morgan struggled to control his annoyance. 'Must be your imagination,' he said thickly. 'I'll be seeing you around, Sergeant.' He made to step around him but the sergeant blocked his path.

'Wait, what's that on your arms?'

Morgan looked down and was startled to see that tracks of blood had spattered the sleeves of his jacket.

'Do you see what's there?' asked the sergeant.

'Yes, I see,' answered Morgan. He noticed that blood had seeped on to his trousers and his shoes. Christ, there might even be drops on his face. 'Can you believe it? I must have cut myself and not noticed.'

The sergeant hesitated. He seemed unsure of what to do next.

'Well, it's up to you, Peter,' said Morgan. 'Whether or not you want to investigate my little accident and your suspicions.'

'What about the screaming?'

'Like I told you, it didn't happen.'

'Just once you could tell me the truth.'

'The truth is I'm heading home to take a shower and get a rest. You can do what you have to do. Feel free to check over my sheds for anything suspicious.'

The sergeant licked his lips, and seemed about to say something, but stopped. They stared at each other without speaking, Morgan in his bloodstained clothing, McKenna in his Garda uniform. The sergeant cleared his throat. The sound of the last lorry leaving Morgan's yard roared and then dwindled away. McKenna contemplated Morgan and the evidence of his bloody clothing, and then he turned and walked back to his station, head down, like a little boy burdened with guilt.

The houses and shops of the village ranged behind him, blind and hearing nothing.

CHAPTER THREE

Maghery, Lough Neagh

The coldness of the water did not fail to deliver its punch of anaesthesia. Stripped to just a pair of swimming trunks, Daly stepped into the pool, a natural formation in the bogland at the eastern tip of his father's farm. During periods of drought, the water level shrank back to a muddy hollow, but in the early-morning light, the pool, fed by the nearby well, brimmed with its spring fullness. Gingerly, he eased his body into the chilly water, a stream of bubbles bobbing up from the black depths.

A month ago, the builders undertaking repairs to Daly's run-down cottage had switched off his fresh water supply, warning him the pipes were full of leaks and needed replacing. Since then, he'd had to resort to the adjoining well for drinking water, boiling it first on the gas stove in his on-site caravan, his new residence for the duration of the renovations. The well had once been crucial to the functioning of the farm, supplying all the water for its inhabitants, human and animal. Mains water had only been extended to this part of the lough shore in the 1950s, and thereafter the well had been used solely to water cattle.

He waded in, sinking up to his chest, feeling immersed in the landscape through the primary sense of touch, participating in the patient miracle of the morning, the lifting mist, the shimmering hedgerows, his cottage moated by boggy fields, the cattle on the neighbouring farm standing in contented stillness and flicking their tails. After the early-morning fog, a dew had descended and he could hear their tails sloshing through the wet grass. Winter was far behind him now, its brooding spirit of loss no longer blowing across the lough.

His feet left the peaty bottom, and then he was moving sedately in the water, his hands pushing forward and parting, allowing him to progress breaststroke fashion to the middle of the pool. There, he angled his body so that he could see the sky, and the clouds that scudded across its expanse. This was deep, solitary water. He leaned back fully, feeling the warmth of the sun on his face.

How far did the water's depths go? How deep were his own roots? He had entered a different dimension, one perpendicular to his everyday existence as a detective and the sole human inhabitant of the dishevelled farm, one that reached into the depths of the past, the layered silences of his childhood. If he dived headfirst into the pool and opened his eyes wide, what would he see in the shadowy caverns below, what ghosts still slithered about in the murk? He lowered his head completely in the water, keeping his eyes firmly shut, and when he emerged with a deep exhalation, he felt renewed, as though embodied into a different morning entirely.

Not since childhood had he felt so aware of his orientation in the landscape, the miles of dense bogland stretching around him, and the endless sky above. No wonder that he had come to rely on these cold immersions, feeling soothed as he lay on his bed after a night shift, rocked and lulled by the wind buffeting the caravan and the rain hammering on its roof. He felt in touch with the farm in a way not possible when he was confined to the run-down cottage, which was undergoing extensive renovations in an effort to find a buyer.

However, this morning, Daly still felt uneasy. His encounter with the fisherman, and the sight of the drowned body had provoked a twinge of guilt in him, as though he were somehow implicated in the stranger's death. The lingering sense of blame had stayed with him. Now, in the pool, it became clear. Commander Donaldson, he thought. The inquest into his former boss's drowning was due to begin any week now. He had not realized how much he was dreading the hearing until the sight of the fresh corpse had rekindled his memories of Donaldson's suicide. He went over his final conversation with the ex-police chief, analysing it for clues to his state of mind.

At the time, Daly had been investigating the cold case of his mother's murder, uncovering a conspiracy between serving police officers under Donaldson's watch and Loyalist paramilitary killers. Confronted by Daly's evidence, Donaldson had promised he would take the initiative. He'd been keen to help Daly launch a public inquiry into the murder, but, somehow, his words hadn't added up. He'd wanted to help Daly but couldn't. He'd been by turns aggrieved, arrogant, sympathetic, imploring. In the end, there'd been no way of working out what had been going on in his mind. Perhaps the commander had had no idea himself. That would be the most sensible conclusion to reach. Donaldson had been torn apart by his conscience and his loyalty to his profession, his former colleagues, and his past. When he'd left Daly's cottage the night before his death he'd been a finished man, his reputation doomed.

Daly took another deep breath, submerged his head and came up for air. He was glad he no longer lived in the cottage. His caravan was insulated and waterproofed against more than the wind and the rain. He thought of the ghosts of the past lingering in the dark corners of the house and the grimness of the silence that lay behind them. He immersed his head again. Thank God for the cottage's ruin, he thought. Its leaking roof and rotten walls had given him the excuse to escape its warren of rooms and the ghosts of his mother and father, who had taken it over to the extent that he felt he was sharing his living space with the past. Not just the memories of his parents, but their noises and smells, too, as if he were a boy again, with no independent existence beyond that of his mother and father.

He adjusted his position so that the white-flowering hedges and the for-sale signs jutting out from his front garden interrupted his sightlines to the lough. He glided back and forth in the pool, feeling a flicker of optimism about the coming summer, the renovation of the cottage and its possible sale.

How much home did he really need? He should sell the entire farm, he decided, retaining just this corner with its pool in the lap of the bog, a place to loaf around in during the long summer evenings.

He was still deep in thought when the sound of a car speeding along the lane to his cottage made him look up. During his swim, there had not been a single human sound in the expanse of fields and bogland apart from his gasps at the coldness of the water and his laboured breathing. He watched the car drive up to his cottage and brake abruptly. A woman stumbled out of the driver's seat and hurried up to the door. He squinted in the low morning sun streaking over the cottage, but could not make out who she was. His estate agent hadn't mentioned any interested viewers and he wasn't expecting anyone himself. Perhaps she was lost and looking for directions.

It must be me she's looking for, he thought as she negotiated her way past the builder's scaffolding and bowed to peer through the cottage's small windows. A sombre tension gripped him as he watched her walk around the cottage, obviously determined to find some trace of his presence. There was something familiar about her walk, the way her dark hair bounced upon her tense shoulders, the slightly offbeat click-clack of her heels on the concrete path. Fortunately, his caravan was hidden from view behind a clump of alder and willow. He remained alert, a prisoner in the pool, feeling an inner chill develop, looking out at the landscape he was reluctant to enter: his father's wild farm, the cottage surrounded by rubble and scaffolding, the dark lough and this impetuous woman trying to track him down.

She returned to the front porch and stood there for several long minutes, rapping at the door with her knuckles. Despite her stillness, there was nothing restful or measured about her straight-backed figure, her long hair flaring in the breeze. She walked round and inspected the windows again, gripping the iron pipes of the scaffolding as though they were a set of prison bars denying her access to the farm's single human occupant.

The ghosts of the past are bad, but the ghosts of the present are terrors, thought Daly. He did not let even a ripple disturb the water. Sometimes the best form of self-preservation was complete stillness. He lowered himself further and watched as his black hen, disturbed from her usual roost on top of the porch, began squawking and flapping around the woman's heels. For a moment, she seemed held in thrall by the bird's attack, and then she retreated, returning to her car without a glance backwards. Daly was sure he heard a grunt of irritation escape her throat.

He felt vaguely embarrassed by the hen's lack of hospitality and his own inertia, as though he had left the most highly strung member of the family in charge of welcoming visitors. Never mind, these days any sudden movements or strange noises were capable of setting the hen off. She was the protecting spirit of the cottage, and for months the place had been overrun by builders and their equipment. They had transformed his quiet country refuge into a zone of invasion and danger.

The gearstick of her car complained as she reversed down the narrow lane, and then the vehicle sped out of view. When he was sure she was gone, he sloped out of the water and back to the comforts of his caravan. He had refrained from greeting his visitor because in a way he no longer belonged to the cottage and its farm. He was in transit, waiting for the right buyer to come along and relieve him of his inheritance. And, if he were honest, the urgency of his unexpected visitor had intimidated him.

The caravan felt warm and snug. Daly put on a clean shirt and trousers, and soon had the kettle singing on the stove. He left the caravan door open and sat on a chair, watching the hen outside, still agitated by the woman's intrusion, rising up and flapping her wings at every gust of wind. He had his tea, keeping the bird in view. He could tell she was still in a bad temper by the way she rustled her feathers and clawed her scaly feet on the ground.

Later, he settled the hen by getting her some food and walking slowly around her, clucking quietly. He moved in slow motion, avoiding any sudden gestures, regulating each step, waiting for the bird's nerves to settle, and then he lifted her gently and carried her off to a coop full of hay. He returned to the caravan and was looking forward to an hour without further fuss when his phone rang.

It was the police station.

'Well?' said Daly.

The constable at the other end started telling him about a fight that had broken out in a local bar, leaving two men seriously injured by broken glass.

Why had the constable rung about such a straightforward matter? 'Who's the duty inspector?' said Daly sharply. 'Why can't he or she deal with this?'

'The duty inspector is you, sir.'

'Are you sure?' But already he was remembering that he'd marked his name down for an extra shift. With a groan, he put on his jacket and climbed into his car, realizing that he had not slept a wink since the previous day.

CHAPTER FOUR

Armagh, Northern Ireland

Daly tracked Irwin down to the canteen in police headquarters, where the younger detective was finishing off the last of his fried breakfast, his face grey with gloom.

'Breakfast not to your liking?' asked Daly.

Irwin ate his mouthful with a frown. 'Food's fine. Feet are soaking wet.'

Daly nodded, sitting down opposite him.

'I slipped on a rock and went into the water while they were bringing out the body.'

Daly tried to muster up some sympathy in his voice. 'Nothing worse than walking about all day with cold feet.' Before Irwin could complain any more, Daly asked was there anything new about the drowned man.

'The pathologist's writing up his report. You'll have to wait a few more hours. But I found out something interesting.'

He paused, waiting for Daly to consider this, before adding, 'Something you need to know. He was a police officer, but not one of ours.' Irwin's frown changed slightly. 'A foreign detective.'

'Then we'll have to contact his embassy. And the Foreign Office. They'll know what steps to take in a situation like this.'

Irwin pushed away his plate and a smile tugged at his lips, waiting for the penny to drop. 'Not necessary. We've contacted his next of kin, his partner, and she's identified the body. Turns out he lived all his life in Northern Ireland. He was a citizen of the UK, just like you and me.'

Daly considered this for a moment. It sounded like some sort of a riddle. Irwin's grin strained at his mouth. Daly was confused until he remembered the twisted logic of living on an island divided by an international border, and that Irwin was a staunch Ulster Protestant with a fixed political bias. The dead man must have worked for An Garda Síochána, the police force of the Republic of Ireland.

'A Garda detective?' asked Daly.

Irwin nodded. 'Strange to have a dead one on our doorstep, isn't it?' he said.

Daly shrugged. Until Brexit took shape, the Irish border was invisible to the people of Ireland. Some of them lived in the North but worked in the South, and vice versa. Why not a police detective, too? Daly could see the advantages of crossing the border every day. For one, it was an effective way of keeping home and work separate. Then there were the security issues to consider. Detectives in the Republic of Ireland seldom had to check under their cars for bombs. But what about the political sensitivities? Had the dead man worn his uniform while crossing the border? And what if he were stopped at a checkpoint? Daly was impatient for more information.

Irwin handed him a printout from a briefcase. Daly read the name at the top, Brian Carey, followed by his DOB and an address. He lived in County Tyrone but was stationed as a detective in Monaghan. *Some bloody foreign detective*, thought Daly, shaking his head at Irwin's description. One thing he was certain of, Carey was definitely not a foreigner.

'What are you thinking?' asked Irwin.

'I'm letting this sink in.'

'Well, here's more food for thought. The pathologist has discovered something he believes might be important.'

Daly waited in anticipation.

'He said that Carey must have been breathing when he first went into the water because of the volume of liquid in his lungs. Which fits with a suicide or an accidental drowning. However, he also discovered contusions around his neck that suggest he may have been forced under.'

'A murder, then.'

'We'll have to wait and see if his full report says anything conclusive. The lough is an easy place to have an accident and drown.'

'But Carey was a detective, which raises sinister possibilities,' said Daly. 'There are questions I need to ask his colleagues. For instance, why did he have a ticket to Spain but never boarded the flight? In the meantime, I want you to check with the forensics team. Ask them to give his clothing and the bag found by the fisherman a thorough going-over. They might find some clues.'

'Shall we put out an appeal to the public for more information?'

'Yes, but first we must liaise with his colleagues in the South. I want to find out more about Detective Brian Carey.' Daly stood up to go. 'This investigation might turn out to have some nasty security implications and we need to get our facts straight as soon as possible.'

'You're probably right. It doesn't seem to be a typical Irish suicide any more.'

'There's no question of that. The cross-border situation alone means we could be on tricky ground.'

'I think we need to call in the help of Special Branch,' said Irwin. He had worked for Special Branch in the past, and he outlined why he believed the case merited their assistance.

However, Daly said it was too soon to involve the specialist agency. 'I'll decide when we need to contact them,' he said firmly.

Irwin let it go at that and agreed to report to Daly any new findings.

Afterwards, Daly rang Monaghan Police Station and got the contact details of a Sergeant Peter McKenna. He was based in a border village called Dreesh, and had been working with Carey on an important case. Daly put the phone down and stared at Irwin's printout. He tried to build up a picture of the dead detective in his mind, his working life, and his daily trips over the border and back again. A UK citizen who wore the policing emblem of another country. How compromised had Carey been? But weren't Daly and many of his compatriots compromised, too? Didn't he own two passports, a British and an Irish one? He could sing two national anthems badly, knew the founding histories of both countries. For his entire adult life he had operated in a murky twilight of national identity, crammed with flags and history, all the time trying desperately to fit in, to find a small place he could call home and just exist, even if it was a dark corner of his father's farm. No wonder Northern Ireland had so many gangs of gloomy men and women, standing shoulder to shoulder, nailing themselves to one flag, clinging to one set of allegiances. Daly thought of the queasy greyness of Lough Neagh. He began to feel that its vast stretch of water resembled a void operating at the heart of Northern Ireland, a vacuum into which politically compromised people like Detective Brian Carey could be drawn at any moment.

A knot of tension tightened in his stomach as he got into his car and headed for the border.

CHAPTER FIVE

The stink of burning rubber tyres and diesel fumes hit Daly as he stepped out of his car. He had been unable to find any sign of the police station in Dreesh, driving slowly up and down the main street several times, before eventually getting out and exploring on foot. In spite of the stench, and the coldness of the wind, he was curious to see how Dreesh compared to villages in the North, which were still stuck in the doldrums of the recession and government austerity measures.

He passed a bar called the Railway Bar, but saw no sign of a railway anywhere. Behind the rows of little shops and houses, he caught glimpses of rubble and buildings in various stages of construction. However, there were no signs of workers or cement mixers, or any machinery for that matter, just mounds of grey clay, pillars bristling with rusted iron rods, abandoned pallets of cement blocks, and piles of weed-strewn sand. A vision of abandoned building sites thrusting through the quaint façade of an Irish village.

He passed a roadside hoarding proclaiming luxurious new apartment blocks, but the paper had flayed and peeled away, like a mask from a skull, and the property investors' dreams of bright rooms filled with happy tenants looked to have flown to the moon. He walked on, a familiar tale of ruin unfolding before him. The housing boom had been a magician's hat, a vast fortune lying within it for the citizens of Ireland to grab, or so they had been tricked into believing. Border villages like Dreesh had been transformed overnight into silent building sites, and the financial advisers and estate agents, who had fanned the heat of the housing market, had disappeared like those flies with gaudy wings whose lifespan is measured in hours.

Oddly enough, he noticed that the cars parked along the main street were top-of-the-range BMWs, Volvos and Range Rovers with the latest registration plates. This was curious, given the impoverished look of the place, or maybe it wasn't. Perhaps the vehicles were more a vulgar display of excessive debt rather than wealth. Struggling consumers trying to persuade themselves and their neighbours that they still had control over their destinies, their cars like sleek distorting mirrors offering a vision of success to passers-by. Daly peered through the windows of a low-slung BMW, staring at the seductive cream upholstery within. He had little idea how twenty-first-century money really worked, its hell-bent sprint around the globe, racing back and forth between financiers in London and New York, and he had no desire to enslave himself to the free-market system of debt.

In the centre of the village, an elderly man sat on a small tractor, its engine idling. He seemed to be sleeping.

Nevertheless, when Daly passed him he felt the old man's eyes wander after him. The people he glimpsed in the run-down shops seemed hollow-bodied, shrunken to the point of ruin themselves. Their faces seemed to say that there was no bottom to the economic recession, that there were still depths to be plumbed, worse hardships to be felt and endured.

At the bottom of the village, he came across a fuel depot and junkyard running into disused farm sheds and untended fields, a stretch of wild country leading back to the border. He assumed this must be the source of the pervading fumes. He caught snippets of someone shouting orders, diesel engines blasting, and a dog barking ferociously in the gloomy hinterland.

This was the sharp end of the village, he thought; this was its thrust, its bleak future. Given the depot's proximity to the North, it was probably a front for smuggling activity. He saw a grimy sign, which read 'Premises closed until further notice', with a name, Tom Morgan. The name was familiar to Daly. If smuggling marked the inhabitants of the border as a tribe apart, then Morgan was their sage and chieftain. A former IRA volunteer turned primitive capitalist, he had earned a shady reputation as a shrewd businessman with his wealth tied up in overseas property and offshore accounts.

A heavily built middle-aged man was parading up and down the yard, roaring commands, seemingly oblivious to the tumult around him. Figures in overalls trudged around him, heaving snaking hoses and attaching them to lorry tanks, while other men in tracksuits loaded factory crates of bottles into the back of vans. No sign of recession here, just the swarming hum of a thriving business.

As Daly watched, one of the bloated hoses burst from its socket, spraying volatile-looking fluids across the yard. The lorries braked to a halt, lights spreading across the yard in a sea of red. The middle-aged man grew animated, arms waving in the wind. Daly stepped back. An old woman carrying a shopping bag had appeared beside him. She watched the spectacle in the yard for a moment before turning to the detective.

'Tom Morgan never stops,' she said, smiling. 'He never slows down. Why should he when there's so much money to be made with the border?'

'What is this place?' asked Daly. 'A fuel depot? Some sort of filling station?'

She laughed. 'No, sir. Those places closed long ago. Mr Morgan's business is the only part of Dreesh still working.'

A whiff of diesel, carried by the wind, made Daly's eyes smart. What was he witnessing, with this urgent replenishment of fuel tankers that bore no company markers, their registration numbers covered in mud? Their anonymity was the key.

Before the old woman slipped away, he asked her for directions to the Garda station. She gave a low laugh and walked on. There was something scornful about the way she turned her back on him.

'Stop,' he called after her. 'I need to find the station.'

'It closed to the public a year ago. There's a station in Monaghan, but it might be shut, too.'

Daly mentioned Sergeant McKenna's name. 'I was told he was based here.'

A half-frown crept on to her lips. 'You want to see him in person?'

'Yes, or whoever's in charge.'

'Go back up the street,' she said, pointing past him. 'You'll find the station opposite the post office. Sergeant McKenna lives there now. He looks after the rose bushes and little else.'

Daly heard a set of heavy gears grinding behind him and the blast of a dirty exhaust. A large lorry rumbled past, forcing him against a wall.

'Get along now,' she warned. 'You don't want to hang around this place for too long, sir.' Her eyes signalled that she had worked out who he was from his accent and clothes, a visitor on police business from the North.

CHAPTER SIX

'On quiet afternoons I take on the mantle of chief gardener,' Sergeant Peter McKenna explained to Daly, putting down a pair of secateurs with his gloved hand. 'There's always something to keep me busy. If I didn't I'd be submerged in weeds.'

Daly and the sergeant were standing in the porch of the police station, now closed to the public but still used operationally by McKenna and his Garda colleagues. After his experience walking up and down the village, Daly felt at ease in McKenna's presence. The sound of his soft accent transported him to his childhood summers, when his father would drive him and his mother over the border to escape the bombing campaign of the IRA and the marching season.

He had found the station not far from where he'd parked his car: a two-storey house overgrown with creeping plants and possessing two clandestine-looking windows on the ground floor, which on closer inspection turned out to be covered in wire mesh. As security measures went it was a far cry from the reinforced steel fencing topped with barbed wire and the watchtowers that surrounded police stations in the North, but then this was the Republic of Ireland, and the only force that threatened to lay siege to the building was nature itself in the form of the clematis and climbing roses.

The sergeant had greeted Daly warmly, shaking his hand and smiling, as though it was wonderful to meet a detective from the Police Service of Northern Ireland, even if the circumstances of their encounter were less than pleasant. The station was not what Daly had been expecting at all, hunkered down in a well-tended garden, concealing any indication of its true function in the village.

Daly had apologized for the interruption, but the sergeant thanked him for making the effort, even if it was only a short trip across the border, and gave him a brief tour of the garden. Spring was in full swing amid the flowering bulbs and well-pruned rose bushes. Daly could not help smiling, feeling like an explorer who had toiled through sleeplessness and worry to catch sight of the luxuriant little island he had always dreamed existed.

The soothing sound of water trickling and birds whistling filled the air. A nearby spring sent a little stream gurgling along the brick paths, splashing Daly's shoes. Somehow, McKenna seemed more Daly's countryman than his Protestant colleagues in the Police Service of Northern Ireland. Daly belonged to the same tribe as McKenna and Carey, Catholic police officers, who had lived and worked during the Troubles, but they had escaped to this slower backwater. He felt he knew what McKenna was yearning for, living and working in this secretive-looking station festooned with roses, and the connection had nothing to do with religion or the community they had been born into. The sergeant was trying to re-create a little corner of peace and contentment, just as Daly had done in his childhood home on the other side of the border. It seemed a fitting reward for a police officer's life of effort amid the murky trail of criminals and their brutal acts, and he could sense McKenna's contentment, living out the last years of his career in the station. As he followed him into the building, he could not help wondering, with a stab of envy, if the sergeant had ever felt disillusioned or betrayed, condemned by his colleagues, or sidelined by powerful political forces.

Inside the station, McKenna removed his gardening gloves and in so doing seemed to emerge from the spell cast by the garden. He shot Daly a slightly apprehensive look. Suddenly Daly felt sorry to be intruding upon this oasis of calm with news of a dead colleague.

'Would you like a drink? Tea or coffee, or something stronger?'

Daly asked for tea.

'I'm not a big drinker myself, but in the circumstances I think I'll take a whiskey. Not a large one, just a drop.' While waiting for the kettle to boil, McKenna brought a bottle and glasses in from the kitchen and poured himself a generous measure.

Daly explained how Carey's body had been discovered on the shore of Lough Neagh along with a bag containing clothing and a flight ticket to Spain. 'It appears your colleague drowned himself at a well-known suicide spot.'

'It's a terrible handling,' replied McKenna. His colleague's death had clearly distressed him. He held his glass tightly in an effort to conceal his shaking right hand. 'I just can't imagine it. Are you completely certain?'

'I wouldn't be here if we had any doubts about the body's identity.'

'No, I'm talking about his committing suicide. He wasn't the type.' McKenna explained that Carey had been looking forward to a well-earned holiday in Spain.

Daly wondered how much of his suspicions to share. 'The pathologist hasn't ruled out the possibility that he might have been murdered,' he said.

Briefly, a wild restlessness took hold of McKenna's eyes, as though Daly had turned into the enemy, a stranger bringing a troubling darkness from over the border. A murdered detective might be old hat for a police detective from the North, but it was still something relatively uncommon in the South.

'Murder?' said McKenna. 'Why would anyone do that to Brian?'

'Did he have any enemies?'

'It's impossible for a police detective not to have enemies.'

Daly nodded. 'How had he been behaving lately? Was there anything unusual about him or his work? Was he investigating anyone dangerous, someone with secrets to hide?'

McKenna took a sip of whiskey. 'Things weren't as they should have been.'

'What do you mean?'

'He was troubled by a case he was working on. A bank robbery in Monaghan town.' McKenna explained how Carey had left to interview the main suspect the day before he had gone on annual leave. Later, the sergeant had found him in

53

his car, parked up at the river alongside the border, sitting at the wheel in some sort of a trance.

'It made me uneasy,' said McKenna, 'seeing him like that, just staring ahead, not moving in any way, looking across the river as though dead to the world. I tapped his window but he didn't see me. He just stared at the water. When he finally noticed me, he gripped the steering wheel and looked frightened. I could have been a machete-wielding maniac for the look he gave me, but then he collected himself. He rolled down the window and asked where I'd come from. I told him the station, but he said that was not what he meant. He mumbled some other things, but they didn't make sense.'

'Who was he meant to interview?'

'A local smuggler. Not one of your petty criminals, I hasten to add.'

Daly raised an eyebrow. Smuggling gangs were no longer the threat they were during the Troubles, when they were closely allied to the IRA. Nevertheless, their influence still counted for something, especially along the border. 'Has this smuggler been known to intimidate officers?' he asked.

'You're not far from the truth. When suspicion for the robbery fell on this individual, his team of solicitors did everything in their power to hamper the investigation, even discredit and undermine Carey.'

'In other words, Carey's death could not have been better timed or more convenient for this suspect.'

McKenna frowned. 'Except that the investigation was closed the day Carey left to go on holiday. The smuggler was in the clear.'

'Why was the case closed?'

'You'll have to go closer to home for that answer, Inspector. It was your lot, not ours, who shut it down. The Police Service of Northern Ireland informed Carey that the individual was not and would never be a suspect in the robbery.'

'What was the reason for dropping the charges?'

'They said they'd had a breakthrough, arrested a gang in Belfast. According to the investigating detective, the gang confessed to the Monaghan robbery.'

'Do you have a copy of Carey's case notes?'

'No. The PSNI requested that the files be handed over to the prosecution service in the North.'

'What about an electronic copy?'

For a moment, McKenna hesitated. Theoretically, the computer files of the Gardai were out of bounds to a detective from Northern Ireland, unless negotiated under higher powers, and Daly's request seemed to unsettle him. They weren't operating at that level of inter-jurisdiction contact, at least not yet.

'I don't think I can give you permission to view them.' McKenna's voice stiffened slightly.

'Then call someone who can. Tell them an inspector from Northern Ireland investigating a possible murder needs to see them.'

McKenna thought about Daly's order and then forced a smile. 'To be honest, Inspector, I've never mastered the ins and outs of cross-border policing. So many political initiatives come and go. But I'm sure I can find the files on the computer system and let you have a look at them, under my supervision, of course. The only thing is it might take a bit of time.'

'I'm willing to wait.'

The sergeant slipped out of the room and Daly was left to his own devices. His eyes scanned the photographs and certificates adorning the wall, his gaze resting on one particular picture. Two police officers, one wearing a blue Garda uniform, the other a dark green Royal Ulster Constabulary uniform, were standing with an old man between them. Oddly, the police officers wore the same dark well-groomed moustache, and their hair was combed the same way. In fact, judging by their faces and general appearances, they both looked to be younger versions of Sergeant McKenna. Daly got up from his seat and examined the picture closely. He concluded that the young man in the Garda uniform was McKenna while the other one must have been an older brother, and the man in the middle their father. Daly was struck by the submissive, mournful expression on the old man's face.

McKenna returned, more sombre than before. There was an embarrassed catch to his voice. 'I've managed to find the files on the computer, but even I don't have the authority to open them. They've been classed as politically sensitive.'

If this had happened in the North, Daly would have been furious. However, he decided to let his anger pass. 'This investigation could become a murder inquiry. I need to know what Carey was working on.'

'Like I said, I don't have the authority to read the file.'

'Then tell me what you believe is in the file.' Daly was eager not to let any silences develop in their conversation, and he had seen the look of withdrawal in McKenna's eyes. 'All I want are your thoughts on what was going on.'

'I can't say for sure what he was doing. I'd rather give you a straight answer, but in this instance I can't. I thought

I knew him well, but perhaps I didn't. Carey was very secretive about his investigations. He kept himself to himself.'

'What about the names of the PSNI officers who requested the file?'

McKenna hesitated, a pained look on his face. Their conversation had felt like a strange hunt for the truth into tortuous crannies. Every time a promising lead emerged, an obstacle appeared, one bureaucratic detour after another to distract him from the fundamental facts. Daly had been slow to realize that McKenna's charming disengagement might have a practical purpose, that he represented a foreign police force with a reputation to protect.

Daly tried again. 'Did these officers ever say who they were, or where they were based?'

'There was one detective from the North whom Carey was urgently trying to contact before he disappeared. His name was Robert Hunter. From Special Branch, I think.'

At last a name, something to work on. 'Did Carey have much contact with Hunter?'

'Quite a lot actually. They were always working on cases.'

This surprised Daly. He was under the impression that police on either side of the border worked separately with only the occasional meeting to share information.

'Hunter seemed to be a big fan of Carey. They both got on well together. They went on fishing trips with other officers from the North. Called themselves the Green and Blue Fishing Club on account of their uniforms.'

Daly would have to track down Robert Hunter and the other members of the club. He needed to find out what role Carey's investigation played in his death, and right now

Hunter seemed the person best placed to help him. 'I'd be interested to hear if you remember anything else.'

McKenna nodded. 'I'll let you know as soon as security clearance comes through on the computer files.'

On his way out, Daly pointed to the photograph on the wall. 'I take it that's you in the blue uniform.'

'That picture's nearly forty years old,' replied McKenna. 'The other officer is my brother, Jack.'

'He's the very image of you.'

'We were the complete reverse of each other, Inspector. I joined the Gardai while Jack took the unusual step of signing up with the Royal Ulster Constabulary.' He looked meaningfully at Daly. 'We grew up in a Republican housing estate in Derry. Jack's career choice wasn't popular with our IRA neighbours.'

'What did your father think?'

'I'm sure he was full of conflicted feelings, but he never tried to persuade or argue with us. No one in our family had ever joined the police force before. During the Troubles, neither of us was safe visiting them in Derry. My parents, God rest their souls, carried their worries to the grave. They're dead a long time now.'

Daly stared at the picture again. Two sons, one dressed in green, the other in blue, standing on opposite sides of history with their father in the middle, wearing an expression that resembled grief or sadness, the face of a man reluctant to influence or show the slightest degree of approval towards either son or their choice of uniform.

'That was the only time we ever wore our uniforms at home,' said McKenna. 'Our police badges made us exiles.'

For a second his gaze left the photograph and travelled back in time, navigating up the dark river of politics and bitter history to the small room in a Derry terrace house where he had posed as young police officer with his grave-faced father. His eyes became present again, acknowledging to Daly the perplexity of the past. He smiled again. 'It was a topsy-turvy household.'

'Wasn't the whole country topsy-turvy?' replied Daly.

McKenna escorted him through the garden and stopped at the gate. They both stood staring at the village, which was empty and dreary-looking in the evening light.

'Poverty is back,' said McKenna. 'You can feel its claws in the air walking down the street. Here I am about to retire, and the village looks poorer than when I first arrived.'

Daly nodded. The village's new economic order was grimly apparent.

'It's all gone,' said the sergeant.

'What has?'

'The money. We never thought emigration would return. Working men having to leave their families and go abroad to find work. And they're the lucky ones. The village is full of men willing to go to any lengths to pay off their mortgage or put food in the fridge, jobless men constantly on the lookout for someone to borrow money from.'

Daly thought of Morgan's yard, the figures swarming around the tankers, the steady roar of the engines and the black voice shouting commands. 'Surely there must be some work, some building going on?'

'Building? You've seen the sites. The village is a wasteland. As soon as the big developers fell into debt, everyone followed.

A chain of bankruptcies that pulled everyone down the drain. The only work now is digging graves for the suicides.' He hesitated and glanced at Daly.

'And smuggling?' asked Daly.

McKenna ignored the question and cleared his throat. 'The banks have turned us down, frozen us out. Nothing will be built here for years. The building sites are a no-man's land.'

And no opportunity to make the same mistakes for at least another generation, thought Daly. The residents of Dreesh faced years of abstinence and gloomy reflection before the next property boom got started.

'I'm camping on a building site myself,' said Daly. 'Knocking down an old house. I never thought it would take so long.'

'Looking to buy somewhere else?'

'I'm not in the market,' replied Daly quickly. 'Never was.'

Dreesh's property market was irrelevant to his visit, unless Carey was betrayed and killed over a property deal turned sour. What if the clue to his death lay hidden within the village itself? Daly noticed how the sight of the main street made the sergeant uneasy. He seemed keen to return to the comforts of his garden and home.

Before they parted company, Daly asked one more question. 'This smuggler Carey was investigating, I take it his name was Tom Morgan.'

The sergeant's look of apprehension returned, and he nodded quietly. He seemed not only scared but also rueful.

They made their goodbyes and Daly left deep in thought. The police station looked to have changed into a hollow grey shell pinned down by overgrown creepers, and McKenna's easy-going hospitality had dissolved away, the station he now guarded no longer full of good cheer. What had Daly seen there earlier? A peaceful refuge or a hiding hole? He had conjured up his own enchantment, endowing the building with the innocent charm that had radiated through his childhood summers escaping the marching and bombing of the Troubles, the garden full of flowers and trickling water strengthening the fantasy.

The gathering shadows reminded him that he was a detective moving through darkness, thinking in darkness. He had thought that by driving over the border, he might leave behind everything that was dark and decrepit, but he had been wrong. It was the same terrain, extending across the divide, haunted by the same ugly monotony of crime, the same perpetrators at large, pursued by police officers who were similar in every way but the colour of their uniforms.

Daly drove down the main street, thinking of Carey's final flight, the aeroplane ticket he had bought, the loose threads of his mysterious investigation dangling behind him. He felt the invisible pull of Carey's death, dragging him back over the border to Lough Neagh. He glanced in the rear-view mirror and saw McKenna's station fade into a silhouette and then disappear. He crossed the bridge, and glanced at the dark water toiling beneath, glimpsing in its depths the exhausted eyes of Carey staring back at him, urging him not to let cover-up and silence do their work, and consign his memory to oblivion.

CHAPTER SEVEN

Aughnacloy police station was only ten miles from Dreesh, but Daly felt as though he'd crossed an ocean when he drove through its steel reinforced gates. He stared at the watchtower, dripping with rain, the deeply recessed windows, and the slabs of fortified concrete bearing down upon him out of the darkness like floating chunks of the troubled past. Security lighting arced through the gulf that separated each ring of security fencing. Daly hurried under its glare, the echo of his feet alarming him, rattling back from the empty walls of steel. At the security hut, he stood up on his toes and tried to peer through the thick glass, but all he saw was a gloomy frogspawn grey. He yelled at the vacant darkness, and eventually a buzzer sounded. Slowly the steel entrance door, its rivets bleeding rust, opened for him, and a pack of dogs began yelping from deep within the station.

A shadow resolved itself into the shape of a young police officer in uniform, who introduced himself as Constable Martin Wilson.

'I didn't realize you were here already,' he said. Daly had phoned ahead after leaving Dreesh, outlining the assistance he needed in tracking down Detective Robert Hunter.

Wilson mumbled something about cutbacks and the lack of staff. It was only when they were inside the station that Daly realized Wilson was the only officer on duty. The air felt dank and slightly refrigerated.

'You wanted a printout of any communications the station has had with Detective Brian Carey and a Robert Hunter?'

'Yes,' replied Daly.

'You're too late.'

The constable was stiff and correct with him. He seemed infected with the station's inflated security and imposing size. Even his voice set Daly's teeth on edge. This wasn't his homeland at all, thought Daly. His return to the North and its policing made him feel painfully exiled.

'What do you mean, too late?' asked Daly. Through a side door, he saw a den of police uniforms and protective gear, neatly pressed jackets and shirts with shining buttons and epaulettes, flak jackets hanging empty and riot gear piled together: a museum of shards and empty shells from the past.

'Special Branch was here this afternoon,' explained Wilson. 'They wanted to see all our files relating to PSNI detectives liaising with their Garda counterparts, and specifically Brian Carey.'

'And what did you show them?'

'Nothing.' The duty constable appeared annoyed, as though he'd been dogged by these questions long enough. 'Any communication with our counterparts in the South is done over the phone or in person. Mostly it's unofficial, otherwise we'd have to get written permission for every meeting and there'd be a mountain of paperwork.'

'Did they ask what type of cases you collaborated on?'

'Yes.'

The heating was off and their footsteps echoed in the dank air. The interior of the station was inhabited by a different gloom to that of its outside, realized Daly, the dead air of policing cuts and austerity measures, giving the empty offices and corridors the proper stillness of a mausoleum. Not even a rat would find comfort here.

'They also asked about this Detective Robert Hunter,' said Wilson. 'I told them we didn't have a detective of that name based here, but they seemed to know that already. They didn't seem to be too concerned about his whereabouts.'

'How did the Special Branch officers behave?'

'They behaved as they always do. They came in and took over the place, asking questions, setting ultimatums. They were patronizing and in a hurry. I didn't get time to do anything else all afternoon but run after them. They acted as though they were the specialists and the rest of us amateurs.' His eyes fixed narrowly on Daly. 'Where did you say you were based?'

'Armagh,' said Daly. 'What did they find?'

'Like I said, nothing at all.'

They reached a metal-barred door, flanked by a grimy lifeless radiator. Wilson heaved the bar with his shoulder and led Daly into a snug office warmed by an electric heater. They sat down and Daly considered the constable carefully, wondering if there was another way of coaxing information from him, one beyond the heavy-handed urgency of Special Branch.

'They even made me sign a form to say that I had never heard of Hunter.'

Why would they have done that? wondered Daly. To gain credit back at headquarters for their thorough approach? The more he thought about it, the greater his desire to track down Hunter.

'You've never met this Detective Hunter?' asked Daly.

'Never.'

'What about Carey, ever had any dealings with him?'

A rictus of a smile appeared on Wilson's lips. 'Funny you should ask me that. I was with him about two weeks ago.'

'How did he seem?'

'Oh, he was very excited. And not at all reticent. In fact, he shouted the place down. Worse luck for me as I had to spend the night with him.'

'How?'

'I was the officer who arrested him. For drink-driving. I pulled him over at the traffic lights in the village. The breathalyser showed a reading of 122 mcg, if I remember correctly. Three times the legal limit.'

'What did he say?'

'He ranted on about an important investigation he was working on with Detective Hunter. One that involved organized criminals. It was going to make his career, he said. He'd found the golden key that was going to unlock all the criminal enterprises along the border.'

'Did you ask him for more details? The names of the criminals, what they were up to?'

Wilson shrugged. 'He just kept asking to speak to Detective Hunter.'

'But did you press him for more information?'

'It all sounded like bullshit to me. A drunk detective away from his home turf and in deep trouble. What he was claiming had no bearing on his drink-driving charge.'

Daly saw something take shape in Wilson's features, his mind working, thinking how much he could trust Daly with the truth.

'To be honest, I wasn't sure if I wanted to hear any more,' said Wilson, frowning darkly.

'How come?' asked Daly. The vague odour of sweated confession that always haunted the air of police stations grew sharp. When Wilson did not reply, Daly spoke. 'If a detective, drunk or not, told me he was close to netting a criminal gang I'd want to know more. Carey might have belonged to a different police jurisdiction but you share the same territory. You're bound to have been interested in who he was talking about.'

'Absolutely. But like I said, I didn't think he was telling the truth.'

'But if you wanted the truth, you should have kept asking questions. You're a police officer. You should have asked the right questions to get the truth out of him. You should have separated the facts from fantasy.'

Wilson lowered his voice. 'What if the true story cannot be told?'

Daly stared at the constable. He was reminded that Wilson operated on his own from this comfortless station, a lonely outcast in a domain of smugglers and cross-border criminal gangs, the dangerous margins of a heavily reduced police force striving to maintain an uneasy truce between former paramilitaries. A badly handled investigation might easily inflame old tensions.

'Carey's behaviour got very strange during the night,' said Wilson. 'He kept demanding to speak to Detective Hunter, and asking to be placed in protective custody.'

'Did he explain why he needed protective custody?'

'No, like I said, he just kept asking for Hunter. He said they had a special arrangement in place. That Hunter wouldn't forget their deal. To shut him up, I rang around but no one had heard of Hunter, and he had certainly never worked out of this station. Apart from the duty officer and traffic patrol, there's just the district's dog-handling team based here now. I even checked with Special Branch but they had no record of Hunter either.'

'Did you tell him there was no trace of his detective friend?'

'Yes.'

'How did he react to that?'

'He looked astonished, frightened, even. As though he'd seen a ghost.' Wilson's tone grew sombre. 'He accused me of being in the pay of the IRA. They had lawyers and politicians in their control, and police officers, too, he said. He seemed rattled. He wasn't as boisterous after that.'

'Did it occur to you to take his request seriously? That his life might be in danger, in spite of his intoxicated state.'

Wilson regarded Daly with evident unease. 'No. Why should I take him seriously, a noxious drunkard who kept claiming he knew a detective no one had heard of?' His unease turned into a glare of defiance.

Daly sighed. 'What about the drink-driving charge?'

'I thought something was up when Special Branch arrived

first thing the next morning. They said they had something urgent to discuss with Carey. Half an hour later, I was instructed to release him without charge.'

Why had Special Branch not mentioned the details of their intervention to him? thought Daly. Surely Carey's drunken claims might have had a bearing on his death? Daly considered the Garda detective's predicament, locked in a police cell with a serious charge hanging over him, hoping that an arrangement with another police detective hatched in the fathomless darkness of border country might absolve him. Carey had pleaded with the unsympathetic Wilson, a stern-faced officer who had not seemed to understand at all, who had never heard of Hunter, which had cast the terms of Carey's special arrangement in doubt, undermining the basis of his rescue, and what else?

It all formed a warning signal in Daly's mind. He wished he had been in Aughnacloy police station the night of Carey's arrest to respond to the signal. That would have been the moment, with Carey garrulous and desperate, to nail the truth, before Special Branch descended in the morning with their cloak of silence. What events had been set in train by Carey's arrest? What had been found out that could not be undone, what had changed irrevocably, sweeping Carey away in its dangerous currents?

'I've one more favour to ask of you,' said Daly. 'I want you to dig out the notes on Carey's arrest and all the paperwork covering his release. If I can't track down Hunter, then I can try searching for the Special Branch officers who let Carey go.'

'If you're so interested why don't you ask Special Branch yourself?'

'I will ask them, you can be sure of that.'

CHAPTER EIGHT

The sound of a car abruptly pulling to a halt disturbed Daly in his sleep. He opened his eyes and stared at the low ceiling in confusion. It had been so long since he had a proper night's sleep. The rosy glow emanating from the curtains told him it was morning, but where was he and what day of the week was it? The bed of tossed blankets reminded him of the one he had slept in as a child, but what age was he now? He could be any age between nine and mid-forties. He waited for the dawn light to reorder his thoughts, restore him to his hectic timetable. Still his bedroom did not feel right. He was not in his cottage, but he could hear, above the idling of the car engine, the familiar babbling cries of the lough-shore birds.

A car door slammed shut and a set of footsteps, strained-sounding, with the click-clack of a woman's heels slightly offbeat, drew near and stopped. He shifted in his bed and the entire room moved, and for an instant he was back in a tree hut from his childhood, imagining that the person approaching him was his mother, come to call him in for breakfast. His career as a police officer was many blessed years away and the overbearing pressures of his career had faded away completely.

But it didn't feel right. Something was wrong. He hadn't managed to cross the gulf of the past at all. He pulled back his curtains and revealed the depths of a hawthorn hedge bubbling with creamy-white blossoms. It was less a window and more a porthole, filled with the dew-drenched light of a lough-shore dawn. The head of a cow trespassed rudely into his field of vision and began straining its tongue to reach the new buds. He wasn't in a treehouse, or any sort of a house. He was in a caravan at the edge of his father's fields.

'So this is where you're living now,' said his visitor when he opened the caravan door.

It was Jacqueline Pryce, the young journalist who had helped him track down the identities of the men involved in his mother's murder. He had no idea what she was doing here this morning. Nevertheless, he invited her into the caravan. He had been intrigued by her, and still was. At times, he had even enjoyed her constant inquisitiveness and hunger for a news story that bordered on bad manners.

'I don't get many unexpected guests these days,' he said. She had aged a little since he had last seen her. Her brow was furrowed and her mouth set in an unhappy frown. For a second, he glimpsed in her eyes tiredness and anxiety, an omen of imminent ruin and disaster. She might be going through a rough patch in her personal or professional life, or perhaps she had just had a late night.

'I'm not surprised,' she said. 'I came early because every time I called you were at work.'

'How long have you been calling?'

'Every day this past week. There was never any sign of you. Just your demented black hen and those builders.'

Daly put on the kettle and fumbled for some cups and teabags. 'Milk and sugar?'

She nodded. 'I never thought you'd make it out of the cottage. I always imagined the walls falling around you some day.' There was little softness or tact in her voice.

Daly waited for the kettle to boil. 'The roof started falling in, so I had to call in the builders and move out.'

When the water was ready, he filled the teapot. 'I like it here; the caravan suits me better than a rented house. Plus I get to keep an eye on the cottage.' He glanced at the view of the old place from the window over the sink. Cables of electrical wiring and copper piping protruded from the empty windows. 'It's a little like watching over a sick relative in hospital.'

'But why the for-sale signs? Why give up on it now?'

'The place felt strange to me,' said Daly. 'Seeing all its insides exposed and with the builders tramping in and out. It just didn't feel like home any more.'

'Got a buyer?'

'Not yet.' He smiled. 'Are you interested?'

It was her chance to humour him, but she replied, 'God, no. Why would I want to live in a place like that?' She looked at him with a trace of pity. A detective trapped in the past. He could read it in her eyes. He must resemble an eccentric relic of the world her generation had left behind. He and the black hen were the only unchanged fixtures left on the farm, if you discounted the old clay chimney pot, which had disappeared from the roof and popped up again at his caravan doorstep in the form of a container full of herbs. She glanced at the rickety table, the disarray of food tins and dirty dishes, the wet clothing hung over the gas stove. So confined was the little kitchen that when Daly reached towards her with the cup of tea, his arm brushed her shoulder. Swiftly, he pulled back.

'Ignore the mess,' he said. 'And you might find that sipping tea next to a budding hawthorn hedge is the closest thing possible to domestic bliss.'

However, this was not what she had come for, drinking tea with a middle-aged detective trying to ward off his personal demons in a caravan going nowhere.

She tasted the tea and put the cup down as though it was not to her liking. 'You're going to need a refuge like this,' she said flatly.

'Why?'

'I've got bad news.'

'Oh.' Disappointment slackened his jaw.

'About your former commander Donaldson and us. Perhaps someone in Special Branch has told you?'

'Told me what?' Daly's mind was a blank. What possible news could there be about Donaldson? The man had drowned years ago.

'You haven't heard what they're saying about us.'

'What are you talking about?'

'You definitely haven't heard?' Her voice softened at his ignorance. 'The story has been going round the courthouse all week. The weekend newspapers are planning to do a special on it.'

He was beginning to understand her defiant trespass of the cottage, her urgent determination to see him.

'Well, you'd better hear it from me now,' she said. 'Special Branch found a suicide note left behind by Donaldson. He accused the two of us of hounding him to his death, of destroying his reputation and his dignity. From their perspective, it's perfect ammunition.'

'Christ,' said Daly. He stood up quickly and banged his head against the kitchen cabinet. He had forgotten the dimensions of the caravan, so distracted was he by Pryce's news. He tried not to think of Donaldson's final allegations as a threat, rather to view them with equanimity.

'Have you seen the note?' he asked.

'Yes, copies were distributed to certain members of the press.'

'By whom? Who authorized it?'

'A contact in the *Irish News* told me it was authorized by Inspector Fealty in Special Branch.'

'Have you checked with Fealty?'

'Yes. He denied any knowledge of it.'

'Do you believe him?'

'I don't know who to believe any more. All I know is that journalists have contacted two of Donaldson's relatives. They know of the note's existence and its contents, and now they're furious. They're demanding a public inquiry once the inquest is concluded. They want their brother's allegations confirmed or refuted.'

Daly wondered should he feel guilty? Was it proper to feel blame over the death of a humiliated man who had taken his final revenge in this unexpected manner? Looking into his heart, all Daly detected was a gloomy sadness. His conscience felt at ease, his battle with Donaldson was finished, but why was his tranquillity now tinged with a feeling of incipient doom? He imagined the former RUC commander's final excursion in his boat, his tall figure leaning over the water, carrying his doomed reputation like a flag at half-mast, disaster inevitable.

'What exactly did he accuse me of?' he asked.

'The accusations were against the two of us. We're in this together, Celcius.'

For a moment, he regarded her suspiciously. What part did she play in this game? Was she in league with forces in Special Branch? She was a determined journalist, but also driven in her career. Looking at her closely, she appeared to have changed. She seemed more menacing, a darker person altogether.

'Are you part of this?' he asked.

'Part of what?'

'This conspiracy against me.'

'No, Celcius. How could you think that? Donaldson has accused me of hounding him to his death, too. I'm a freelance journalist. I'll never get another assignment if this goes the wrong way. You have to trust me, Celcius. We're on the same side.'

Daly nodded. 'I'm sorry. I don't know what to think right now. How could this note exist without my knowledge?'

'From what I heard, Special Branch had been hoping to keep it under wraps.'

'Probably so they could smear me at a time of their own choosing. What did it say exactly?'

'Donaldson made a long list of personal offences and insults received from you over the years. He expressed incomprehension as to why you targeted him for character assassination. Among other things, he said you had attacked him repeatedly and he could no longer bear to fight any more.'

'But these are all lies. Donaldson was out of his mind, deranged. Did he mention his wife's role in my mother's murder?'

'No, but you never went to the press, or allowed me to write your story. Now Donaldson has written the only script of what happened.'

'What else did the note say about me?'

'He addressed you personally. He asked were you proud of your conduct. He wanted you to examine your conscience in the light of responsibility to a colleague who had done his best during very difficult circumstances, who had placed the defence of democracy and the rule of law above personal interest. Those were some of the phrases he used.'

'But he's accusing me of undermining his reputation as an end to itself. As though I behaved maliciously and irresponsibly when all along I was trying to solve my mother's murder, nothing else.' Unable to hold back, Daly's voice began to rise. 'If anyone is the persecutor in this, it's Donaldson, not me. And like all persecutors, he was unable to face up to the consequences of his own actions.'

'The newspapers are going to publish the contents of the note.'

He knew he should control his tongue but anger made him reckless in his condemnation. 'Oh for God's sake, don't they know the type of police chief Donaldson was? A bigoted old fool, clinging to the crest of the RUC. He knew he was politically finished and broken, and this suicide was his final bluff, his attempt at regaining the moral high ground. He's dead and buried, and should be forgotten, not wheeled out by the press like a pathetic old ghost.'

What had he done, destroyed Donaldson's dignity? A feeling of dread, not unlike guilt, uncoiled from his heart and swelled in his chest. He had confronted his superior, a police chief impervious to criticism, with the dark deeds of the past. He had taken on a man full of fight, of polished outward appearance, who moved in important political circles and bristled with indignation at Daly's investigation into the murder triangle of the 1970s, and, having wreaked his vengeance, having won the battle and exposed the truth, he had transformed Donaldson into a hollow-eyed shadow of himself, a clumsy old man unable to manage the repercussions of his bad leadership. In a moment of painful lucidity, terrified at the collapse of his reputation, the shine of his professional charm dimming, Donaldson had applied the final blow himself, writing this bitter note and taking his own life. In that masochistic act, he had transformed himself into a martyr and made Daly the persecutor, not Donaldson and his cronies. *I am the persecutor; I am the persecutor.* The publication of the note would ensure this terrible new truth would be repeated over and over again. It alarmed him to think that right now there were journalists primed with the scandal of the note, discussing his behaviour with people he did not know, formulating the story for their readers, measuring him up for the fall.

He lifted his eyes and saw that her demeanour had changed. She had discharged some of her distress, and now a look of enviable serenity was taking hold, her eyes watching him closely. He lowered his eyes, feeling scrutinized, hemmed in by her interest. He released his fists with a sigh. He hadn't noticed he was clenching them so tightly, as if at any moment he might need to defend himself. A thought crossed his mind. The cranky old fisherman at the lough shore, whose grey face had blazed with anger when he recognized Daly, who had made him play blind man's buff with the past: was this the terrible crime he had been talking about?

'Did Donaldson have a brother?' he asked.

'Yes. And he knows about the note. From what I hear, he couldn't be more different from Donaldson. Hasn't the slightest interest in anything but his old fishing boat, and one or two nastier habits. He has links to some Loyalist paramilitaries based in Portadown.'

Daly took a large gulp of tea to hide his dismay.

Pryce was watching him closely. 'I don't expect you'll be hearing much from him. Or his sister. They're conducting everything through their solicitor.'

'How do you know about his friends in Portadown?'

'I'm a journalist. I have a network of contacts. I'll let you know if they hear anything else. Think of them as your contacts, too.'

'I might need their help. I think I met the brother yesterday morning. He seemed to know a lot about me, more than he was willing to tell. He said he would be seeing me soon.'

'Then you'll have to tell your story. Every single episode of your hunt to find your mother's killers.' Her gaze flickered across his face, as though she were systematically reading every thought and emotion expressed in his features, alert to every single drop of his anguish and self-doubt. 'It's your duty to set the record straight.'

'Somehow, I don't think his brother will be interested in that dark tale.'

'I don't mean Donaldson's relatives.'

'Who then?'

She leaned forward, her eyes gleaming, her knees almost touching his. 'I mean the public. The people who read the news. I could arrange for a set of interviews in all the main newspapers. Donaldson's inquest and suicide note will be widely reported. Editors will be hungry for follow-up leads.'

Amid the physical distraction of her closeness and the attention of her green eyes, Daly began to harbour suspicions about her visit again. She stared at him with an absorbed look, eyes that saw something more than a troubled detective. She was not reading his face any more, he realized. She was reading fragments of his story, constructing them into the narrative that had obsessed her ever since they had first met.

'You have to tell them, Celcius. Just tell them the truth. That's all you have to do.'

Daly grew reticent. He rose and put away the cups. Anything to obtain a measure of detachment from this impetuous journalist. He gazed at her from the sink. His silent answer reached her, and her eyes dulled with disappointment.

He explained to her that he wanted to protect his freedom, specifically his freedom from the past. It was why he had moved out of the cottage and organized its renovation in the first place. He no longer wanted to be subjected to its painful memories: his father's tactful silence, his mother's murder, and their abandoned dreams. He wanted to be freer than he had ever felt before, and he had entrusted those dreams to this caravan sunk deep in an unruly field, an abode with wheels rather than foundations, no roots to clutch at earth and stones.

'I got you into a bad mess,' said Pryce. 'This will make things difficult at work.'

'Not to worry. I'm used to feeling ostracized.' He thought to himself that perhaps deep down he enjoyed stirring suspicion. He had thrived on it as a form of self-imposed loneliness, pointing an accusing finger at his superiors, rather than playing the political game of protecting the force's reputation and advancing his career. But now he was the one entering the spotlight of blame. If the public inquiry went ahead, the note would be recited in court, brandished in the press, displayed constantly on the internet, its accusations carried everywhere. It would always be a stain on his reputation; not the lifetime stink of betrayal and cover-up that marked the careers of other police officers, but an indelible mark, none the less.

He said nothing, feeling the darkness of the lough all around him, stretching to every point on the horizon, and Donaldson standing in his pitching boat at its centre, about to topple into the great deep. His newfound freedom from the past was priceless, but it had been tricked away from him. Donaldson's note had done the damage. Now Pryce had brought trouble to his door, and he would have to pay again and again with the sweat of his brow.

After a moment of silence, Pryce changed the subject. 'There's another story doing the rounds among journalists. About the Green and Blue Fishing Club. It was a secret association of police officers from the North and South. Ever hear of it?'

'No.'

'Two detectives, a Brian Carey and a Robert Hunter, were its principal members. You don't have any way of contacting them, do you?' A half-hopeful, half-shameful gleam had taken hold in her eyes.

'Why do you want to know?' He was suddenly on his guard. Did she really think he could be persuaded into releasing confidential information so easily?

'I'm doing a news story on the club. I've some questions that need answered.'

'Questions for Carey?'

She flashed him her strange, impertinent smile. 'Carey can't answer any questions. His body was found yesterday morning. You're the investigating detective; you should know that.'

'I'm glad you've finally revealed why you came here.'

'Come on, Celcius. I just need to speak to Detective Hunter. No one will give me his number. Just one little interview.'

'Do you expect me to just hand it over to you?'

'Yes... please.'

'I can't on any account.'

'OK, what about a brief comment from you about where the investigation is going?'

'That would be highly irresponsible of me. You'll have to go through the press office.'

'I've tried. They're stonewalling me. I need a comment from somebody close to the investigation to make the story stand.'

He stared through the window above the sink, watching the builders arrive in their vans at the cottage. He thought of the trouble ahead, the certain trouble to be stirred up in the media. Pryce was honest, but scheming, a journalist with a quota of stories to write every day, always toiling away at a lead, trying to disentangle the web of truth and lies that made up his country's painful history. But the more he thought about it, the more he grew convinced that her brand of journalism was an unfit medium for telling the truth about Northern Ireland. How many revelations had reporters like her pressed into the mould of an attention-grabbling headline? How many more could their readers take before anger and surprise dissolved into indifference and an aversion for the truth? He shivered inwardly at the thought of what her colleagues would make of Donaldson's suicide note: the emotive headlines, the accusing first paragraphs, the glossed-over background. Pryce's request for Detective Hunter's number reminded him that writing was her vital element, her primary focus, and that she was rushing back to a world of ruthless editors and hungry readers, a roiling pit from which he, as Donaldson's persecutor, could not escape.

'Come on, Celcius,' pleaded Pryce. 'Don't be angry with me. This is a big story. A detective from the South found dead in the heart of Ulster. From what I hear, he was investigating corruption within the police.'

'Your contacts are better than mine. That's the first I've heard of corruption.'

'This is going to hit the front pages soon.'

'And naturally you want it before anyone else.'

'Someone's going to get their byline on it. Why shouldn't it be me?'

'Not with my help,' he said, and opened the caravan door. He escorted her outside. The horizon had brightened, but on the lough the darkness of the waves still rolled in thickly. The wind moved, testing the hawthorn hedge, releasing the scent of blossom. Birdsong dipped and rose. Glimpsed through the hedgerow, which was fluttering with life, the lough seemed more an augury of trouble than real, the contrast between its mass of gloomy water and the brightly lit fields was so strong. Then a mechanical drill opened up the morning like a tin opener, unsettling the cows in the next field and triggering a stampede. The builders had started working.

Daly walked Pryce to her car. At the last moment, in front of the gaze of the builders, she turned and touched the side of his face with her fingertips.

'Goodbye for now, Celcius,' she said.

Her words instilled a sharp feeling of anxiety in him, but also a strange gladness, implying that they had already taken the first steps of a journey together.

CHAPTER NINE

At police headquarters, Daly found himself forced to attend a dismal meeting on future cutbacks to the police service, with more border stations earmarked for closure. He sat hunched over a briefing paper with his colleagues, rubbing his eyes numbly. They were expected to pass comment on the reorganization plans, even come up with suggestions as to how to manage the changes, but his mind was a blank. A detective from one of the doomed stations whispered darkly about another extension to the retirement age. Daly felt tired with the rounds of pointless consultation over such relentlessly bad news.

The previous evening, he had asked the police archivist at the central records office to carry out a little research work for him. She rang him back after the meeting to say she had checked the police graduation lists right back to the early 1970s, but found no mention of a graduate called Robert Hunter. However, the graduation files for 1980 and '81 were missing, she pointed out. Daly frowned.

It was strange, said the archivist, and she promised to investigate the matter further.

When Daly pressed for possible explanations for their absence, she was at a loss.

'But you must have some record of Hunter's training,' said Daly, 'where he was posted after graduation, his discipline record, his leaves of absence.'

'You can come over if you like and see for yourself. If he works for a special unit, then those details can only be accessed with the permission of the unit commander.'

Daly nodded. Many officers had been promoted to intelligence teams over the years, and it was normal for their details to be given the strictest security protection.

She said, 'Perhaps in the basement of some half-empty police station there is a file on Hunter's early career, but it would be impossible for me to locate it. Completely impossible.'

Daly was not happy to leave the matter. 'Is there any indication of when the missing graduation files were removed?'

There had been a similar search for Hunter's details a few weeks earlier, she told him. They had been listed as missing then, too.

'Who would have given permission to take them?'

'Officially, it would have had to come from the archive director's boss.'

'And who's that?'

'Chief Commander Spence.'

Before Daly could ask anything more, she tried to finish the conversation. 'So there you go, Inspector, another little mystery from the past.'

'Wait, there's something else you can do for me. I need some details on another police officer. His name is Jack McKenna. Originally from Derry.' In his head, he went over the conversation with the sergeant from Dreesh, and did a rough calculation. 'He would have graduated in 1976 or 1977.'

She sighed.

'It would help me very much with an important investigation.'

When she reluctantly agreed, Daly said he would wait on the phone. It did not matter how long the search would take. After about ten minutes, she returned.

'What did you say his address was?'

'Derry, the Bogside.'

She sounded triumphant. 'Got him. His postings are all listed here. Most of them along the border. As well as his professional record. He retired two years ago. From Special Branch. It says here he was a liaison officer with Gardai in the South.'

Daly asked her to scan and email the records. It was only a hunch, but in Daly's world, everyone was potentially a suspect, everything hinted darkly at something else. He operated in a heightened arena of suspicion, and McKenna's description of his brother had struck him as odd: *We were the complete reverse of each other, Inspector.* What exactly had he meant by that? Was one police officer the dark negative of the other, two brothers operating in parallel along the border?

He kept frowning as he walked to the canteen for lunch, his entire mental force concentrating on the memory of the photograph, and the haunted expression on Sergeant McKenna's face when he gazed up at it, as though he were peering into a distorting looking glass.

CHAPTER TEN

'The poses he's striking, it's as if he suspects someone is watching him,' murmured Daly, staring at the computer screen alongside Detective Veronica O'Neill.

They watched expectantly as Carey's rain-jacketed figure moved slowly along the shelves of the airport bookshop, fingering the spines. The Garda detective opened one of the books, examined a page, and then placed it back. Daly squinted at the images, another camera catching Carey as he sidled towards a display of perfumes. A woman stood beside him. When she looked up and saw he was staring at her, she moved away quickly. The detective's wariness provoked uneasiness, a more nervous speed in the figures around him.

Daly and O'Neill were sitting at a computer, watching CCTV footage from the airport on the day before Carey's drowned body was found. O'Neill had sifted through the reams of images and managed to collect a considerable amount of footage tracking Carey's movements in the departure lounge.

Not for the first time, Daly felt grateful for her diligence and expertise.

Other pieces of footage showed Carey trailing after random groups of travellers, keeping them in sight, before changing direction and targeting another group. Daly and O'Neill watched the same movements altered by different camera angles, Carey foreshortened or in the distance, always wary and mysterious-looking, with his untidy beard and rain-coat, as the crowd rippled around him. He was doing what solitary people do to hide themselves, thought Daly, he was following others.

But Carey resembled a bad dancer faking it to the music and hoping no one was watching. He glanced around too much. He failed to walk hurriedly enough. People flowed past him as he wandered along the check-in points, a detective with a deep secret studying the movement of passing figures as though trying to imitate their pace and gait. At one point, Carey quickened his step and joined the bustle of people hurrying for their flights. At the last moment, he turned towards an exit sign. He had no intention of catching his flight.

Daly thought of Sergeant McKenna innocently encouraging Carey to take a well-earned break. Even your closest colleagues might not see enormous changes in you until it was too late, how one course of action might conceal another, how a secret version of yourself might flow beneath the surface of your life and, one afternoon, carry you off in an entirely unexpected direction. Carey had perplexed those incapable of detecting the shift, double-crossing those who believed everyone was borne along by the same currents. That day in the airport, the Garda detective had been searching for a crowd, a mass of people flocking so thickly together they swallowed up his secret.

Daly stared at the flickering screen, his mind sifting through the images. The important thing was to pay close attention and be patient. He watched the last recorded hours of Carey's life unfold in their mystery, the detective walking back in time, forward in time, appearing and disappearing in the crowds, the continuous wave of travellers drawn to the check-in gates. He searched for the moment of transformation.

After Carey had disappeared towards the exit sign, they picked up footage on another camera and found him staring at his ghostly reflection in a shop window.

'He's checking for any shadows behind,' said O'Neill.

The next piece of footage showed a swarm of figures at the exit doors. Amid the throng of relatives greeting their loved ones, a man in a cap emerged carrying a sign. *A taxi driver waiting for his fare*, thought Daly. An overweight figure dressed in a brown raincoat drifted in front of the taxi driver, the daylight from the automatic doors shimmering around them.

'That's our detective,' said Daly. 'About to leave the airport.'

For a few moments, Carey stood before the man with the sign, and some communication seemed to pass between them. There was the brief flourish of a handshake and then they walked through the doors into the bustling curtain of people.

'Who's the driver?' asked O'Neill.

'We'll have to check with all the taxi companies. Someone must remember picking him up.'

They ran through more footage of the departures exit hall in the minutes before Carey had appeared.

'There,' said Daly. 'Freeze the video.'

With bated breath, they scrutinized the image. The driver who had walked off with Carey had just appeared in the hall and raised his sign.

'Zoom in.'

The pattern of light and dark expanded on the computer screen, making the writing on the sign just about visible. The two detectives stared at it in silence, trying to place the name in context. 'Mr John Andrews', it read.

'That's strange,' said O'Neill.

Strange it was, a secret life exposed in such a way, sealed forever in the frozen moment of a video.

'An alias,' said Daly. 'Someone must have instructed Carey to look out for a driver bearing that name.'

'Why?'

'To throw anyone looking for Detective Brian Carey off the scent.'

Daly went back to the scene of Carey meeting the driver. Staring at the images, he felt the appearance of another mysterious presence, a man playing a role that was unexpected of him. *I must be mistaken*, thought Daly, his attention transfixed by the smiling face of the driver. Carefully, he compared the image with the one that had flashed into his mind. He could not be certain but he thought he had seen the same smiling face in the photograph at Dreesh police station. The face had been younger and thinner, sporting a thick moustache, a figure dressed in an RUC uniform. The brother who was the reverse of Sergeant Peter McKenna.

However, Daly needed more proof before he could be positive the driver was Jack McKenna. A suspicious mind tended to do that to people; it made them simplify things, see things that weren't there, or misread what they did see. The similarity might never have occurred to him had he not been intent on tracking down the retired Special Branch officer. The driver appeared once more in the footage, this time in an underground car park, pointing Carey towards a blue-coloured Ford saloon, the expression on his face changing as Carey climbed in, watching him with what looked to be a grotesque smirk. Daly felt a shiver of fear run down his spine.

They checked the car number on the registration database but no results came up. It did not exist, at least officially.

'A false number plate,' said O'Neill. 'The car must belong to a criminal gang.'

Daly did not voice the more sinister explanation that ran through his mind.

An hour of searching for the number plate through all the police databases produced a single tenuous lead. A concerned member of the public had rung Portadown station on the same day as Carey's flight, and reported what he believed was suspicious activity involving two cars and a group of men in a forest close to Lough Neagh's southern shore. He had taken down the vehicle registrations, one of which matched that of the car at the airport. Daly checked the time of the report. Roughly an hour after the car carrying Carey had left the airport. It must have gone straight to the rendezvous in the forest.

'What are you going to do?' said the constable who had taken the report. His voice at the other end of the phone sounded a little concerned at the intensity in Daly's voice.

'Assuming that the eyewitness is to be believed, the report raises several important questions,' said Daly.

The constable summarized the call. An elderly man out

walking his dog had thought there was something odd about the meeting he had just witnessed. He had spotted the vehicle parked in a remote lay-by in the forest, and another car pulling alongside. However, the witness's account was disjointed and the constable on duty had not believed it was linked to anything serious. He had thanked the old man for getting in touch, but neglected to take his mobile number or any other contact details.

There was one particular detail in the description that made Daly's stomach knot up. According to the elderly caller, an overweight man, dressed in a brown raincoat, emerged from the first car and appeared elated, shaking hands with two men from the second car, but then when he stepped into their vehicle, his expression had changed. He looked disappointed and bewildered, as though he had been the victim of some sort of a practical joke, while the driver of the car had taken off at speed, grinning behind the wheel.

'What conclusions did you draw?' asked Daly.

'None at all. I thought there was most likely an innocent explanation for the meeting. Perhaps they'd exchanged a joke that backfired in some way.'

'Did you mention it to anyone else?'

'No one. Like I said, I had no concerns.'

'I need to know more of the conversation you had with him. I want to know every single word.'

The officer remained silent.

'Think back,' said Daly. 'Did the caller say anything else? Perhaps it seemed irrelevant at the time, but this meeting could turn out to be the last known sighting of Detective Brian Carey before he drowned. Every detail is important.'

A sigh was the only response.

'Did he hint at anything else? It's easy to let slip something when you're writing it down afterwards.'

'How was I to know?' said the constable.

'Know what?'

'That he was going to drown himself.'

Daly had no answer to that, but it was clear to him that Carey had been the victim of a deeper, darker joke than the one the constable suspected, a sudden reversal of fortune, the significance of which not even Carey had fully understood. Moreover, the men in the two cars weren't his friends playing a little trick on him. The figures had toyed with him, wielding the power of a criminal gang. An image of Carey's face as he stepped into the back of the second car stayed with Daly, the face of a man stumbling towards his death, the waters lapping the nearby lough shore and a sense of utter abandonment descending upon him.

Why had he looked elated when he first met the men from the other car? Why had he gone along with the subterfuge of the trip to Spain and an alias in the first place? Who had picked the meeting place? Obviously, they had not wanted to be seen or traced in any way. Was it because they were intent on arranging Carey's death? But why have Carey meet the occupants of the other car? Something must have been exchanged, a message or an object, and a decision made. But what exactly? It was pointless, he realized. He needed a lot more information before he could speculate on what exactly had occurred in the forest.

They ran the number plate of the second car through all the databases, but again there was no record of it. Daly stared at the registration numbers. No doubt this was an important breakthrough, but its implications were shrouded in mystery. O'Neill repeated her belief that the cars must be connected to a criminal network. Daly said nothing. He was unwilling to voice the fear that floated through his mind. The suspicion struggling for expression involved another murky entity – the cars might belong to undercover intelligence services.

O'Neill stared at him, trying to read his thoughts. He was about to confide his suspicions when his mobile phone buzzed into life. He sighed when he saw who the caller was.

CHAPTER ELEVEN

'Is that you, Celcius?' It was Pryce, speaking softly at the other end of the phone.

'Of course it's me.' Daly was irritated by the intimate tone of her voice. He walked away from O'Neill to the window.

'I've a special request to make. It's on behalf of Detective Carey's girlfriend.'

'You've been speaking to her?'

'Of course I've been speaking to her.' It was her turn to sound irritated. 'Do you think I can read her mind? I thought I'd pay her a visit.' Her voice returned to its oddly soothing tone. Daly remembered that her telephone manner was a digging tool. In the competitive world of journalism, reporters had to learn how to mask the threat posed by their questions.

'Why did you visit her?'

'What do you mean why? I just did. I'm a reporter and her partner's death is a news story. Remember? She wants to meet you.'

'What's so special about that? I've been planning to speak to her.'

'She wants to meet you urgently. No later than six p.m. She says she knows something important about the Green and Blue Fishing Club.'

Daly glanced at his watch. It was already 4 p.m. He had not a single free moment these days.

'By the way,' continued Pryce, 'the papers are still going to run the story about Donaldson's suicide note this weekend. Your name is going to be in the headlines.'

Daly tried to feign indifference. 'I hope they spell it correctly.'

'The whole thing stinks, Celcius. The top brass are going to use you to scrub the toilet. There's nothing you can do but sit down and write your account of what happened, how Donaldson erected a wall of silence around the murder of your mother.'

He made no noise and simply closed his eyes, troubled by the image of Donaldson's boat, anchored in the middle of the lough, and his suicide, which had brewed up this cyclone about to engulf him.

'You make it seem like the simplest of chores. The truth is, I wouldn't even know where to begin.'

She lowered her voice again. 'You sound tired. Been working overtime again?'

'I'm always tired. Doesn't matter how long the hours are.' He wondered had he turned into a workaholic just to avoid the fact that his life was running in a completely aimless direction. He looked up and saw a face looming at the window in the door. It was Detective Irwin, his eyes fastening on to Daly's with a look of insolent anticipation.

'Remember, Celcius, it's just you and me,' said Pryce. 'Just you and me against your enemies in the police force.'

'You're right,' said Daly, glancing away from Irwin. 'You and me and whatever newspaper you happen to be pitching this story to.'

'All right, there's no time to go into this right now. Like I said, Carey's girlfriend needs to see you. As soon as possible.'

Daly ended the call and pocketed his mobile phone. He was distracted again by the sight of Irwin's face at the door, hovering like a gleeful messenger with bad news.

'What are you waiting for?' said Daly as he pulled the door open.

'To tell you the latest developments.'

'Which are?'

'The pathologist's report was inconclusive. He said the bruising to Carey's neck and shoulders could have been caused by a boat or even rocks. He's not sure if there was foul play or not. So he's ordered an official inquest into his death.'

He remained at the door with an amused expression, watching Daly return to his computer. When he hadn't left after a few moments, Daly asked him what he was doing.

'Waiting on you, Celcius.'

'What do you mean?'

'That's the other development in the case. Special Branch has instructed me to shelve everything else I'm doing and wait on you.'

'I don't need your company.'

'It's not company I'm offering,' replied Irwin with a cheery air. 'I'm awaiting your orders.'

'Have they sent you to help me or keep an eye on me?'

Irwin shrugged. 'I'm just obeying orders.' He allowed himself a grin.

When Irwin still had not moved from the door, Daly asked, 'Is that all?'

'One more thing. Special Branch aren't the only ones expressing an interest in the case. Someone else has been in touch.'

'Carey's Garda commander?' said Daly.

'How did you know?'

'Sometimes my hunches are correct. What does the commander want?'

'Regular updates, and advance notification whenever you cross the border. Special Branch would like the same.'

So he was right. Keeping tabs on officers, that was something Special Branch specialized in these days. Daly thought for a moment, speculating as to what other instructions Special Branch had given Irwin. He was used to having the younger detective lurking around his investigations with unknown and usually negative intent. He tried to appraise him as a genuine colleague, wondering what talents and abilities he might possess worth putting to the test. Daly decided to take a risk and asked Irwin to contact the intelligence agencies. He wanted Irwin to seek their co-operation in finding the owners of the vehicles involved in Carey's disappearance. Daly also instructed him to dig out any references to the Green and Blue Fishing Club and Detective Robert Hunter in Special Branch files.

A stomach pang reminded Daly he had not eaten since breakfast time. He should really take a break, he thought, as he heaved himself into his car. He felt its engine come alive and wondered why he had agreed to months of overtime and weekend shifts. A motor had to be kept running to keep it clean and oiled deep through, but he was not a machine. He drove absent-mindedly to a fast-food restaurant, queued in his car, and allowed himself to be handed a paper bag of food by the teenage attendant.

Somehow, the cold discipline of all these hours on duty was not having the desired effect. He felt run-down and confused, but also cheated. It came as a surprise that the harder he worked, the more free his mind was to wallow in darker thoughts, free to ponder the things he was trying hardest to avoid. As though the flurry of police work had created a cell of privacy and remoteness around him, into which floated countless memories: his mother's blue nurse's shoes, his father's fireside silences, Donaldson's frowning face, as well as the habitual reminders of the purposelessness of his life, his lonely caravan, his past divorce and childlessness.

He finished his meal and drove into South Tyrone, searching for the address of Carey's partner. He felt as though it had become his conscientious duty to drive along the same silent border roads every evening. He switched on the radio and picked up speed, gripping the gearstick, going through the changes. A strange sense of liberation took hold. The blackness of the road repeating before him, the trees leaning out of the forests, seemed oddly soothing. Every now and again, his eyes scanned for a side turning, searching for a sign of his destination.

An image rose out of the undergrowth. A deer emerging from the forest, its eyes gleaming gold in his headlights. He swerved, fearing that it might bolt into his path, and another image flashed before the windscreen. A woman with blond hair and stricken eyes running towards his car, the flowering of her disarrayed dress, her outstretched arms jolting him with shock.

He braked sharply and closed his eyes, as if he might drive into a deeper darkness, and avoid this wildly staring woman, but it was too late. He jerked forward with the force of the brakes, and felt the sickening thud of her body against the bonnet and then the windscreen.

Suddenly, the evening blurred and disappeared into a hail of flickering images. He remembered climbing out of the car and rushing to where her body lay on the road. Already, blood was seeping from her neck, forming a thick pool on the tarred road. He tried resuscitation. He pumped her ribcage and breathed into her mouth until his lungs wheezed with the effort. He sat down beside her and tried to staunch the flow of blood. Where was it coming from? He had never seen so much blood at the scene of a road accident. He stood up to make several phone calls, turning to describe the scene, his head buzzing with interfering thoughts and images.

When the ambulance arrived, he ran to its reassuring blue lights, as if seeking shelter from a gathering storm, abandoning the body and his car, with its smashed windscreen and door hanging open. The squeal of the stretcher scraping along the ambulance rack made him start. The faces of the paramedics peered at him as if they were going to tell him something, but were in too much of a hurry to formulate the words. The stretcher squealed again.

A police car pulled alongside him, and the driver and

passenger doors swung open. Two uniformed officers joined him at the side of the road. They explained to him that they were taking him back to the station.

'Two officers for me?'

They did not reply.

'Why?'

'In your own time, sir,' said one of them. 'We need to breathalyse you and get a statement.'

Daly stared at the pair, not recognizing either of them. They stood in front of him, bulked out by their uniforms, as impersonal as deep-sea divers on a routine underwater mission. He did a double take of the scene, which other officers were now cordoning off with tape. He saw how it suggested a different crime altogether, a ghostly ribbon of road, a woman bleeding to death, her killer frozen at a safe distance, and the shadows of the forest yawning all around them.

He looked back at the officers with his estranged detective's eye. They were fresh-faced but the lines around their mouths and eyes deepened as he stood still, trying to overcome his inner resistance. He had the unpleasant feeling that something new and dangerous was about to disrupt his monotonous work-filled existence.

'She came out of nowhere. I didn't have time to stop or swerve,' he said, but his protestation sounded feeble.

The ambulance floated in space, bathing everything in its blue light, and then it swung away and accelerated down the road at dizzying speed, its sirens screaming. He whispered a prayer to the woman, hoping that the paramedics would save her, and climbed into the police car.

He was still dazed when he walked into the police station,

accompanied by the two officers. He felt sweaty in the interview suite, as the police doctor, laboriously slow, took a sample of his blood for alcohol testing. Traces of the woman's blood were still on his hands and clothes. The poor thing, who or what had she been running from? He thought of the strange day he'd had. First Pryce calling to his door, demanding his story, reminding him of the things he would rather forget, and now this strange woman, who was probably dead already and whose blood was drying on his hands. He had not expected his path to cross with either of them, but he felt a sense of grim inevitability about both encounters that he could not shrug off.

Then they told him what he feared and suspected, that the woman had been declared dead.

'It all happened so fast, I barely had time to react,' he repeated to the doctor, but already he felt as though he was deviating from the truth. He knew that the accident must have been over in a flash but when he replayed it in his mind, it seemed to pass so slowly. A shadowy disturbance amid the trees, the woman's stricken face moving into his line of sight, his foot lunging towards the brake, the flash of her eyes and her arms stretching towards him, her body straining within the fluttering dress, and then a thump like the kick of a horse, and the sickening second impact upon the windscreen, before the road whisked her body away.

However, time never slows or lets up for an instant. It had pulled Daly in its unstoppable wake, in the police car behind the ambulance, and now in this sterile interview suite, where he carefully constructed the events of the evening and wrote them down in his statement. It seemed an affront to the dead woman that his version of the accident should be the only official description of her demise.

His sense of disorientation remained when Detective O'Neill came over to him, her face drawn and pale.

'Are you all right, Celcius?' she asked.

'I'm all right but the woman I hit is dead,' he said flatly. 'Find out her name, please, and tell me. And anything else you can find out about her. She's still a stranger to me and I don't like that.'

'It was an accident. Don't blame yourself.'

'True. I didn't expect her to rush out like that. But I'm still responsible for her death.'

When he had finished and signed his statement, Commander Sinclair was waiting for him in the corridor.

'Take a few days off, Daly,' he said.

Sinclair was putting him on notice, realized Daly. Already the commander was considering the damage the accident might do to the reputation of the police force. 'Do you want me to issue an apology to the family or explain what happened?' he asked.

'Right now, neither. It's enough that you take some leave.'

'I've a lot of work to do,' Daly explained. 'Detective Carey's death. I can't take time off.'

'Up to you, Daly. But this accident is going to cause a nasty stink when it gets out to the media. It would be better if you stayed out of the public eye.'

Daly nodded. He had to force himself to remember what he was doing in the time leading up to the accident. Already the evening had an air of unreality about it, as though it had been a piece of theatre, a grotesque performance that he never wanted to witness, let alone play the principal role in. Again, the thought nagged him: who or what had she been running from?

CHAPTER TWELVE

Dreesh, eighteen months previously

The totality of his life's misfortunes Tommy Higgins traced back to a drunken encounter with a woman who turned out to be the wife of an IRA man. When word got out about his mistake, four men in balaclavas lured him to a car park behind a pub, interrogated him in a makeshift court and then subjected him to a violent beating, covering him with his own blood. That brief kiss and fumble in the darkness invoked the unlucky demons from the Republican underworld that tormented him for the rest of his life.

The wounds soon healed but the attack left him with a permanent limp and a bitter taste in his mouth that worsened as the weeks went by. He felt burdened with a sense of humiliation. He had been the innocent party but his limp, the permanent sign of a punishment beating, now marked him out for public condemnation. Mangled rumours circulated about his misdemeanours. He began to feel trapped and defeated, his every movement and gesture noted and talked about by his neighbours, as though he were a sub-human who had to bow to every degradation. To make matters worse, his torturers soon forgot about the incident. They greeted him as though nothing had happened, but for Tommy everything had changed. The village of Dreesh became the opposite of the village he had grown up in, a sullen community where no one cared whether he lived or died, a pit of closed minds, rumours, and suspended violence.

Like most of his young friends, Tommy knew very little about spying or informing. The words and deeds of his hitherto uneventful life had never led to another person's arrest or murder, and any informers that he knew were either dead or on the run. He had never seen the inside of a police station, let alone met a detective or spoken to an intelligence officer. What he knew of these shadowy things, he had learned second-hand through rumours and gossip.

So when Detective Brian Carey's car pulled alongside him one evening and offered him a lift, he jumped in without thinking. From the look on the detective's face, he thought Carey was about to come on to him. He was ready to defend himself if necessary, but instead the bearded detective asked for tittle-tattle about Republican dissidents and smugglers, promising generous payments if the information led to arrests.

'All we want is a little information on some bad boys,' the detective said. 'We'll look after you; set up a bank account in your name, sort things out if you get into any trouble.'

Tommy told the detective he was wasting his time, and got out immediately.

'No harm done, son,' said Carey. 'I'll see you around.' He gave Tommy a sad half-salute and drove off.

But there were more encounters on empty roads, with Carey sitting in his car, giving Tommy a frozen salute whenever their eyes met. He seemed to be biding his time, lulling Tommy into a false sense of security before striking, keeping a discreet distance in his car, drawing just enough attention to remind Tommy of his constant presence, his detective's loneliness, which was without cure and would never be alleviated in a border village where almost everyone had benefited from the illegal trade of smuggling and the paramilitaries still held sway. Tommy's limp had drawn the detective's attention, and now, it seemed, he could get rid of neither.

Carey followed him for six weeks. Perhaps it was because Tommy did not want to be lonely either that he was strangely comforted by the detective's presence. Looking for his car was a welcome distraction from his own train of thoughts, an interesting game of cat and mouse that lifted him out of the shadows.

One evening, he accepted Carey's offer of a lift and they drove out of Dreesh and into the mountains. The clouds thickened and enveloped the road in a grey drizzle. Neither of them spoke and the car filled with a sense of frustrated anticipation. After several miles of driving, the detective reached into the glove compartment and retrieved an old glass bottle. Without slowing down, he removed the stopper and took a heavy glug. The smell of illicit booze filled the car. He handed the poteen to the teenager, saying, 'We have to stop the bastards, you know that, don't you, Tommy?'

Tommy took a nip and felt his throat burn. He looked

through the windscreen at the rain-shrouded road and realized that Dreesh's air of suspicion and bad omens weren't going to clear of their own accord, that this encounter with the detective was his only chance to set things straight, and that he had been blindly stumbling between anger and self-pity for far too long.

Without warning, Carey brought the car to a halt in the middle of the road. It felt as though the detective had not planned to stop, that he had come suddenly upon an invisible crossing point. Droplets of mist clung to the windscreen. It took a while for Tommy to notice the obstacle that had made Carey stop. Hunkered on the road before them was a young hare. It seemed to have prepared itself for this moment, crouching on the lonely road, ready to leap away, but in reality, it was frozen with fear. Carey turned his head to the right and Tommy, following his gaze, saw a fox peering back at them from the side of the road. It lifted its head and sniffed, its panting mouth grinning at them. Tommy's skin prickled, sensing the brutality of what was about to unfold.

The hare did not move. Its bulging eyes glistened in the wet air. Silhouetted against the encroaching mist, the detective also seemed frozen in place, chained to the moment, a prisoner to fate. The fox took a step forward, paused and then padded across the road. It pounced on the still hare, grabbing it by its slack neck and shaking it in one quick ghastly motion. The hare convulsed slightly, its eyes enlarging. There was a sad stiff grace about its death throes, and then the fox vaulted the roadside bank, dragging the limbs of the dead animal, disappearing into the brown and red bracken.

Carey rubbed his eyes and leaned against the steering

wheel. 'That was an unlucky sign for us, son. We'll have to be careful.' He shook his head.

What was he talking about?

'The stunned hare was him, you know,' said Carey.

'Who?'

'The ghost of the poor boy those IRA bastards murdered up here.'

Carey turned to him so that Tommy could see his full face, the darkness in his eyes, the corners of his bearded mouth, the whiteness of his sweating skin that shone like chalk in the dim evening light.

'The grace of Jesus on his lost soul,' said the detective. 'Everyone in the village knows who did it, but no one will come forth with their names. Those bastards still boast in the pub about how they tortured him.'

Tommy knew the men he was talking about but said nothing.

In the quiet that followed, in the blindness of the mist descending with absolute whiteness, Tommy felt his body grow weightless, as though he too had been carried away by the fox to its infernal den in the bracken, his arms and legs trailing in the mist. Any capacity he might have had to struggle or escape his fate had deserted him, leaving nothing behind but the calm pumping of his blood, his unblinking gaze and a mysterious lack of awareness of the dangerous border he was about to cross.

That was the moment Tommy began talking. He told the detective everything he knew about his torturers. He felt elated, surprised by his confidence; then, remembering the threat posed by his enemies, who had eyes and ears everywhere, he peered behind at the lurking mist, worried that a car might have followed them. But the little road was empty. He glanced at Carey and gave him an uneasy grin. He was unwilling to confront the detective's face for too long, his steady gaze, the beads of perspiration on his forehead, his eyes as fixed as the tiny countless pearls of mist suspended on the windscreen. He smelled the alcohol on the detective's breath and heard the upholstery creaking as Carey adjusted his position in the driver's seat.

Tommy kept talking. The poteen and the mist-shrouded road, the intoxication of the revenge he was about to seek, blinded him to any sense of danger. He felt close to tears, but it was not sadness that welled in his heart but a feeling of release. He had been handed a way out of the frustration and humiliation of village life. For months, it had been so difficult to imagine any form of escape.

'A plan will be put in place for you,' said Carey afterwards. 'It is important that you understand we'll always be watching out for you. The precise details you won't be aware of, but…'

Only afterwards did the thought strike Tommy that something had been left unexplained, the fox running with the dead boy's ghost in its mouth, the smell of alcohol in the detective's car, and Carey's sombre warning that they had been cursed with bad luck.

CHAPTER THIRTEEN

The gravest error Tommy made was assuming his role as an informer would have a limit, an imminent expiry date, and that when the police had successfully acted upon his information, the curtain would fall on this sad little chapter of his life, that he would no longer have to live in subterfuge, passing himself off as someone he was not.

However, when his information led to a number of arrests, Carey introduced Tommy to the enigmatic Robert Hunter, the PSNI detective with the arrogant stare, who quickly became his mentor and self-appointed bully. Carey's role, as far as Tommy could work out, was to supervise the flow of intelligence to his Northern Ireland colleagues. Whereas Carey had been distant and sad, Hunter was motivated and professional, taking him under his wing, buying him a new car, setting up a bank account in his name with regular deposits. Hunter showered him with praise and encouragement, as well as money, as if they were gambling partners at the lucrative casino of cross-border intelligence. The only problem was that the stakes very soon grew dangerously high. Tommy found that he was betting with his own life to keep up with Hunter's insatiable desire for information.

Hunter and Carey encouraged him to get closer to Republican dissidents. He started fundraising for prisoner societies and then branched into moneymaking scams including smuggling. His efforts helped him gain credibility among senior figures in the criminal networks along the border. He had an aptitude for computers and, under Hunter's guidance and special training, he helped the gangs set up encrypted files, anonymous email accounts, and messaging systems. He helped them erect firewalls against spyware, and warned them not to use smartphones for security reasons. The criminals thought he showed enterprise and know-how. He began to move in shadier circles, mixing with professional smugglers, disaffected former IRA men, dissidents, and organized criminals.

Hunter's bravado and charm helped reassure him that, in this netherworld of intrigue and danger, he was not hopelessly out of his depth. The detectives promised him a new identity and relocation when his work was over, and a fat pension for life.

'You'll never have to do anything you don't want to,' Hunter told Tommy. 'Get as close to the pack as you can, that way you'll do the most damage.'

When the smuggling boss Tom Morgan recruited him to encrypt his secret accounts, Carey seemed uncharacteristically over the moon, Hunter a little less so. On a USB stick, Tommy downloaded a mountain of data, which revealed details of Morgan's financial dealings, his property transactions, evidence that he was laundering money through legitimate businesses and hiding it in offshore banks. Tommy told the detectives how the trail of money led to prominent politicians, professionals in law and accounting, and even elderly relatives and neighbours in Dreesh, who appeared to be sitting on bank deposits worth millions of euros. Morgan had given loans to the villagers of Dreesh that would probably never be repaid, including mysterious transfers of property and companies. It was remarkable how much the smuggling boss moved his money around, and how many people were caught up in his convoluted financial web. Tommy handed the USB stick to his handlers, and told them he had only scratched the surface.

He expected that it would take weeks for computer experts to work their way through the data, unpicking the contracts and companies one by one, but the months passed, and still there was no sign of the police raiding Morgan's premises. Perhaps they were investigating Morgan behind the scenes, he thought, waiting for the right moment to expose his corrupt financial dealings.

He was reassured to see his bank balance inflate in line with the agreed bonuses for delivering top-grade intelligence. However, he would have liked more encouragement from his handlers. The fact that the money was deposited meant that the detectives were not dissatisfied with his information, but the lack of police arrests did not feel like a suitable response to the risks he was taking and the scale of the corruption he had uncovered, whatever the reason behind the inaction. He phoned in tip-offs about Morgan's smuggling runs, the bank robberies he was behind, the punishment beatings, and the locations of secret fuel-laundering plants. Every evening he turned up at Morgan's yard, he expected to hear the wail of police sirens raiding the plant. Any day now, he reasoned. But nothing of the sort happened. His detailed descriptions of Morgan's law-breaking drew no response from his handlers, yet the money kept appearing in his account.

He began to toy with the idea that the detectives were protecting Morgan. He tried to arrange a face-to-face meeting with them, but to no avail. At first, the brush-offs were polite, carefully worded. *Sorry, Tommy, you've called at a bad time. Look, we can't talk to you right now, give us a ring tomorrow evening.* The excuses should have put him on his guard, made him alert to the dangerous eventualities that lay ahead. He pestered his handlers for two weeks, even turned up at the police station in Dreesh, risking his own safety. *We got your messages, Tommy, and we agree we need to talk.* Carey promised to arrange several meetings with Hunter but nothing ever materialized.

Now he suspected they had been improvising furiously to gain time. 'It's Hunter you need to speak to, not me,' Carey told him. 'He's the one in charge.'

Then a rumour went round that Morgan was searching for a mole, someone who was talking to the police. The crime boss began taking in his employees and interrogating them, one by one. Soon it would be Tommy's turn.

He managed to speak to Hunter on the phone. 'You're meant to be my protector,' he told the detective.

'Of course.'

'Just promise me I'm safe.'

114

'You're safe.'

'I don't feel safe.'

'Just brazen it out. Act like you've always done. Morgan has no proof you're an informer.'

Days passed and time seemed to slow down. He was overwhelmed with the feeling that his life had come to a dangerous brink, that he was standing on a set of railway tracks with plenty of time to step off, but was frozen to the spot, waiting for the impact of the train. Like the hare on the road, something within him had decided on death, or at least the end of his life as an informer. It wasn't that he was paralysed by the looming danger, the possibility of an ugly death at Morgan's hands, it was more a matter of deciding his own fate, or willing the final moment to arrive.

Morgan and his henchmen interrogated him twice. They had only vague suspicions and he was able to deny everything. However, they told him to come back for a third interrogation. He was rattled now. No one else had been asked to come back for a third grilling. He demanded a face-to-face meeting with both Carey and Hunter; otherwise, he would go to the media and blow the lid on everything.

'You're working hard, Tommy,' said Hunter, 'but trust us on this. Morgan doesn't suspect you. We've got the inside track. He thinks the informer is one of his lorry drivers, not you.'

'Don't worry about Morgan's suspicions,' Carey joined in, 'they'll keep you alert, on your toes, ready for anything. Nothing wrong with that, is there?'

'In the meantime, take a little break,' Hunter suggested. 'Stop offering to do as much work for him, be less obtrusive. Morgan will calm down soon.'

Determined to do what was asked of him, Tommy lay low, stopped sending the detectives tip-offs, but Morgan's suspicions did not abate. One of the lorry drivers rang and warned him that Morgan had him in the frame as the informer, and that he planned to interrogate Tommy in one of his cowsheds when he turned up for work that evening. That set him into a panic. Informers, once exposed, never got second chances. It was time for his handlers to step out of their passive role and intervene. He wanted to be relocated, he told them at a face-to-face meeting.

He was shocked when the detectives told him they were going to do nothing of the sort.

'I think we have to consider decreasing the scale of your operations,' said Hunter.

'You've done that already.'

'I mean cut it drastically.'

He did not reply. Several moments passed. For the first time in his career as an informer, he did not trust what they said. 'There's something I'm been meaning to ask you,' he said.

'What's that?'

'Why haven't you arrested Morgan?' He heard their breathing change. 'Here I am, working in the greatest danger, with nothing but the threat of death hanging over me, yet you haven't done a single thing to that bastard.'

'You've received all your payments,' said Hunter. His eyes seemed disconnected from what he was saying. They looked odd and icily intense. 'We're preparing to swoop any day now. We have to organize the evidence. Everything has to be meticulously planned.'

'Tell me when?'

'It's not your job, Tommy, to set guidelines,' said Hunter. 'Or issue ultimatums.'

Tommy noticed the dangerous tone of condescension immediately. The harsh truth it masked. He was completely expendable, while Morgan was being protected. Carey could not even look him in the eye.

'That's cologne you're wearing,' Tommy said, addressing Hunter. 'You've slapped on too much of it.'

The detective stared at him blankly.

'You're trying to hide the truth,' said Tommy.

'What truth?'

'That this stinks.'

'I think we've heard enough, Tommy,' said Hunter. 'Remember, if you run now, you'll blow your cover for good, and eventually Morgan and his men will track you down. We can't look after you forever. You just have to lie low, stick it out; Morgan can't prove a thing.'

Tommy decided to act on his own and did not turn up for work that evening. Instead, he booked a flight to London. He expected his handlers would help him locate there, set him up with a new identity, but instead his whole world fell apart.

A week after he arrived in London, he tried to contact his handlers to let them know he was safe. He rang the number they had given him. Immediately, it went through to a taxi company in Enniskillen. He tapped the numbers again. This time, the woman from the taxi company was annoyed. He asked her if she was connected to the police or intelligence services.

'Are you taking the piss?' she said.

He rang Scotland Yard and hesitantly explained his situation to an inspector. He described the torment he was experiencing, and was given another number to ring, and then another. He told his story repeatedly. He went round the bureaucratic loop, talking and mumbling on his phone, deep in monologue. They listened to him, but he grew weary of his own voice, his litany of deception and betrayal. In their silences, their deep pauses, he felt the weight of long corridors and thickly carpeted offices, where grey men plotted secret battles in the intelligence war. He was put through to Special Branch in Belfast, but no one there had heard of Detective Robert Hunter.

A terrible truth began to dawn upon him. Carey and Hunter were the only people who knew the truth about his life, the secret role he had been playing. With everyone else, even his own mother, he had to be careful and remember his lines, not to slip up in any way. He needed his handlers more than they needed him. Not just for the money that rolled into his account, but to make decisions for him, and to work out what to do when things went wrong.

In desperation, he rang every police station along the border, pleading for any information that might help him track down Hunter, leaving his number so that his handlers might call him and fix things again. He felt disorientated, travelling along the London Underground, knowing that he was about to disappear from sight and memory. He wandered the streets, trying to find refuge in the overflowing crowds. This was a new loneliness, he realized. Not the self-imposed solitude of an informer living and working among criminals. This was a loneliness without any certainty whatsoever, without a centre to hold things together. Those bastards had cut him off in a manner so stark and cruel that he began to lose his sense of what was real, which parts of his identity were true and which were false.

I'm on my own now, he thought. *No one else to rely on*. He felt the stuffing had been knocked out of him. He went to the Irish Embassy and told them who he was, the life he had been leading. They gave him a number to ring at Garda Headquarters in Dublin, but no one there had heard of him or knew anything about intelligence-gathering operations along the border. He fell more steeply into despair. He sat down and wrote a long detailed letter, outlining his predicament and asking for advice. He sent it to politicians in the Houses of Parliament and the Northern Ireland Assembly. He included his mobile number. He endured a bad stretch of days waiting for someone to contact him. He stared at the phone for a fortnight with a gloomy obsession, pinning all his hopes on it buzzing into life.

Slowly, he worked his way out of the darkness. He was resilient. He still had plenty of money left in his account. He stopped looking into himself, stopped thinking about home. That corner of Ulster was a conflicted place, betrayal running in every direction, shadowy figures exerting opposing forms of deception, the stress lines running through every layer of society. Who was Morgan secretly working for? Why were his handlers protecting him? It was the layers of deception that made his life disappear without a trace. In the circumstances, what could he expect his handlers to do? Utter some miraculous truth down a crackling phone line and bring him back to the world of the living?

He made one final call – a goodbye to his mother, telling her he was safe, but that he could never return to Dreesh. He boarded the next flight to Spain. He took a seat next to the window and stared through the scored glass, waiting for the sunlight to split the sky.

CHAPTER FOURTEEN

Dreesh, present day

When Sergeant McKenna opened the door to the police station, a cat slipped through his feet like a thief and disappeared into the shrubbery of the garden. Everywhere he turned, he had the sensation of shadows evading him. Footsteps sounded harshly behind him and the shape of his commander, Sean Halligan, emerged and pushed past into the building. His voice rumbled ahead, complaining about the lack of heating, prowling the confines of the little office. They had just returned from Detective Carey's wake, and the experience had left both men restless and uneasy.

'The older I get the more I hate going to wakes,' said Halligan. 'All that sitting in a room with an open coffin, strangers groping through the family's grief, not knowing what to say about the deceased, and, let's face it, Peter, Brian Carey was always a bit of a cold fish.'

'Would you like some tea or coffee?' offered McKenna, thinking that in the circumstances it was an unfortunate metaphor for Halligan to use. True, the wake had been more awkward than normal, held in Carey's sister's home, with the detective's partner, Brigid Donnelly, mysteriously absent.

'Something stronger, Peter,' replied the commander.

Neither of them took off their shapeless dark coats, which they had donned over their uniforms for the spot of off-duty formality. Halligan was not often cast down by tragedy, but tonight he looked rattled, staring intently at McKenna, sipping the glass of poteen the sergeant handed him.

In McKenna's own mind, he could still see Carey's drowned face mingling with the pale faces of the mourners, the hypnotized stare of Carey's sister, and his elderly mother beside her.

'I didn't know he had that much family,' said Halligan.

'Cousins and distant relatives, I believe.'

At the wake, there hadn't been much else for them to do when the conversation dried up but sit transfixed in the corridor, leaning back to allow the shuffling visitors through. Awkward neighbours nodded at McKenna, whom they recognized, before shifting on to the room where the coffin lay. The two of them had paid their respects and offered their condolences. McKenna had even whispered a prayer to the corpse. A light had appeared to emanate from Carey's face, a cold light offering no comfort. Mentally, McKenna had reached towards it, as though it were a faintly glowing ball, the final icy vestige of the detective's consciousness, as if he might draw it up into his hands and guard it there before the darkness swallowed up his secrets forever.

Commander Halligan cleared his throat and stared gravely

at the wall behind McKenna. He hadn't invited himself back to the station to talk about ordinary police matters, and McKenna couldn't help feeling resentful of his brooding presence. He'd had enough of death and intrigue and wanted to return to humdrum matters, to chat about the latest village gossip, like the church renovations and the cache of old Civil War rifles that had been found in the roof space.

Halligan took another sip of the poteen. He struggled to come up with some sincere words to mark the occasion, but McKenna intervened to save him the trouble.

'If it was suicide, then Brian's death was a release. He hadn't been in his right mind for months.'

Halligan stared at him. 'What did you know about his frame of mind?'

McKenna chose his words carefully. 'He didn't say anything but I could see he was tormenting himself.'

He gave Halligan a brief rundown of the cases Carey had been working upon, skimming through the files he had been able to access, and the information he'd dredged from personnel about the detective's career and health record. He tried to reconcile the brief biography with his image of the bearded detective, bulky and vulnerable behind his desk, staring at some paperwork in a strange way, or more often than not, in the last weeks, sitting in his car parked by the bridge leading to the North, his face barely discernible amid the shadows, eyes staring fixedly at the border, as though it were a mirror full of distorting reflections that only he could see. Again, he conjured up Carey's blanched face in the coffin, a face that would no longer have to give an account of itself.

He told Halligan how the dead detective's secrecy had been

driving everyone to distraction. In the last month, he had skipped team meetings, ignored run-of-the-mill investigations, cancelled interviews at the last minute, and disappeared in his car for hours on end without telling anyone where he was going. It was as if the Garda station had acquired a resident ghost. And now his death by suicide had added a darker hue to that secrecy.

After ruminating on what McKenna told him, Halligan asked, 'Ever been involved in intelligence work yourself?'

McKenna stared at his reflection in the darkened window and took a sip of his poteen. There were houses and shops beyond the glass, but from here, the village looked like a sea of darkness.

'I mean you personally,' said Halligan, when McKenna did not answer directly.

'In what sense?'

'Direct recruitment of informers.'

'I've acted on tip-offs but never as part of any formal arrangement.'

'This Detective Hunter, tell me about him. I take it he and Carey ranged the length of the border, an informer in every hole of the hedge?'

A block began to take shape in McKenna's mind. The dead detective, his colleague, was a mystery to him, but the living Detective Hunter was a mystery within a mystery. He was aware of Halligan staring at him intently. With effort, he managed to come up with a few brief details.

Halligan asked, 'What department does Hunter work in now? I take it he's no longer a rank-and-file detective?'

'No, no.'

'Seconded to MI5?'

'I don't think so.'

'Some sort of intelligence specialist, then?'

McKenna shrugged. 'Carey once told me Hunter belonged to a secret department working within the Northern Ireland police service. Top-level security clearance. There were other detectives involved but Hunter was the leader. The unit's sole task was to co-ordinate the flow of intelligence between the criminal underworld and the police on both sides of the border, as well as politicians.'

'Politicians, police and criminals,' said Halligan. 'Did he ever use the word conspiracy?'

'Not to my knowledge. I think he believed that Hunter was in step with the times, the era of post-ceasefire policing. The expectation that police on both sides of the border should work more closely with each other and political leaders in the interests of sustaining peace.'

But McKenna had delicately skirted around the facts. In truth, detectives like Hunter were men of shadow, without coherence or substance, police officers who operated in the insomniac territory of informers, detectives with the guts to extend themselves across the border and roam with psychopaths and murderers. In Carey, Hunter had found another detective brave enough to join him, willing to let himself be stretched as thoroughly as the war against crime and dissident terrorists would allow, far beyond the paltry boundaries that commanders like Halligan or village sergeants like himself could ever envisage.

Halligan squinted at the look on McKenna's face with a slightly bemused look. 'All very dark, isn't it?' he said.

McKenna resisted the temptation to pass judgment on Carey's detective work and his state of mind. He avoided any interpretation whatsoever.

'You look worried, Peter,' said Halligan. 'Don't be.'

'I hear the press are already on Carey's trail, and Detective Hunter's, too.'

Halligan winced.

This was how policing crises developed, thought McKenna. A dead detective, an investigation with no centre, and senior commanders on the prowl, intent on covering their backs.

The commander finished his poteen, and reached over to the bottle for a refill. He took a fresh sip. 'Detective Robert Hunter,' he said, savouring the name as if trying to drag up a vague memory. 'Was he based in Crossmaglen? Around the time of Inspector Mills?' He repeated Hunter's name to himself.

'I think you're right,' said McKenna.

'I ran into him a few times on fishing trips with colleagues from the North. He was close friends with that Detective Ian Cunningham, who was blown up in a bomb. He took it very bad, I remember.'

'Those were bad times,' said McKenna.

Both men's eyes watered a little. The effects of the poteen were taking hold.

'Christ, I remember every time one of their men was killed by the IRA,' said Halligan. 'Having to go up North and pay our condolences. I was drunk on almost every occasion.' He gulped at his poteen. His voice sounded more sincere than it normally did. 'Do you know what comes into my head every time I think of the Troubles?' he asked.

Halligan waited but McKenna said nothing.

126

'The bloody Angelus bells.'

McKenna stared at him blankly.

'Every time the Ulster Television bulletin came on at six in the evening, and the newscaster started reading about another bomb or shooting, I'd switch immediately to RTE, and those bells were always ringing out like the furies.'

'Of course,' said McKenna. 'They still do.'

'Now the two things are connected in my head. The carnage over the border, all those lives trapped in violence, and the bells of the Angelus racking the conscience of holy Ireland.' He sighed. 'Those demented bells can't be stopped now. They keep ringing in my head.'

McKenna felt he should say something. 'The Virgin Mary ran out of miracles for the North a long time ago,' he murmured. Deep down, he wondered if Halligan was hiding from a painful conscience, that in reality it had been too easy to ignore the suffering over the border and that the bells had been a symbol of the obtuseness that perpetuated itself through their society.

Halligan leaned forward, lowering his voice. 'Did Hunter ever tell Carey anything about his unit, who his chief was?'

'If he did, Carey never repeated it.'

Halligan frowned. 'What do we really know about Hunter, other than his name and the fact that he was a PSNI detective?'

When McKenna did not reply, the commander leaned back and sighed. Perhaps it was the effect of the poteen and the low lighting, but Halligan's eyes closed slightly, as though he had grown sleepy.

McKenna said, 'I know one important thing about him.'

'What's that?' Halligan roused himself from sleep.

'He had a dangerous influence over Carey.'

'How?'

'He offered him ambition, the chance of career glory, a way out of this humdrum police station.'

Once again, McKenna saw the corpse, this time carried by the currents along the perimeter of the lough, played on by wind and rain, drifting towards that lonely shore made out of mist and mud like some sort of floating bomb ready to detonate its secrets. Why of all places did he have to commit suicide in the North? In spite of the poteen, he felt chilled all over. Carey's death had left behind a fuse, a very fine, almost invisible fuse but one he would have to snuff out quickly.

'Another glass?' he asked the commander.

'I'd love some.'

It was only 8 p.m. and the night stretched ahead of them. In the morning, they would both have a hangover and no clear memory of how their conversation ended. They would seek a restorative from the drinks cabinet before attending Carey's funeral, convinced they had accomplished something together, negotiated their way through tricky and contentious territory.

Halligan leaned forward and stared at McKenna, his eyes shining. 'You've always been a top-class police officer, you know,' he said drunkenly.

'Don't feel you have to say that.'

'I'm serious, Peter. You've a cool head and you've kicked around this dangerous border even longer than me. You've always been the soul of discretion.'

McKenna shook his head, but Halligan continued, undeterred. 'You're the one colleague I feel I can talk to. I've never confided with anyone else. All these young upstarts determined to further their careers. None of them is interested in the grind of community policing. A village like Dreesh needs a pragmatic police sergeant. Someone who gets along with everyone, gives them the time of day. They don't care that you've never cracked a big case or collared a criminal like Morgan.'

McKenna nodded. It was true that he had turned down promotions in order to hang on to his post in this dreary village with its comfortable station house and garden. Nor had he paid much attention to Morgan's criminal dealings, apart from the occasional oblique glance at his fuel depot and farm. But the rise of Morgan's empire had disturbed him, no question about that. The border bred men like Morgan – its market and political forces. The flow of money that lavished vast wealth on some and drove others to suicide. He watched the poteen slosh in the glasses as Halligan poured another round. And what if he'd stood up to the horror and death of Morgan and those capital forces he now controlled?

As if reading his thoughts, Halligan said, 'You've always understood what's important.'

'What?'

'It's the people of Dreesh that count, their livelihood, their fight against the poverty of their ancestors. Men like Morgan not so much. They want their police sergeant to be interested when their livestock goes missing, or when a drink-driver crashes into their gate. They think the world of you; you know that, don't you?'

Halligan was veering beyond sentimental eulogy. *I'm going to need more fortification for this*, thought McKenna, topping up his glass.

'We're police officers,' said Halligan with a slur creeping into his voice. 'We have to uphold law and order, but we have to be careful of throwing the baby out with the bathwater.'

Christ, he's completely crocked, thought McKenna. He wanted to stop him before he said something irrevocable. 'I'm not sure I like your compliments,' he said with a painful grin, 'or where you're going with this.'

'Perhaps I'm not saying it right. What I mean is… you're one of the few police officers left that I respect. You've been through it all. Nothing ever rattled you. You're a breed apart.'

What sort of breed was he then? A faithful hound eager to obey its master, too faithful for its own good?

'I'll tell you why everyone in this bloody village respects you.' A note of bitterness had crept into Halligan's voice. 'This station is your life.' He waved his hand vaguely, as though the village beyond the four walls were his invisible audience. 'And the people of Dreesh walk straight in. They know you personally. So many things change. Neighbours and friends are unpredictable. But you're not. You never change. You and this station stay the same.'

'We're getting drunk,' said McKenna.

'True.' Halligan glowered at him with what looked like angry jealousy.

'The public respects you, too, and your officers look up to you,' said McKenna.

'As their commander. But they don't know me personally. How do they know what kind of man I really am?'

'I know.'

'And do you respect me?'

'Not just respect.'

'But do you respect me?'

'Very much.' McKenna felt as though all the energy had drained from him. It was the stress caused by Carey's death, the increasing worry that there had been something frantic about his last days, and now these drunken emotional signals from Halligan. He rose and walked to the window, gazing out at what he could see of the village. The commander's patronizing words felt like the last straw. Only a police officer so smug and crassly careerist as the chief could afford to indulge such a sentimental view of the border village. He gulped the last of his glass, the poteen tasting sour. Whom did Halligan think he was kidding? Getting drunk in this lonely station, going on as though his sergeant's post were somehow vital to the well-being of the village.

The commander raised his eyebrows at McKenna and said, 'And now this Inspector Daly has turned up. Thinks that Carey was murdered.'

'That's the crux of it,' McKenna said.

'Did you tell the inspector your misgivings? About Carey?'

'Only slightly. Daly's from a different police force. That information is confidential.'

Halligan nodded in agreement. 'And what kind of detective is Inspector Daly?'

'A good detective, but I get the impression he's confusing the investigation with another case. A few times, he called Carey by a different name. Donaldson, I think it was. I seem to remember a police chief by that name drowning on Lough Neagh a while ago.'

McKenna moved a little unsteadily to a cupboard and retrieved a bottle of whiskey. Halligan held the glass up to him as though to make a toast, but in reality, he was waiting for another top-up.

'Cheers, Peter,' said Halligan, 'you've always given it to me straight. The view from the ground through the eyes of a seasoned professional.' He knocked the contents of his glass back.

McKenna stared at Halligan's bulging eyes, his half-smile, and his tie awkwardly protruding from his shirt collar. He understood it clearly now: the commander's glib words of praise, the comfortable lies, the feigned confusion about what Carey and Hunter were up to. *What secrets are you hiding?* he thought as he filled Halligan's glass again, listening to him hold forth on the reputation of the police force, the safety of law-abiding citizens living along the border, the core values of An Garda Síochána, the words bubbling up around him, the half-truths and deceptions forming and dissolving. *Perhaps I really am a breed apart, lost in a herd of a different species,* he thought.

The alcohol dulled McKenna's brain, and all the suspicions and fears he had been harbouring towards Carey faded, as if he had suddenly understood the real reason for his disappearance and evasive tactics, his lack of a proper goodbye. He knew perfectly well that Halligan and the rest of his Garda colleagues could not help him now, but at least they provided companionship and the illusion that a miracle might happen, something unexpected that would save the village of Dreesh from damnation.

He forced a shallow smile at Halligan, the one he wore most days to hide his sense of failure and shame, and stared at his chief, so full of authority in his gleaming uniform even when drunk, his epaulettes and his brass buttons. What was the point dressing up like that? he thought. In Dreesh, no one respected the uniform any more.

Detective Carey's determination to arrest Morgan had made McKenna angry and jealous inside, because he had once felt a similar fervour, to be thorough and persistent and one day surprise his commander with a shrewdly worked-out analysis that would crack an insoluble case, but he didn't have that any more, and Carey had kept reminding him of the painful truth. Reminding him that he was the longest-serving police officer along this part of the border, a man who could no longer say boo to a goose, who drank several glasses of illicit booze every evening to numb himself from the humiliating truth: that he had allowed Morgan and his greed to seep through the entire village, to fill the lives of its failed business people, its struggling farmers, even the children who constantly demanded from their parents the things they could not afford – the latest smartphones and sportswear.

The police station had been McKenna's life, and his home, but something much worse. The young IRA man, Morgan, had begun as a burden to put up with, turning after the ceasefire and recession into a darker thing altogether, a biblical curse from which there was no escape. He convinced himself it was the law of the border, the price to pay for a monotonous and safe existence in the heart of the village, shut up in this police station that was his home, and prison, too. How could he stop being the policeman he had ended up being? If he could find a way to blurt out the truth to Halligan, what would his commander say, how would he react?

Halligan must have seen the expression of dismay on his

face. He leaned towards him with a kindly look, and took a while to formulate some words. 'Don't worry, Peter, things are looking up. Retirement beckons, yours and mine.' He replenished their glasses. 'Did I tell you about the little boat I've bought? I keep it down at the marina. Just perfect for a little fishing trip around the lakes. You should come down some weekend and check it out. A little motor boat for you and me to enjoy in our retirement.'

The mention of retirement felt like Halligan's coup de grâce, adding a final blow of sadness to McKenna's pain and envy.

CHAPTER FIFTEEN

The morning after the traffic collision Daly was summonsed to the mortuary to view the body of the woman he had knocked over. To his further dismay, she turned out to be Brigid Donnelly, Detective Carey's partner, who had been so desperate to speak to him. Commander Sinclair had left Daly a cryptic message on his phone, insisting that the detective liaise with the pathologist. Apparently, the post-mortem examination of the body had thrown up perplexities about the woman's death.

Normally, killers weren't called to see their handiwork, thought Daly as he made his way to the forensic suite. Did Sinclair want him to wallow more deeply in his guilt? Or was there a more sinister reason: to ensure Daly could not claim later that the evidence against him was flawed or prejudiced in any way? If his commander viewed him with such distrust, Daly did not know whether to be hurt or disgusted.

There was no sign of anybody at the glass doors to the

autopsy room. A sign instructed visitors to press a buzzer for entry, but Daly noticed that the door hung slightly ajar. He entered the room slowly.

The dead woman lay on a table, her body covered by a blanket, her face turned slightly to one side, her blond hair shining in the morning sun that slanted in rays from the high windows. Glinting beside her, on a little table, was a tray of surgical instruments, arrayed as if for a final breakfast.

She seemed diminished and defenceless, her head resting on an ugly plastic block, her eyes wide open as though dazzled by the invisible afterlife. One of her false eyelashes was slightly detached. Daly's stomach churned with guilt. He was not up to this, he realized. He should have told Sinclair he did not feel in a fit state to view the corpse.

A figure, appearing at the door, exclaimed a welcome. Daly blinked and stepped back from the body.

'Just having a tea and sandwich,' said the pathologist Ruadh Butler, his pink scrubbed face beaming at Daly. He stretched his impeccably clean hands into a pair of surgical gloves, and clenched and unclenched his god-like fists over the tray of instruments. 'At first, I thought we had the wrong body,' he explained, pulling a long fluorescent lamp over the table.

'Why?'

'Even on a cursory examination I could see you hadn't killed her, at least not with your car.'

Butler grinned at Daly and whipped back the blanket. Daly stared at the woman's sharp bones and luminous skin. For a moment, words evaded him. He felt numb. He had held her dying body in his arms but he had lived the scene so many times in his head that its details were now completely blurred.

'Have you brought me here for an autopsy lesson?' asked Daly. 'Because if you have, I don't think I'm equipped. Mentally, I mean.'

'Take a look. The injuries she sustained in the collision were minor and not sufficient to have caused her death so suddenly.' Butler spoke with total certainty, as if he had been an eyewitness at the accident.

Daly had entered the room in a kind of trance, but now his heart began to beat unevenly. What was the pathologist implying? He wanted to blurt out that he wasn't feeling good, that he hadn't slept well at all. Every time he had nodded off, the memory of her face had jolted him awake. And now, here he was, in this room without shadows or dark corners, translucent, exposed in every possible way. No wonder Butler exuded such an air of comfortable self-possession, inhabiting this stage of hyper-real light where nothing was left hidden, while detectives like him floundered in the side wings, wrestling with half-submerged horrors and the pale ghosts of their suspicions.

'You've looked at the dead before, Daly. Don't be so morbid.'

The pathologist was correct. In the circumstances, morbidity was an indulgence, and he shouldn't indulge himself. Daly turned and examined her body more closely, every contour, muscle and bone.

'She died from a bullet wound in the left side of her neck,' said Butler. 'The bullet severed the right subclavian artery.' He gave Daly a sympathetic smile, as though he were no longer a killer, just a disastrously bad detective. 'Did the profuse amount of blood not strike you as odd?'

The bleeding *had* struck him as unusual, but it seemed improbable that she had been in the act of dying when he struck her.

'The scene-of-crime officers found a track of her blood leading back through the trees. It appears that she dragged herself on to the road in a futile attempt to get help.'

Sure enough, Daly saw a gouging wound amid a large maroon discoloration covering her upper left shoulder and neck. Just the sort of wound a bullet would have left behind. He had been too quick to take the blame. In a flash, he saw the accident in its proper light. He had been so distracted and tired with overwork that he had failed to absorb her strange, unhinged flight from the forest. He remembered the visible effort in her body as she struggled to stay upright, her hands groping at the air, before the bonnet of his car, in that sickeningly raw moment of physicality, flipped her into the darkness. His conscience had rushed in too harshly. For a moment, he savoured the relief at his misunderstanding.

But the woman was still dead, not sleeping or in a coma. It was far from being a false alarm. The guilt he had felt about her demise, the anger at his carelessness began to evaporate away, and was replaced by a burning desire to find out the identity of the killer who had delivered her into his path.

The suite began to fill with laboratory assistants and forensic experts. All about him were voices and quick foot-steps. He felt the steadying hand of professional routine return, demanding that he gather himself and muster his forces of reasoning and intuition. He had a crime scene to find, and a killer. Thank God for murder, he thought, and the way it filled his life with a ready-made labyrinth into which he could lose himself day by day.

CHAPTER SIXTEEN

'You know that I don't approve of your methods, Daly,' said Special Branch Inspector Ian Fealty, 'the way you secretly disappear into border country while going about your normal detective business.'

Not for the first time, the stern gaze of the inspector took Daly aback. Several times over the past year, his strong and weak points as a police officer had been cold-heartedly discussed in the heavy light of Fealty's bare office, analysed and exposed not only in professional terms, but also in personal and political terms, for with Fealty you could never separate one from the others. It was not easy to keep the Special Branch officer at bay, and Daly usually came out of the meetings feeling worse than expected.

Fealty continued, 'Nor do I approve of the way you follow clues that aren't really clues, confusing your colleagues and disorientating your superiors.'

Daly blinked. What was a clue that wasn't a clue? A riddle

or a red herring? Fealty was referring to his detective skills as though they amounted to little more than amateur guesswork.

'However, sometimes your oblique and unconventional methods have an uncanny knack of getting results. And in the current circumstances your tactics might prove advantageous, as we are all struggling in the dark.'

Daly let the criticism pass. 'What do you propose?'

'I'm going to provide you with the full resources of Special Branch.' Fealty's gaze was still unblinking and severe. 'Irwin will be your subordinate. He will follow your orders, as long as you are clear in your instructions, and don't compromise the investigation in any way.'

'And at the same time, Irwin will report everything back to you.'

'It's true that Irwin will operate as an observer for Special Branch, but that shouldn't prevent you from taking advantage of his expertise.'

'Does that include access to Special Branch files?'

Daly had demanded the meeting with Fealty to help shed light on the investigation into Detective Carey and his partner's deaths. Earlier, a stir had gone through the police station, when the scene-of-crime officers, tracking Brigid Donnelly's final flight through the trees, found that her house had been ransacked, furniture upended, drawers emptied, and files scattered everywhere. A botched burglary or something more sinister? Daly wished he had spoken to Donnelly earlier, before her killer had struck.

Fealty stared at Daly thoughtfully. 'What exactly do you want to know?'

'The details of a group of detectives who may or may not

have been operating under the Special Branch banner,' said Daly. 'They were given the responsibility of liaising with their counterparts in the Gardai, who included Detective Carey.'

'You need to give me some names before I can proceed.'

'Why don't you give me the names? From what I can gather, their identities are being protected. One of them used the name Robert Hunter, but that may be an alias. I've searched the police records. There's no trace anywhere of an officer with that name.'

'Tell me what you know about this unit of detectives, and then I might answer your question.'

'You *might* answer my question?'

Fealty consulted his watch. 'Look, Daly, I've a meeting with the Justice Minister this morning. I can only give you another few minutes of my time.'

'OK,' said Daly. 'According to his Garda colleague, Carey had been close to apprehending the smuggler Tom Morgan, but the file was sent back up North and the investigation suddenly dropped. Detective Robert Hunter had been working closely with Carey, too closely by the sound of things, and had been co-ordinating the flow of intelligence information over the border. Apparently, they met on regular fishing trips.'

'They were friends?'

'I'm not sure. The picture McKenna gave of Carey was of a loner, obsessed with his work. I don't think he confided in anyone, which is also interesting.'

'I don't follow you.'

'You'd think that in handling a difficult case like Morgan's he would seek support from his colleagues. But according to McKenna, he didn't. Was that because he didn't trust them?'

'You think you're on to something?'

'I'm only speculating. Perhaps it's far-fetched to say that Carey suspected there was a traitor among his colleagues.'

'You mean in the South?'

'South or North. Sergeant McKenna said that Carey was annoyed when the charges against Morgan were dropped by the PSNI. Carey thought he had a case against him. You can interpret that in different ways.'

'Can you? When the prosecutors say there isn't a strong enough case to bring, then the charges have to be dropped.'

'Nor can we overlook the fact that Carey had been trying to find Hunter in the days leading up to his death. Perhaps he had urgent questions to ask him.'

'This is just speculation.'

'At the moment, yes.'

'Daly, the problem with you is you've been conducting the same speculation over and over again. There is no end to it, no summing up or conclusion. There is always this logjam of conspiracies but nothing to reveal, no hope of clarity or resolution. Here you are, rehearsing the same paranoia, afflicted by the same itch, and this makes me question your underlying motives. Whose side are you really on? Who is pulling your strings in the darkness? Why do you keep raising the same suspicions about your Special Branch colleagues, the same unending questions? What am I supposed to do with them? What am I supposed to do with you?'

Daly did not reply.

'And what does all this have to do with the murder of Carey's girlfriend?'

'Donnelly knew something important about the investigation, something incriminating. I believe that's the reason she was murdered.'

For a moment, Fealty looked as though he was tempted to get rid of Daly, but somehow he resisted the urge. 'How do you know this?' he asked. 'I thought you ran over the woman before she could be interviewed.'

'A journalist spoke to her first.'

Fealty's eyebrows rose. 'You're talking about Jacqueline Pryce, aren't you?'

'She told me she'd asked you about this cross-border group of detectives. According to her, they called themselves the Green and Blue Fishing Club. She said you ignored her calls.'

'Of course I did. Journalists like Pryce have stirred up enough shit about my officers without me volunteering to drown in it.' There was a stillness in Fealty's gaze, a determination to keep Daly under scrutiny. 'What do you intend to do now?'

Despite Fealty's professional manner, Daly detected in his eyes the shadow of a secret. 'I want to find Robert Hunter. With Special Branch help.'

Fealty explained that a team of his staff had scoured the entire records and questioned police officers in stations along the border. They, too, had found no trace of Robert Hunter.

'Which confirms my belief that he's using an alias,' said Daly. 'What do you have on Morgan? Is he an intelligence asset?'

'Let me be clear on this, Daly. Morgan is not being protected by anyone in Special Branch. He is not and never has been an informer. These days, we have fewer resources for intelligence-gathering but we have the advantage of being more astute and better co-ordinated. We do not cross the moral line. Unlike many of the arrangements with informers in the past. We have to be aware of the political attitudes to the people we recruit. We don't go down the old paths. That hinterland is strictly out of bounds.' Fealty stopped talking and coughed. It was not a spasm triggered by any bodily irritation. It was the cough of a man telling Daly it was time to go. He gestured towards the door. 'Normally, I'd allow you a week to produce some definite leads,' he said, 'but you're such a hesitant detective, I'll allow you a fortnight. I'm prepared to support you in any reasonable way if it means that we can find a chink in Morgan's defences. It goes without saying that, at this moment, I completely subscribe to your theory that Morgan might be behind Carey's death and that of his girlfriend. Currently, he is our prime suspect. It's up to you and Detective Irwin to find the evidence.'

Daly stared around at the impeccably white walls one more time. He wanted to thank Fealty for his admission that he might be on the right track, but he did not know how to without breaking the code of their relationship. He thought of shaking hands with him, but he had already done so at the start of the meeting. He got up and left the room, his head brimming with dangerous questions. What was his journey as a detective but a flouting of the political? He thought of his relationship with the Special Branch inspector as being, like all long-lasting partnerships, founded on tension: Daly pushing against the political constraints, and Fealty hemming him in; Daly desiring the freedom to operate according to his suspicions, and Fealty compelled to crush those suspicions.

Daly thought that in criticizing his methods Fealty had

inadvertently given expression to something profound. That in trying to connect to the mysterious life of a dead detective, he had found another shadowy place to distract himself, to try out his powers of deduction and stumble towards a solution that might not exist. It wasn't a thirst for justice that drove him on in this particular quest, but the unanswered questions that Carey had left behind, the blank of his final days that had compelled him to follow the trail of another lost creature.

CHAPTER SEVENTEEN

Tommy dreamed that he was flying towards home, his body carried over swells of air, rising and falling through vast heights in the clouds. He felt happy and giddy, yet also pained at the thought that he was airborne and free at the expense of the countless fugitives below, as though only he had been saved to make this dangerous flight back to Ireland. He had taken the place of so many lost and wandering men and women, not because he was the best or strongest, but because he was the worst, an informer, betraying everyone and usurping the places of that army of leaden exiles trapped on the ground below. He picked up speed and rose higher but still he could hear them shouting for deliverance as they jostled together. How had he escaped the turmoil of banishment, the hands waving for help, the yearning faces boiling up from the depths? Why did he deserve to be saved? It was more than chance or the power of circumstances that had lifted him to these heights. It was because of his mother that he had been singled out for this return journey home. Her letter had formed the basis for his rescue. A mother's love for her only son.

He flew with determination back to the place that had reared him, eager for redemption, but the feeling of shame would not go away. It nestled deep in his heart, gnawing away at him, weakening his resolve to return to his old life. Why had he been saved and no one else? What responsibilities lay waiting for him back home? What exactly did his mother mean, writing in her letter that he would be a marked man and would have to bear witness to the truth? The shadows of suspicion and shame began to trouble him as he drew closer to the northern dusk.

Almost within sight of home, he hit a wall of turbulence. His body thumped downwards, his bones quivering in the violent air, and he braced himself for the long fall into darkness.

He gave a start, jerking from his dream. A woman leaned towards him, tapping his shoulder. For a second, he thought it was his mother. It was time to fasten his seatbelt, she told him. He realized she was a flight attendant. Tommy glanced blearily around the plane. The economy-class flight to Belfast, full of sleeping commuters and holidaying families. He checked his watch. He had been out for most of the journey. A little girl stared at him from the seat on the other side of the aisle. She was stuck to her mother's side, listening to her reading a story from a picture book, behind her a round window of cloudless air. He felt empty and remote as the plane circled above patches of glinting water and then descended towards Belfast.

Right on cue, it began to rain as the taxi took him into the city. At the station, he caught a bus, which carried him at speed along a new motorway, and then down dangerously narrow roads, the windows blindfolded by high hedges. He stayed on the bus to the very end of the line, the very end of the country, a black bridge leading over a river that marked the border with the Republic of Ireland. No matter how you approached this place, it always felt secretive and fortified. Gone were the military watchtowers, the barbed wire and cement blocks obstructing the roads, but still there remained a sense of remoteness, an uneasy relationship with the outside world.

I'm mad to have returned, he thought after the bus deposited him by a lane too muddy to drive anything but a tractor along, the only living things in view a flock of starlings wheeling above a row of roofless cottages. He walked the final mile home. The gloominess of the rounded hills and the tangle of roads deepening in the twilight surprised him after the blazing light of Spain. He stopped at the little lake below his mother's house, and stared at the smoothness of the water in the last of the evening light. He felt as though he were peering into an interior landscape trapped beneath glass, another tier in the labyrinth.

His mother was not expecting him when he walked through the kitchen door. He had thought about phoning her, hesitated, and then decided against it. Her back was turned to him as she worked at the sink in her familiar way. He could see her shoulders bracing at the sound of his footsteps.

'I'm back, Mum,' he said. He had practised saying the words in a normal voice.

'I know,' she replied. 'I heard you disturbing the lake with your thoughts.'

She turned to him with a sudden movement. He thought she was going to embrace him, but, to his surprise, she slapped him firmly on the cheek.

'You made me so angry,' she said. 'I can't help it.'

However, he saw the relief in her shoulders as she turned and set about making tea.

'You messed up your life, working for that criminal Morgan, without even thinking of me or your poor dead father,' she said, slamming the cupboard doors and running water into the kettle. 'Do you know what your father thought on his death bed?'

'I don't want to know.'

'He thought you were ashamed of us. That we were one more secret in your life.'

She waited for the kettle to boil. The sensation of return did not feel as comforting as he had imagined. It felt distorted and unreal, as though he had fallen into that other landscape, the one trapped in the interior of the lake. He had thought he would be able to tell her everything about his career as an informer, wash his soul clean and turn over that dark page in his life, but he had been mistaken.

'Why did you send me the letter?' he asked.

'Because it's my punishment to bring you back. I'm serving a sentence, too.'

'What did you do wrong?'

'I let you fall into such bad company.'

She walked around the kitchen, rearranging objects, closing and shutting drawers. Busying herself was her weapon of mental aggression. Eventually, she produced an apple tart, his favourite, from the fridge, her mouth set in a narrow frown. Her temper seemed to have cooled. Later, he realized it was the apple tart that gave her away. Her movements and her words had felt so natural and unrehearsed, but she had meticulously prepared them in advance. Apart from the freshly cooked apple tart, she had been flawless in her performance.

'For months, I denied your existence,' she told him. 'All the neighbours were asking me questions. About my son, the smuggler and criminal.'

He thought of telling her everything, but she probably knew already.

'I never imagined the trouble you'd land me in. The shame of walking home from Mass and seeing the look of suspicion on neighbours' faces. Crossing the street when they saw me coming, as if I was the criminal.' She sighed with a sharp edge to her breath. She glared at him without the usual wavering that had met his teenage misdemeanours.

'And then to hear from poor Detective Carey that you were an informer, on top of everything else. Christ, what were you thinking?' She stared at him with a look of desperation. It was not aversion he saw there, nor was it love. It was as if a part of her were trying to give him some sort of forewarning.

He wondered what was the point in seeking her sympathy when he was so far beyond it. He moved from his uncomfortable post at the table to the sofa. He was tired after the long journey. He lay down and drifted in and out of sleep while she sat in a chair by the fire. From time to time, she rose and came close to him. Afterwards, he realized she had been tidying the room, preparing the place for their visitor.

He awoke to hear a low voice in the porch. His mother's chair was empty. A man was speaking in hushed, respectful tones. He was not interested in who had called at the door and he dozed again. It was a dreamless sleep, and then his mother woke him.

'Someone's here to see you, Tommy,' she said. Her introduction was strangely posed. She sounded afraid.

He took the hand offered by the visitor and shook it.

The man spoke in a deep voice. 'Well, Tommy, you've come back like a calf to the fucking slaughterhouse.' The voice had lost its polite tones. It was vulgar and brazen.

His mother spoke. 'My son wants to help put Morgan behind bars.'

'Well, I'll be damned.' The visitor looked at Tommy critically, as though he had come to bid on his carcass.

'Look at him,' said his mother. 'Under my roof with his life in danger, his friend Detective Carey dead, his life hanging by a thread. I hope to God I have the strength to help him.'

She began making more tea. He could tell from the manner in which she lifted out the cups and saucers and placed them on the table that she was agitated again.

The man sat down opposite Tommy and grinned. He needed no introduction. He was Paddy Leadon, the IRA chief along this part of the border.

'Stay where you are, Tommy. I've only just walked in the door. It would be bad manners to get up and leave now.' He looked into Tommy's eyes, his large hands twitching with suppressed violence.

To Tommy's relief, his mother quickly placed a china cup brimming with tea into Leadon's hands. The IRA man focused his attention on sipping noisily from the cup. Then he leaned back and breathed in deeply. 'That's an apple tart I smell. Armagh Bramleys, if I'm not mistaken.'

'Yes,' said his mother. 'Armagh Bramleys.'

She put a slice before Leadon and, for a while, nothing else was said. When the IRA chief had finished eating, he smeared his hairy hand across his mouth and smiled at Tommy's mother, who did not seem to mind his bad manners.

When she had returned to the kitchen cupboards, Leadon leaned closer to Tommy. 'I've met a lot of informers in my time, son,' he said.

Tommy's heart thumped in his chest.

'And none of them ever took their secrets to the grave. Even the most hardened bastard feels an inner need to tell the truth after I've got my hands on him.'

Tommy forced himself to stare at the look of dark glee mounting in the IRA man's pupils.

CHAPTER EIGHTEEN

Daly drove along the Birches road, glancing at his rear-view mirror, taking in his stray fatigued eyes and the shifting stretch of road behind. It was the first time in weeks he had looked into his own eyes, and they resembled those of an exhausted stranger, a man whose feelings he was too busy to care about any more. But he had not looked into the mirror to confront himself or gauge his inner state of mind. He was checking the car that had pulled out from a hidden lay-by and was now tailing him.

Still looking in the mirror, he braked suddenly and watched the car swerve at the last moment to avoid a collision. The driver pulled alongside Daly and rolled down the window.

'So there you are, Celcius,' said the journalist Jacqueline Pryce.

'I spotted you in my mirror. You were driving too close.'

'I need to talk to you.' She had that impatient no-nonsense expression she wore when under the pressure of a deadline.

'First you keep calling to my house, and now you try to ambush me while I'm driving. Are you stalking me?'

'No, I just wanted to hear if you'd discovered anything about the Green and Blue Fishing Club.'

'Nothing.'

'What about Detective Hunter?'

'The same.'

'You look tense.'

Daly blinked at her. 'I had a rough night's sleep.'

She nodded sympathetically. 'It must be hard going, dealing with what happened to Brigid Donnelly.'

'What do you know about that?'

'I heard you knocked her down. You shouldn't blame yourself for her death.'

'I don't blame myself. I blame you. You're her killer.'

She gave an incredulous laugh. 'Are you joking? I was nowhere near her last night.'

'But you killed her all the same.' His eyes maintained their heavy accusing look.

'You're being ridiculous. Stop this.' She released her handbrake. 'I'm not your suspect.'

'You're not my suspect, but you're in the frame. You told me she wanted to speak to me urgently about the Green and Blue Fishing Club. Who else did you tell?'

'Apart from you, no one.'

He toyed with the possibility of calling her a bloody liar, but he failed to summon enough rudeness. 'You must have told someone.'

'I don't know what you're talking about,' she said with a brazen look of defiance.

'You let it slip to your colleagues. You must have.'

'If I were you I'd concentrate on what your own colleagues knew about her.'

'What do you mean?'

'Far be it from me to meddle in your investigation, but I can tell you the name of a Special Branch inspector who knew about my conversation with Donnelly.'

'Who?'

'Talk to Fealty. He'll put you in the picture.'

'I just have.'

Pryce watched Daly closely, clearly enjoying the look that now clouded his features. 'I've another tip-off for you,' she said. 'Morgan's travelling across the border tomorrow to present a fat cheque to a GAA football club at Drumkillen near Aughnacloy. He's funding a new stadium and training facility. I'm covering it for the local papers. Got any questions you want me to ask him?'

'You never give up,' said Daly. 'Sometimes I think you should have been a police detective instead of a journalist.'

'Really?' she asked, smiling.

'Promise me you'll stop interfering in this case.'

'I can't do that.'

'Then, good luck with your interview. I'm sure you'll want to tell me how it went.'

'I will,' said Pryce. 'By the way, I'll be thinking of you tomorrow.'

'Why?' Daly stared at her blankly.

'The newspapers are publishing the story of Donaldson's suicide note.'

Daly turned and gazed at the windscreen, saying nothing.

'Well, I just wanted to tell you,' said Pryce. 'I'll go now. Goodbye, Celcius. Next time we meet I hope I'll have some good news.'

Good news. He grimaced at the term.

At police headquarters, Daly remembered Brigid Donnelly's dead body in the morgue. He had yet to hear from the forensics team that had been tasked to search Carey's house for clues to her killer. He rang Detective O'Neill's mobile number. She was at the house and answered the call immediately. It struck him how confident and in charge she sounded. She summarized the details of the search so far.

The intruders had emptied drawers and cupboards, and upended furniture, she told him, but forensics had yet to find any clues to their identity. In what appeared to be the study, Carey had installed his own security measures. He had given his computer and hard drive its own lockable housing, which he had chained to the wall. A thief could not simply have walked away with the equipment. However, whoever had ransacked the house had spent time using a crowbar to open the housing and free it from the wall. Interestingly, the screws which stored the housing had been covered in glitter nail polish.

'What was the purpose of that?' asked Daly. 'To check that no one had tampered with them?'

'That's what forensics believe,' she replied. 'Carey would have noticed if anyone had tried to access the data on the hard drive or tamper with it in any way. Clearly, he didn't expect someone to take a crowbar to the unit and remove it wholesale.'

She had also found several phone books, earmarked at the name Hunter, with all the numbers listed under the name underlined. 'I've rung all the numbers; no trace of a Detective Hunter.'

Daly thanked her for her diligence. He told her that reporters were interested in the story, and to be careful. 'I want you to warn everyone there that they have to be discreet and professional at all times. We have leaks.'

'What do you mean, we?'

'The police team here in Armagh. Including Special Branch.'

'Who's doing the leaking?'

'I intend to find out,' he said and hung up.

Afterwards, he went off in search of Inspector Fealty, but the Special Branch Inspector was nowhere to be seen. Daly cornered Detective Irwin in his office as he was shutting down his computer and preparing to leave. He was humming a tune and obviously in a good mood.

'Sorry, I haven't been much help today,' said Irwin. He pointed to a stack of boxes crammed with dusty files in a corner of the room. 'I found the Special Branch files you wanted. I've scanned through them and can't find any reference to this fishing club or Detective Hunter.'

Daly raised an eyebrow. Could he trust Irwin to have looked carefully enough? Might he have ignored important clues in the files? The questions were irrelevant. He would have to sift through the boxes himself.

He lifted out the files and saw that the notes were not arranged in any alphabetical or chronological order. He groaned. There were sections and sub-sections, reports of meetings, coroner's reports, even individual murder files and case notes. Somewhere within them, a record of Hunter must exist, he told himself. He scanned page after page, seeking the name but finding no trace of it.

He was not even sure what he was looking at most of the time. The security force operations along the border had always been shrouded in secrecy. For decades, there had been rumours of rogue intelligence agents operating on their own, and lingering fears of betrayal and collusion between the police forces and paramilitary organizations. A mood of suspicion and a fear of giving anything away dominated the reports. He got sidetracked reading about the watchtowers along the border and their surveillance platforms, as well as other static observation posts, known as OPs. During the Troubles, a mythology had built up around the capabilities of the all-hearing, all-seeing gadgets deployed by the intelligence forces. He was surprised at the depth of information they had gleaned from the border communities. Although the army manned and ran the OPs, all the intelligence gained had been passed to Special Branch. He was amused to read that sometimes the army set up fake aerials and mysteriously shaped boxes at border sites to keep the IRA guessing about what they might be.

He skimmed through the army intelligence reports, reading any files he could find relating to cross-border policing, the manoeuvrings between intelligence officers from the different jurisdictions, and the recruitment of informers. A recurring theme of the confidential reports was Special Branch criticism of the rift between the police forces in the North and South. Liaison between them had always been problematic. One Special Branch detective inspector accused the Gardai of showing a degree of reticence in co-operating at an official level. However, he noted that at a local level with established contacts there appeared to be a more congenial relationship and a little more assistance was forthcoming.

A coroner reporting on an IRA bomb detonated in the Republic was concerned that the Gardai had failed to supply any evidence. He expressed grave doubts over claims that the Southern force had stepped up border security. However, the coroner had scored through these remarks and they were absent from the official inquest report, perhaps in anticipation of the political storm they might have caused. Elsewhere, Daly came across speculation from junior detectives that members of the Garda Síochána were in league with the IRA and had helped set up police officers. However, their lines of investigation were usually quashed by senior commanders.

Daly saw evidence everywhere of fragmented detective work, fear of betrayal, and a lack of cohesion and direction to investigations into criminals like Morgan. The reports presented a picture of decent, hard-working officers doing their best to police the border while weighed down with paperwork and hampered by bureaucracy. On numerous occasions, the Northern Ireland security services chased IRA suspects and smugglers to the border, where they were forced to stop and watch them disappear. The Gardai would only deal with the British Army through the Northern Ireland police service, and the Irish Army refused to take part in any cross-border operations at all. Valuable time was lost when army commanders in the North had to contact their police counterparts to ask them to request a border crossing point be sealed by the Gardai.

He came across a file outlining concerns about individual Garda officers and their links to the IRA. Important DNA evidence that might have implicated an IRA bomber had been thrown on to a skip at the back of Dundalk police station and destroyed. Afterwards, a retired sergeant had been arrested for helping the IRA acquire false passports. However, it was a delicate time in the Northern Ireland peace negotiations and the charges were quietly dropped.

Joint task-force meetings had been set up between the police forces to address the numerous problems, but the reports provided very little detail. Only the highest-ranking officers took part. He flicked through the minutes of meetings spanning the past decade. As time went on and the threat of IRA attacks diminished, the meetings grew less frequent and shorter. There had not been any at all for the past two years.

He wrote down the names of the chairpersons and the supervising committees, wondering if any of them would speak to him privately, or admit to knowing the truth about Detective Hunter. He also made a note of the different locations of the meetings, the names of Gardai officers in attendance. However, the more he read, the more he suspected that these official meticulously recorded meetings between the two forces were just an empty shell, and that intelligence must have been secretly channelled through informal contacts with operatives on the ground. That way it would leave behind no trace.

He looked at his watch and saw that he had been searching for just over two hours. Surely, he should have found some reference to Detective Hunter by now. As far as he could make out nothing had been redacted or removed from the files. 'What else is there?' he asked the stack of boxes. 'What else have I not yet read or seen?' There must be a hiding place for Hunter somewhere. A place impregnable to prying eyes.

He forced himself to keep searching, making a silent plea to Detective Carey for guidance. Protection and darkness, he thought. What secrets had been gathered in the name of both police forces? He started reading over the files again to penetrate the veils of bureaucracy, the private fiefdoms of senior commanders North and South, and finally he found a chink. He stepped out of the tunnel his mind had been racing along, and stared at the bottom of one particular report. He peered at it closely. There was an innocent-seeming reference to recreation costs. He followed the reference back into the main body of the report until he found the details he was searching for: a fishing trip to an undisclosed location in Donegal, the cost of security to protect the high-ranking attendees from both sides of the border, and a list of names. The only one he recognized was Detective Jack McKenna from Special Branch. There was no mention of either Carey or Hunter or any suggestion that the officers had called themselves the Green and Blue Fishing Club. However, it was the first hint of intrigue, of a mysterious secret gathering. The report mentioned a commitment to make the trip an annual get-together, but Daly could find no reference to other trips in the files for the following years.

Daly made a note of the details and folded the piece of paper into his wallet. Two police forces operating across the same terrain: he could see how all manner of betrayal and confusion might be generated by a border and political suspicion, especially the worst, the most terrible betrayal of all.

CHAPTER NINETEEN

Paddy Leadon leaned his big-boned body towards Tommy, his physical bulk menacing, a horrible half-smile lingering upon his face.

'It's time you loosened your tongue, Tommy.' His eyes glinted like a farmer who had pulled off the deal of the market. 'It's time you told me the truth.'

Tommy ought to have said a quick prayer, an act of penance, but instead he stayed where he was on the sofa, still as a hare in a set of headlights, subjecting himself to the IRA man's penetrating gaze. He would have to watch what he said and did, as if he were in a court presided over by a merciless judge. An unfortunate nod of the head or slip of the tongue would be enough to condemn him in the eyes of this violent man to whom he was not a real person, but just a shadow, another informer to be exploited and manipulated.

'What age are you, son?' asked Leadon.

'Twenty.' He tried to avoid looking into Leadon's dangerous

eyes. He had always imagined that an interrogation with the IRA would take place in the dingy back of a Republican pub, or an abandoned cowshed along the border, somewhere redolent of torture and secrets, not in this sitting room with a cup of tea in one hand and his mother hovering mysteriously in the corner.

Leadon ducked his head out of sight of Tommy's mother and winked. 'Christ, I wish I was twenty. Just back from your travels?'

'I was in Spain. I had to get offside.'

He patted Tommy on the shoulder. 'That's the boy.' He glanced back at his mother. 'Tell me, what's your fucking set-up?'

'What do you mean?'

'Look me in the eye now, Tommy, and tell me who's in charge of you? Who pulls your little strings?' Something wild and dangerous blinked in Leadon's face, like a fox peeking from its hideout.

For several moments, words abandoned Tommy; his mind abandoned him. He braced himself.

'You're shivering, Tommy. You're missing the Spanish sun.' Leadon was smiling again, but his presence filled the room, driving out the last of the evening light. His mother's pale face slipped into view.

'His handler was a PSNI detective called Robert Hunter,' she said.

'I'm not acquainted with a Detective Hunter,' said Leadon. 'I've never heard that name before.'

'He works in Special Branch,' said Tommy.

'Believe me, I know all the detectives in Special Branch.

They're like old friends to me now. This Detective Hunter must belong to the intelligence services. What else can you tell me about him?'

Tommy gave Leadon the special phone number Hunter had given him, and all the details he could remember about the detective, the cars he had driven, and the secret location of their meetings. The more he talked about him, the more he realized Hunter belonged to the shadowy war, the unending battle of subterfuge and propaganda, surfacing here and there in operations, his identity little more than a carefully honed silhouette. Leadon listened closely and asked several more questions. Afterwards he leaned back and stared at Tommy with a look that almost amounted to commiseration.

'So you reported on Morgan's operations to this detective, even downloaded all his financial files, but none of your information ever led to his arrest. That's not a good reflection on your intelligence-gathering skills.'

'I didn't get caught. That's the best test of an informer.'

His mother appeared with a fresh teapot and took her time pouring more tea into Leadon's cup.

'I want to know what information you gave to your handlers,' said Leadon.

Tommy told him how he had downloaded details of a string of secret bank accounts on to a USB stick and passed it on to Hunter.

'Tell me about the accounts.'

'I didn't get time to analyse them, but I could see that Morgan was recruiting elderly relatives and neighbours in Dreesh. He signed them up as directors of fake companies. These people have no idea about the world of finance. If they did, they'd be shocked by the fortunes attached to their names. The files contained lots of documents, backdated contracts, large transfers of cash, blank documents with the signatures of Dreesh residents placed in the middle or bottom of the page. I counted up the money flowing through the accounts, and it came to millions of pounds.'

'How does he rely on their secrecy?'

'He pays them large amounts in cash, and uses fear and ignorance to finish the deal. He keeps gathering names and addresses, spinning the money around.'

Leadon smiled, drank, and wiped his mouth. 'The IRA's ruling council have long had suspicions about Morgan,' he said. 'Every time one of his operations is raided he's nowhere to be seen, and afterwards any charges are mysteriously dropped. We've come to the suspicion that he must be a member of that rare protected species, an informer. Unfortunately, there are rules in the organization that can't be broken, even over a criminal like Morgan, and we're reluctant to launch an official investigation. We'd rather work with the meagre resources on the ground. People like you, Tommy.'

'What do you mean?'

'The IRA wish you no harm. You have my word. We have our code of honour, even though you're a tout, a little worm wriggling in the belly of a pig. Your mother came to me and her story moved me. I helped her write the letter that brought you home. We've arranged a little deal for you. I will do everything in my power to keep you alive, and you, for your part, will do exactly as I ask.'

Tommy contorted in his seat. 'The letter never said anything about working for the IRA.'

His mother spoke in irritation. 'For the love of God, son, shut up and listen.'

'Your mother has made a bargain with the IRA to save your life,' said Leadon. 'It's time you pulled yourself together. We want to get our hands on Morgan, this bastard who's caused you and your poor mother so much trouble. The scumbag poses a far greater threat to the IRA than an informer like you ever will.'

'I've cut my ties with Tom Morgan and the security services. What use am I to you?'

'The other side aren't going to allow you to walk away just that easily,' said Leadon. 'They won't let you pick up your old life as though your career as an informer was some sort of bad dream. These men are full-time professionals, and their raison d'être is intelligence-gathering. When Hunter finds out you're back, he'll want his pound of flesh. He'll come calling for you.'

Watching the movements of his mother in the corner of his eye, Tommy felt disturbed by her silent, watchful presence. She was no longer a shadow merging with the background. She was a woman with force in her body and direction to her movements. Leadon had offered him the deal, but somehow, she had recruited them both. They were hers to direct. There seemed to be no steps she would not take, no deal she would not broker, to ensure he would extricate himself from the mess he had created.

'Your mother thinks the world of you, Tommy. She thinks you have it in you to make something of your life, to do something important.'

The mention of his mother's belief in him made him feel

sad and ashamed. She stood in the background watching him with such intensity that he thought she was speaking through Leadon, explaining these things through the IRA man's grim lips.

'We understand you don't have a high opinion of yourself right now,' said Leadon. 'You've done things that neither you nor your mother are proud of and, all things considered, you've placed yourself and her in great danger. You're an informer, back among the people you betrayed. And the person you betrayed most was your own mother. She's right, you little bastard, your life hangs by a thread.'

Tommy stared back at her. She had matched him in his betrayal. 'What do you want of me?'

'We want to know why Morgan is being protected, and we want to know who exactly he is working for: MI5, Special Branch, or some more shadowy unit. Tomorrow, you will go back to Morgan's yard, and tell him you want your old job back.'

Tommy almost laughed in shock. 'But he'll interrogate me first. He's bound to smell a rat.'

'We'll know if things go wrong and pull you out. Nothing to worry about there, son.'

'But how?'

'We have eyes and ears on the ground. We'll get him to hand you over.'

'He won't do that.'

'He will if we ask him to. All you have to do is turn up in the morning and ask for some work. Don't volunteer a reason for your return or an explanation.'

'And what happens afterwards?'

Leadon shrugged. 'You leave Dreesh, and get a proper job.' He rose and walked over to Tommy's mother. 'This woman has been watching out for you, but a little tout like you needs more than his mammy.' He placed a hand on her shoulder and grinned. 'What a pair we make, the two of us, your guardian angels.'

Tommy stared at them. They were both linked together, belonging to the same chain of betrayal. He sank back into the sofa.

'You shouldn't confuse the IRA with beasts like Morgan,' said Leadon. 'I admit that in the darkest days of the Troubles we made mistakes. There were far too many innocent casualties. But in the end, the British were desperate enough to come to the table and negotiate a deal with us.' He went on to boast about the ruling council's power and influence, its years of experience and strategic planning. He talked as though the IRA were still an invincible force, and tried to convince Tommy that no harm would come to him.

But this was border country, thought Tommy, and Leadon was out of his depth. London, Dublin, and even Belfast might as well be on the other side of the earth. This was a world where men and women were killed for knowing other people's secrets. He thought of all the informers who had been tripped up by Morgan's humourless grin, defenceless young men interrogated and tortured until they vomited up the truth.

'What if the truth about Morgan is too dangerous to discover?' asked Tommy.

'What if it's too dangerous to keep secret?' replied Leadon.

CHAPTER TWENTY

Daly rose early on Saturday morning and took a quick dip in the bog pool. Now that he was confined to a caravan, submerging himself in the bubbling spring water that had once sustained his ancestors was one of his few remaining home comforts. He moved slowly, his hands pushing forward and then parting in a sedate breaststroke fashion. The swim made him feel virile in a way his workday existence and clothes, filled with the reek of frustration and doubt, could not. What a difference in the way the water carried his middle-aged weight. How dignified and purposeful he felt in this element, and how clumsy in the other, all those days and nights ambling down the endless corridors of police headquarters, or crouching over a computer screen during the graveyard shifts.

Deep bog pools with their slightly acidic waters were dangerous but merciful places. They washed things clean, gobbled then up, or purified and preserved them. Nothing decayed here, unlike old police stations and border villages mired in debt. Those places slowly rotted everything, stinking the air around them, he thought. They should be drained for the health and economy of their occupants.

Daly swam back and forth in the pool, reviewing the investigation in his mind. As he moved under the cloud-filled sky, his thoughts grew troubled. The unease he had felt since first hearing of Carey's frustrated investigation into Morgan had not dissipated, nor had he progressed a single step closer to tracking down the mysterious figure of Detective Robert Hunter. A recruiter of informers, a man whose face and name did not appear in any official documents, a no-man operating in the no-man's land of the border. Why was he convinced that only Hunter could explain the mystery of Carey's death and that of his girlfriend? His paranoid suspicions were seldom wrong, and when this haunted state of mind came over him, he could not be dissuaded or deterred. On the other hand, he had been mistaken before, badly, when his paranoia about Special Branch had blinded him to the corrupt role of a senior detective, and disastrously so when he had agreed to give refuge to the former IRA spy Daniel Hegarty.

It intrigued him that there had been a secret group of detectives calling themselves the Green and Blue Fishing Club. He had heard rumours about associations of police officers, but he had never been invited to any. He had not moved in the right circles, played enough golf, or taken up the offers to join fishing trips to Donegal. He had heard the gossip about legendary feats of intoxication, and close friendships struck up with detectives from the South, as well as politicians and journalists. He had listened to stories about cross-border alliances and betrayal, too. Hiding out on his father's dishevelled farm with a bottle of whiskey had been all the escape he had needed on weekends and when he was off-duty.

He was a recluse, a lough-shore recluse, preferring to spend his free time trying to prevent the small back garden from going to ruin, tending to his father's sole remaining hen, overseeing the dying enterprise of the farm, content to appear odd to his colleagues, and, worse than odd, anti-social, one of those sorry ageing police officers trapped in the past. However, he was who he was. A detective who tried to be good at his job, and if he sometimes slipped from the highest professional standards, he wasn't the only one. He had tried his best, but on too many occasions he had been found wanting. He was a flawed detective, a real, human detective, condemned to repeat the same mistakes. A detective who had fallen in love with his own shadow, hunting his own doubts and suspicions, gathering their darkness around him in an attempt to ward off the demons of Donaldson's suicide and his own dispiriting domestic life.

Feeling a chill set in, he climbed out of the pool, dried himself with a towel, and got dressed. When he walked back through the field to his caravan, a builder in dusty overalls was waiting for him.

'That's us done,' he said.

Daly stared at him, confused.

The man pointed to the cottage with a satisfied look on his face.

Daly was thrown by what he saw. The builders had cleared away the scaffolding and building material around the cottage, fixed the truncated piping and loose wires, and covered them with plaster. The completed building came as a surprise to Daly, even though he had seen the new dimensions drawn on plans that lay buried beneath invoices and delivery notices. The builders had added a striking new sitting room, one side of which was a large sheet of triple-glazed glass aimed at the view of the lough. Gone were the constricted little panes that made up the old cottage windows. In fact, the builders had transformed the entire building into a house full of vistas. The new roof of sleek black tiles rose higher than he had expected, fitted with skylights, its shadow extending further across the wild garden.

Preoccupied with work, he had not noticed the steady advance of electricians and plumbers, plasterers and roof tilers. His caravan had been positioned far from the cottage and at such an awkward angle, estranging him from the renovations. How many months had passed since the builders began knocking down the internal walls? Six or seven? It felt like an unfathomable amount of time. But the days had passed one after the other, and the seasons had changed. What had he been thinking of every morning and evening as he passed the old place, huddled under builder's plastic and rusted scaffolding, barely raising his eyes to check on the progress as if it were a stranger's old ruin. It reminded him of the inadequacy of his vision, his inborn tunnel vision, a lough-shore man bred to ponder the inner frailties that might break him any day now, the questions of self-doubt bunching up in his mind like brooding ghosts.

Before leaving, the builder walked Daly around the outside of his new home. The detective lingered in its shadow, a little hesitant, feeling like an intruder.

'We've fitted strong locks on the doors and downstairs windows,' the builder told Daly. 'In a place this remote you'll need them.'

Daly wondered should he confess that he had not locked the doors of the old cottage in years, had let the black hen and other creatures wander in and out, and kept the windows open night and day, except in winter. He had developed bad habits all round. When they walked round the back of the house, Daly noticed that the builders had removed all the roof-scratching branches from the trees. The house no longer looked like a humble habitation moulded into the folds of the lough-shore landscape.

A breeze picked up, blowing gently from the lough with a hint of coldness. However, at the south end of the gable, the wind grew louder and rushed under the eaves. A strange whine came intermittently in the gusts, like that of an electricity generator or a nest of wasps. The sound seemed to emanate from the sleek new roof. Daly stood still and tense, expecting the expensive new tiles to fly off.

'What's that noise?' he asked.

'Just a trick of the wind,' said the builder.

'If it keeps up I'll think the new house is more haunted than the old.'

'Don't worry,' said the builder. 'The walls are well insulated. Once you're inside you'll not hear a thing.' His tone was the one builders used all over the country to deny the obvious. 'You look worried. You should be happy not to have to spend another night in that old caravan.'

Daly looked at him sceptically. 'You're telling me the strange noise is not important.'

The builder shrugged. 'It won't bring the house down upon you, put it that way. And even if it did, I'd be down first thing to fix it for you.'

Daly thanked him for his reassurance, and the builder handed him a set of keys.

'What are these for?' asked Daly. There was something oddly unspecific about the bunch of shiny new keys, as if they might open all the locked doors in his life.

The builder explained the locks on the windows, the double locks on the front and back doors, and the boiler-house and electricity-meter locks. He told him the code for the burglar alarm and handed him a set of instructions. The complexities of modern home ownership began to dawn on Daly, the intricate task of keeping out intruders, and the securing of heat and electricity. How much simpler it had been to live in a crumbling old cottage. The thought of all the renovations that had been done, the modifying of his childhood home to modern comforts, made him feel uneasy.

'Cheerio,' said the builder. 'And thank you.'

'Why thank me?' asked Daly.

'I can't remember having a client who made so few demands.'

'My father was happy with the old place,' said Daly. 'He never wanted to leave it, not even, you know, when... he was dying.'

When the builder had left, Daly felt reluctant to enter the house. Through the windows, he peered at room after room of empty space. He feasted on the views from the new sitting room, but failed to connect with it as a place of habitation. Under his orders, the builders had removed all the old furniture, the Welsh dresser and stove in the kitchen, the worn settee and armchairs in the living room, and the net curtains and rugs, but he could still see their shadowy imprints, the hollows and dark patches they left behind. All this empty space inside the cottage was the start of something new, but what Daly experienced was an ending, and the sense of peace that filled the renovated rooms bore no resemblance to the agitation in his heart. He did not care any more that the furniture had been full of woodworm and falling apart. He'd have kept it in the new house even if it stank like a collection of corpses. He would have suffered the entire rotten legacy just to cling on to the memory of his parents. How could he replace that inheritance? It would take more than a trip to Ikea to ease his sense of loss.

He dropped the bunch of keys into his pocket and went back to his caravan. Behind him, the stunted trees stirred in the wind, their branches parting and coming together again. The noise from the roof increased like a warning sign from the past. It struck Daly that the strange roar of the wind was the landscape's revenge, a token of his ancestors' displeasure at the way the new house disturbed the topographical order, the way it privileged visibility over protection from the elements.

The whitethorn trees in the hedge next to the caravan were dense with blossom. He shivered, hearing the branches whispering in the wind. They seemed to be hinting at something, calling to the very roots of him, just as the waves of Lough Neagh also called to him, rolling like ripples in a gloomy flag on the horizon. He stood still, imagining that he heard an old man hoarsely coughing. There was something more to the hedge than he would ever understand, something ghostly waiting to be illuminated as the wind hurried through the black branches and twigs. For a long while, he stared at the blossom and at his caravan bedded into a corner of the field, its rotting wheels niggling to be somewhere else.

CHAPTER TWENTY-ONE

Like infiltrators, Jacqueline Pryce and her photographer colleague slipped into the back of the community hall at Drumkillen. The room was hushed and packed with parishioners, the parish priest and club chairman about to speak on the stage. However, the dominating spirit was that of Tom Morgan, pacing up and down the aisle, a ripple of attention following his progress as he waited for an introduction from the priest. Along the walls, tall windows afforded a view of a fallen landscape, broken-looking hills, a football pitch sunk under rainwater and grey clouds bruising against the horizon.

The chairman appeared pale and sweaty for a man about to be presented with a cheque for a million pounds. The priest looked equally miserable, all colour draining from his face as he spoke into the microphone. He talked hesitantly about Morgan's great generosity, his love of GAA and the Catholic Church, the two traditional cornerstones of Irish society. He sounded and behaved like a man clearly aware Morgan had built up his vast wealth through smuggling and violence, but hopeful that this did not necessarily make him a monster.

If Morgan was trying to rehabilitate his reputation, thought Pryce, he was clearly on the road to success. Poverty seemed to have made the parish less sceptical about the reputations of criminals. The church and the football club were deeply mired in debt, and the community no longer cared if their new benefactor's money stank. They did not mind if his largesse came from a variety of criminal enterprises. In their desperation, they would have defended his generosity tooth and nail to the highest judge in the land.

When the priest finished thanking Morgan for his help repairing the church roof, the club chairman took to the microphone and also paid homage to Morgan's generosity, the donor of their new football stadium and the state-of-the-art training facility with hot and cold showers, an ice bath, and even physiotherapy rooms.

In spite of their gratitude, Pryce detected behind the uniform smiles of the audience a mood of secret shame. She surveyed the faces – businessmen and -women who had probably taken out multiple mortgages in more optimistic times, bankrupt builders and unemployed tradesmen desperate for the work that Morgan's donation would provide, young couples who had bought overpriced houses and adorned their marriages with unpayable debts, all gathered in this cold hall that echoed to the thud of Morgan's footsteps as he walked slowly towards the stage. The former IRA man and lawbreaker, legitimized by the peace process and now the recession, the only man in the room still on the socio-economic rise, powered by his mysterious business interests.

Morgan ambled alongside the priest, his presence like a magnet, deepening in power, pulling the attention of the entire room with it. He cut a cleaner, sharper figure than the one Pryce had seen in blurred newspaper photographs. His face glowed in the spotlight, his eyes looking exhilarated. He angled his large body towards the audience, his overweight belly, the excess of it, full of swagger and self-assertion. By comparison, the other figures on the stage looked crumpled, almost slovenly. The faces of the audience seemed to whiten as Morgan confronted them with his blank stare.

After a tense moment, Morgan patted the priest on the back and referred to some shared childhood anecdote from the playing field, one that painted the priest in a very poor light. There was scattered laughter from the audience and then Morgan told them how humbled he was to be able to help a community whose values were so close to his heart. His voice boomed to the back of the room. 'Tell your children and grandchildren they will have the best sporting facilities in the country right here on their doorsteps,' he said.

He invited everyone to examine the new plans, which were housed in a glass-panelled box at the back of the hall. Pryce saw computer-generated pictures of an impressive-looking building and football stand, scale drawings from all elevations and angles, land maps showing the extent of the work, mocked-up pictures of happy-looking families standing on the terraces, cheering on their local team.

Morgan bathed in the warm applause of the audience. For a moment, he looked almost human, desperate to be liked and respected. As soon as he stepped down from the stage, Pryce and her photographer ambushed him.

'Where are those pictures going?' he grumbled, turning to the red-faced chairman hurrying behind. 'You told me there'd be no photographs. No journalists sniffing for a story.' He stared with contempt at Pryce.

'Your name won't be mentioned anywhere,' said the chairman. 'I can assure you of that.' He seemed just as keen to keep the name of the parish's new donor out of the newspapers.

'Why not?' asked Pryce. 'It's a free press. We can mention whoever we want.'

'Why are you here?' asked Morgan. 'You haven't come to give me free publicity or report a good-news story.'

'I came here for the headline: "IRA murderer bankrolls a church roof and new sports facility with his dirty money".'

'I doubt your editor will have the balls to stand over that,' snorted Morgan.

When the photographer snapped another set of pictures, the chairman intervened, his hands clasped in an imploring, nervous way. 'The new stadium will give much-needed work to local businesses and support to our young people,' he told the journalist. 'Were it not for Mr Morgan's generosity we'd have to close the club.'

'Can I quote you on that?' asked Pryce.

'Yes, of course,' he replied. Desperation had driven him into Morgan's company, like a lost soul forced into the inner circle of hell. The banks were no longer giving out loans, and bankruptcy had spread like a contagion through the parish. If it had not been for Morgan's fat wallet he would have had to wheedle contributions from the local community for years, organize parish draws, sell countless tickets, even seek a helping hand from rival parishes and teams.

'Why throw money at this particular parish?' asked Pryce when the chairman had hurried away. 'Why spend so much here when there are clubs and parishes up and down the country in desperate need of funds?'

'If it wasn't for me places like Dreesh and this parish would be empty of everyone but children,' said Morgan. 'Every adult on the run from their creditors. Even the priest is in debt up to his eyeballs.'

'The people of Drumkillen might applaud you now but they'll condemn you as soon as your back is turned. They know your history and where your money came from. They'll make fun of your generosity. The way you're burning money as if there's no tomorrow.'

'I haven't come here for the approval ratings,' said Morgan, his eyes glinting. 'Come here with me and I'll show you something.'

Outside he pointed at a set of dilapidated-looking football terraces, and the backdrop of bogland and pine forests, so sodden they looked to be underwater in the evening light.

'The new club stadium and football pitch will be built about a mile away,' said Morgan. 'In the meantime, I'm going to pull down this old sports ground and develop the site into a multi-million-pound business.' He reached over and squeezed Pryce's arm. 'Can you see what I'm talking about?'

'But there's nothing to be developed here,' she said. 'There's only the border,'

'You've hit the nail on the head. With Brexit looming, the big money is on the border. No one on this island will stand for a hard border with customs posts and high security. Think about it. That would be like asking Germany to build the Iron Curtain again. In a year or two, this place will be awash with financial opportunities. I've already submitted plans to build a fuel depot and filling station.'

Morgan's shining black eyes reminded Pryce of a primordial predator. He had come to the community hall on a hunting trip, she realized, and his donation was nothing more than a calculation based on pure financial efficiency, devoid of any generosity or communal feeling.

'The people here see me as a champion against unemployment,' he said, grinning expansively. 'I can devise all sorts of ways to keep them in jobs. I can create miracles out of dirt. Give me a few years and all this murky bog will be filled with the colour of money.'

CHAPTER TWENTY-TWO

Driving home from work, Daly had meant to get something to eat, but instead he pulled in to a petrol station and bought copies of the three newspaper titles published daily in Northern Ireland. He left them on the passenger seat, resisting the temptation to read them immediately. When he pulled up at his cottage, he rolled them up and walked into the garden, treading carefully among the rubble and spare lumps of scaffolding that the builders had overlooked. He used the tightly rolled newspapers to knock back the young nettles and thistles, gritting his teeth as he flayed the weeds, the bringer of bad news to his own door. The path petered out at an ancient garden seat. In the evening light, the place was thronged with deep shadows, and a pervading sense of disconnection and unsettledness.

He sat down and read the papers, surprised that only one of them, the Belfast *News Letter*, had covered the inquest and suicide note. His entire body grew tense as he skipped over the introductory paragraphs to get at the details. Once through, he read the article again, this time slowly. A preliminary hearing had taken place outlining the coroner's investigation, with the coroner quoting a line directly from Donaldson's suicide note: 'My blood will be on the hands of Inspector Celcius Daly and his accomplice Jacqueline Pryce.' He shuddered to the core of his being.

Below the main article was an opinion piece from a retired police commander. He pointed the finger of blame for Donaldson's death at the media, its insatiable desire for new scandals and conspiracies, and police officers who made dubious alliances with investigative journalists. Inspector Daly and Pryce had driven Donaldson to take his own life, the ex-commander had written. They had killed him indirectly. The determination that made them blind to everything but exposing the next conspiracy theory had been their murder weapon. Daly put down the newspaper and stared blankly ahead. He thought of a newspaper-waving mass of people, brandishing the facts of Donaldson's death, chanting Daly's name and the lines from the suicide note. How could he have known that Donaldson's death would end the search for his mother's killers and declare checkmate on the entire tawdry game of silence and cover-up?

He was grateful at least that neither article had mentioned his mother's name, and that she had not been hauled out into the public gaze for the satisfaction of the readership's burning curiosity. He feared this most of all – the tragic account of her death passed into the hands of the baying crowd. In spite of the media interest, he would resist Pryce's encouragement to tell his side of the story. It would never bring his mother back to life, and another part of him would die there and then, he was sure of that.

He gritted his teeth, thinking of Donaldson's words, the final bitter lines of a dead man. The temperature dropped and his empty cottage looked abandoned, no sign of life or noise, now that the builders had gone, the new roof and windows enveloped in wispy trails of evening mist. In the corner of his eye, he caught a glimpse of Donaldson's adamant grey face looming towards him, a loose piece of the past fleeing from the darkness. *What does his ghost want from me?* he thought. *Why won't he give up and go away? Why isn't he put off by the truth, that his wife and other police officers colluded with Loyalist killers, and that at least part of the blame for the cover-up rested on his shoulders?*

The lough shore was full of ghosts like Donaldson's, hiding from the truth, unwilling to resign themselves to the repercussions of their past deeds. Donaldson's words ran through his head. *My blood will be on the hands of Inspector Celcius Daly and his accomplice Jacqueline Pryce.* The corners of his eyes filled with ghosts, or were they just his thoughts projected on to the watery film of air? He saw Donaldson's face again, mocking him. Daly had always behaved like the silent outsider, but now he was in the frame, identified in the press, the threat of a witch-hunt and pubic hate hanging over him.

He leaned back in the seat and heard it creak. It was beginning to rot in its fixtures; its metal legs so entangled in weeds that not even a tug-of-war team could uproot them. He was a fixture here, too, stubborn and unyielding. All the cover-ups and lies in the world could not shift him. Not even the accusing words of dead men. They would never uproot him. It was a trial of strength he was determined to win.

The only thing that might shift him now, a divorced forty-something living on his own, would be the promise of family life, a partner and children to guide him by the hand from this garden of decay, a chorus of laughing voices to lighten his heart. In the meantime, he had his detective work to occupy him. It did not unduly trouble him that his long hours produced so few results, and that his night shifts felt so stupefying. He knew that this did not matter. The work itself mattered. Even if it felt as though he were nailing his soul to nothingness, night after night.

He read the newspaper report again, and convinced himself that he would manage, and everything would be all right.

CHAPTER TWENTY-THREE

Daly woke in the middle of the night, breathing hard. He had heard someone shouting his name in agony, a ghostly mouth wincing in a dream. He sat up in bed, seeking comfort in the caravan's cramped furniture, its nooks and crannies reassuringly familiar in the moonlight shining through the little window. The voice had sounded so real it remained fresh in his mind, shrill and accusing. He tried to recall the precise details of his dream and the mouth he had glimpsed, to clutch at some clue his subconscious might offer, and a way out of this sense of dread, but the dream had faded completely.

He was spooked when he heard the voice call his name again. He peered through the window. The moon added deep shadows to everything, and the cottage and farm looked eerie in the silver light. In the distance, he sensed as much as saw or heard the shifting of waves across the vastness of Lough Neagh.

He pulled on his clothes and stepped outside, his senses alert.

A figure waited for him at the walls of the cottage. It swayed slightly in the wind, not uttering a sound as he approached. At first, he thought it was his loneliness and anxiety, making him see ghosts again, but the figure turned out to be real, an old man dressed in a fisherman's jacket and watertight trousers tucked into black boots. It took Daly a moment to identify him. It was Commander Donaldson's brother.

'What do you want?' asked Daly. He gave the old man a searching glance.

'Just a little chat, Celcius Daly,' the fisherman replied, studying him in return. Neither of them seemed able to read the other's face. 'So this old hidey-hole is where you've lived since a boy?'

It was not entirely the truth but Daly nodded anyway. 'Yes. I've always lived here.'

In the poor light, the fisherman's face might have been smiling or sneering. 'But have you really lived here?' he asked. 'Is it possible for a police officer in this country to lead a normal life, do ordinary things, and go to certain places? Take my brother; he ended up a hermit, just like you. He always complained that he hadn't lived properly, but I thought he was just being stupid. Now I realize he was right. He never lived the life he should have had.' He gave a sarcastic little laugh. 'Did it feel like murder, Daly? Getting away with driving a good man like that to his death?'

Daly strongly resisted the accusation. 'No way,' he said, but his voice shook slightly.

'But you and my brother were colleagues. On the same side. Upholding law and order. Was it fair to hound him with threats of a public inquiry?'

'I was pursuing an investigation into the past. I uncovered evidence of mistakes made by senior police officers, including your brother. What he did can't be wiped away by the note he scribbled down before he died.'

'But words matter, you bastard. History comes down to words and the public record. Come with me, I've something you need to see.'

With a swift jerk of his arm, he beckoned Daly and took off. The moon disappeared behind a cloud and the shadows grew deeper. Daly felt compelled to follow him, orientating himself in the darkness to the harsh sound of his breathing. When the moonlight returned, the old man had reached the bog pool. He was aggressive now, his shoulders dropping into a boxer's crouch, his eyes glinting.

'You're a marked man, Daly, now your name is out in the public arena. You will never be forgiven for what you did to my family.' As he spoke, he walked around the black waters of the pool, Daly following him, cautious of slipping on the muddy banks. The detective decided not to bother asking for forgiveness. What could he say that would change the old man's opinion of him?

The fisherman began pacing up and down in an agitated manner. 'I'm sure you tell yourself all sorts of stories to justify what you did,' he said. There was something vulnerable yet dangerous about his frail body, his rubber boots slipping and squelching in the boggy ground, giving him the reeling movement of a fighter about to collapse but trying to deliver the killer blow. 'You and that journalist friend, spurring each other on like dogs in a pack. But remember you're still alive and my brother is dead.'

'Listen, you can't come to my home in the middle of the night and harass me just because your brother took his own life. There is no justification for this.'

'But there's a price you have to pay for killing him. Think of me as a debt collector come to gather my brother's dues.'

'What do you mean?'

'Why should you be allowed to live without suffering in any way?'

From his coat pocket, the fisherman took out an envelope containing several handwritten sheets. He unfolded them with reverence. Daly recognized the heavy cramped writing of his former commander. Christ, he thought, the old man was determined to see the thing through, to inflict the maximum amount of punishment.

'How did you get the note?' Daly asked sharply. 'I thought Special Branch had the only copy.'

'My brother wrote several letters before he died. This one was addressed to my sister and me. It contains a full report on your character, and what he calls its deficiencies. You can read it if you like and tell me what you think.'

'No thanks.'

'He said he watched you at work and you often looked unhappy.'

Daly felt a sick feeling in the pit of his stomach. The comment unnerved him. 'I wasn't unhappy,' he said. The last thing he wanted was a dead man's pity.

'He said he often wondered why you chose the profession. Why you wanted to be a detective.' He looked at Daly closely. 'Did you ever think like that?'

The question surprised him. The true answer was not every

day, but often enough. Policing was never a career choice he had considered growing up during the Troubles.

'Was it because of women that you felt unhappy?'

'Because of women?' Again, the question jarred Daly.

'He wrote that women were your downfall and the crux of your unhappiness.'

The sick feeling began to crawl through Daly's stomach.

'He mentions how you compromised your investigations because of your relationship with vulnerable women.' The fisherman opened the pages and scanned their contents. 'Here we are. These are the lines. I want you to read them.' He thrust the letter towards Daly, pushing the loose leaves into his hands.

Stupefied, the detective stared at the lines, but in the weak moonlight, the words danced across the page in a demonic scrawl, the gibberish of a ruined old police commander.

'Well,' said the eager, gloating voice. 'Do you see what he's written?'

'I can't read anything.'

'What did you say?'

'I said I can't read anything.'

'Here, let me read them then.' The fisherman took the letters back and began perusing the pages. 'He mentioned a trafficked woman and the wife of an informer. He says that your desire for these women made you unhappy. He uses the words "lonely fantasies" and "dishonourable intentions".' The fisherman shifted about in the mud, waiting for a response from Daly. When Daly did not reply, he pressed on. 'He said that you were fixated on your mother. She died when you were a boy and you never recovered.'

'What does all this have to do with my desire to be a detective?'

'You wanted to rescue your mother. That's what he wrote. You wanted to save her through these women who came under your influence.'

Daly felt dizzy, the blood draining from his head. The pool below him was still and dark. He stepped back from its brink. What bothered him most was that Donaldson had taken time to reflect on his failings, trying to come up with an explanation for his discontent, to fit the pieces of his life and career together in a way that made uncanny sense.

'What about this journalist Pryce?' asked the fisherman. 'Why were you so vulnerable to her charms?' He stepped back and forth in the mud, clearly excited by the knowledge he'd got under Daly's skin. 'Why did you let Pryce meddle in your past? You're a detective. You should have known better. You demeaned yourself and the memory of your mother.'

'Pryce was not responsible for your brother's suicide. Leave her out of this.'

'Not responsible? Of course she was responsible.' His breathing grew harsh and anxious, his boots shuffling and sucking in the mud. 'My brother blamed her and he blamed you. The two of you pursued him with questions in a disgraceful way. It was disgraceful and ruthless.'

Daly could take no more of this. He wanted to get away as quickly as possible from this old man whose knowing sneer threatened to drag him back to the degrading past. He swiped at the letter, wanting to destroy it, the sad disgusting finale to Donaldson's career in the police force. He was seized by the notion that if he ripped it into pieces and flung it into the pool, he would escape the fisherman's net of blame and debasement, the unnerving curse of the dead, and the scorn of the living.

The fisherman sidestepped him, saving the letter. He plunged into the shallow end of the pool, shaking the letter at Daly, inviting him to draw closer.

'That was your brother's private note,' said Daly. 'I'm sure he didn't want its contents spilled all over the newspapers and the internet. He was an old-fashioned officer who kept his feelings to himself.'

'But we live in a different age, Daly. What's private is public business. And people are prone to judging harshly.'

He was right, thought Daly. These days, the internet was awash with high emotion and puritanical sentiment. 'What do you want of me?' he said. 'A public spectacle of guilt, breast-beating?'

'And allow you to save your own skin and salvage your reputation? If you think that would give me satisfaction then you misunderstand why I've come here tonight.'

'What are you talking about?'

'You drove him to suicide, and now I'm going to do the same.' He splashed out of the water and began weighing down his pockets with stones and loose bits of rubble. 'Your torture is only beginning, Celcius Daly.'

Daly watched in alarm as the fisherman strode back into the pool. What was he doing? Was this his ultimatum, his final feint to get Daly to admit his guilt? Was Daly going to end up with another suicide on his hands?

'Wait,' said Daly. 'We can go back to the caravan. Talk things through over a glass of whiskey.'

'Not if I can help it,' said the fisherman, taking a large downward stride into the water. 'Why don't you join me, Daly? Failed police detectives have an extremely high suicide rate.'

Daly's voice froze at the breathtaking nihilism of the old man's intentions.

'Death will improve your situation immeasurably,' said the fisherman, now up to his shoulders in the water. 'Everyone will love you at your funeral. Who knows? All those journalists might start penning tributes to you. Isn't the thought of that more satisfying than spending your days hiding on this farm with just your shortcomings for company?'

He is prepared to destroy me at all costs, thought Daly. *Not just my reputation and career as a police officer, but my belief in life itself.* 'For God's sake, don't do it,' he pleaded. 'You can't drown yourself. Get rid of the stones in your pockets. Don't be a coward.'

'Sorry, Daly,' said the fisherman. His eyes were shining with euphoria, his face tinged blue with the cold, as he immersed his head in the water.

Daly plunged in after him, grabbing him by his coat, but the old man was too heavy to haul on to the bank. He felt the fisherman's shivering arms lock around him, his face snuggling into his flank, pulling him down through a doorway to his brother's watery grave. In desperation, Daly thrashed against his deathly hold, but he could not escape the net of guilt, the sordid history of suicide in Donaldson's family, this unnerving invitation to doom. He saw the fisherman's underwater face staring up at him, magnified in the moonlit gloom, silvery bubbles clinging to his hair and eyebrows, eyes glittering greedily, his tattered coat and rags swelling around him like an old mummy unwrapping itself.

Where does he get his determination and strength from? thought Daly. *It must be his dead brother's ghost*, he realized. Fear penetrated his heart as he grew weary and sank beneath the surface. A fear greater than he had ever felt before. Furiously, he pushed against the fisherman's foul old body. Hatred made him frantic, confused his movements. He struck at the fisherman's face and managed to writhe out of his embrace. He swam upwards with all his strength, emerging at the surface, gasping for breath.

The fisherman's head reared up beside him, spitting water and curses at Daly. His eyes grew wild as he struggled for another hold on the detective. Eye to eye, they fought, arms thrashing.

'Enough,' cried Daly. It was not just the downward pull of the fisherman and his dead brother. It was the gravity of his entire life working upon him, the degradation of his divorce, the troubles he'd had at work, the discovery of the truth behind his mother's death and his father's silence. Wasn't it true what the fisherman had said? Even if his words stemmed from hatred? At last, he thought he understood the attraction that death exerted over the guilty and the lost, and a blank calm came over him.

The fisherman fixed him with a surprised stare. He gloated at Daly as if the matter were settled, as if they had wasted enough words and physical effort.

'Your guilt, Daly,' he said, his lips shivering. 'Your guilt. There's no cure for a guilt that deep.' His icy hands extended and gripped Daly's shoulders. 'Even a dog has more honour than you.'

As they slipped underwater, Daly felt the coldness of the water numb his mind and ease his beating heart. He closed his eyes and wiped his internal slate clean, expunging the burden of the past, the unanswered questions, and the paranoid and unreasonable suspicions that had dogged his career as a detective.

Now that they were sinking towards death, all enmity between them seemed to dissolve, and they united in harmony, a tangle of tired limbs descending through the levels in a slow embrace, until finally no ripples perturbed the dark surface of the pool and the night was as silent as the judgment of God.

CHAPTER TWENTY-FOUR

Drowning in a bog pool was the most vivid image of disaster
from Daly's childhood: the murk of the water, the mud that
could trap you like sinking sand, the sucking down into the
abyss. Bog pools were treacherous places, death traps, the
lurking, resident monsters of the farm. He had heard stories
of old men drowning in them, confused by inundating
weather or alcohol. The mire of the past was very much like
the downward pull of a bog pool. It got you into the same
kind of trouble. The safe negotiation of those pitfalls was the
first requirement for survival on his father's farm, but he had
failed to find a sturdy and negotiable path. The undertow of
the past was too strong. It took the legs from under him and
dragged him down without mercy.

Sinking down to the bottom of the pool, Daly no longer
had any sense of orientation, no sense of depth or direction
of escape. Even his consciousness wavered, his senses sliding
towards oblivion. Blood boiled in his ears, and a sharp pain

took hold in his ribs as though he had been violently kicked. How had he ended up here, at death's doorway with the ghost of Donaldson waiting for him? He should not have to bear the entire responsibility for the past; it was too heavy a burden to take to his grave.

Out of the murk, the fisherman's face loomed, his violent eyes staring at Daly, his hands pulling at his body. Daly retaliated with greater force, pushing back the grasping hands, lurching sideways and wrenching at the fisherman's collar. With all his strength, he worked the coat off the man's shoulders, tugging his arms loose, rolling it down his chest and back. At last, the weighted garment fell away. Flight was once more possible. He no longer had to plead for mercy in his enemy's ear. He kicked upwards, dragging the fisherman behind, and out of the deathly darkness they climbed.

Daly emerged into silver moonlight and the seething surface of the pool, gasping for air along with the retching creature beside him. The fisherman's face was white as chalk, his blue lips spluttering water and vomit. Daly felt the pain in his lungs and thought he was going to vomit, too.

It was hard work, pulling the old man's body across the water. Daly's feet sank in the mud along the fringes of the pool, and then he slipped and slithered on to the bank. The fisherman's body grew heavier, but Daly was not discouraged, nor did he feel the cold seeping through his clothes. They sprawled and shivered together on the bank, a chasm opening between them in spite of their physical proximity. When Daly got his breath back, he went to the caravan and returned with a bottle of whiskey and some blankets. He offered the fisherman a drink, but the old man pushed it away. Daly took a hearty slug himself. It tasted fiery and strong. He wrapped the blankets around the fisherman, who did not flinch or move his face in any way, just gaped back at Daly, his breathing ragged, water and phlegm still gargling in his throat. The essence of life was heat, but there was nothing warm-blooded about this old man. His thin, cunning body seemed to have its own currents of coldness, his face blank as a stone. Daly felt the blast of bitterness and grief emanating from him.

The fisherman blinked and swallowed, his eyes rolling with hate. He flung out a clawed hand at Daly, grabbing him by the shoulder. He clung on, levering himself to a half-standing, half-crouching position. Then he stumbled away with an angry sigh, so groggy with the cold he looked to be drunk. After a while, Daly heard a car engine start up, and a set of headlights light up the lane. Soon the vehicle and its driver had disappeared into the darkness.

The surface of the pool, which had been seething moments before, was smooth and black again.

CHAPTER TWENTY-FIVE

Daly had always feared that life might make him the victim of one of those relentless media witch-hunts on which journalists preen themselves. When he glanced cautiously though his bedroom curtains the next day, he was relieved to see no reporters camping outside his caravan. The farm was silent and peaceful-looking. Nor did it bear any traces of his altercation with Donaldson's brother the night before, as though their near drowning had been little more than the supernatural fabrication of his guilty conscience.

There was no sign of the press at police headquarters, either. Daly had been wary of turning up to work as himself, without resorting to some form of disguise, a hat or a pair of sunglasses, but had decided against it. Knowing his luck, the disguise would have fallen off or a colleague would have waved and greeted him by name, right in front of the pack of reporters.

He slipped into the building through a back entrance. There were other detectives and police officers drifting through same doors. They seemed not to notice Daly, or each other, their heads hung low, their eyes withdrawn. They trudged up the stairs together. It struck Daly that he and his colleagues were all a little paranoid, a little bit guilt-ridden, emerging from decades of fear and loathing, their justice system still shuddering with the after-effects of the Troubles. If only their debts to society were straightforward, he thought, the kind that are easily paid and forgotten. He tried to convince himself that the debt he owed over Donaldson's death was more honourable than the debts of others, but that judgment no longer lay within his power. It was in the hands of the media now.

To settle himself, he made some tea, and sat at his desk. He pushed from his mind his feelings and the memories of the night before. He took stock of the investigation into Carey's death and that of his partner Brigid Donnelly. It was imperative he find Hunter and Jack McKenna. He had to work out the connection between the two detectives, and the point at which their paths crossed with Carey's. The search for that connection was the only possible route forward. He would do everything he could, he vowed. No one would accuse him of indecision or reluctance to probe the shadowy dealings of intelligence officers along the Irish border.

Someone knocked the door of his office. It was Detective O'Neill. Her face looked pale.

'Has something happened?' he asked. His voice was sharp and defensive.

'No. I'm sorry to bother you.'

'You're not bothering me at all. Any news about Jack McKenna?'

'No trace of him, but there was a fire at his last-known address about a fortnight ago. According to reports, the house was completely gutted. Since then, none of his neighbours has seen or heard of him.'

'That's strange.'

'There were some vague sightings of a car with a Southern registration visiting the burnt-out house a few days ago. But nothing definite. Nothing to give us a clear lead.'

'Anything of interest inside the house?'

'We gave it the once-over. Everything had either been destroyed in the fire or cleared out.'

'What about his police records? Any mention of cross-border intelligence units? Anything that might connect him with Detective Hunter or Carey?'

'We're still digging away. He moved around a lot. That's all I can tell you right now. Sorry, I haven't anything more to give you.'

'Not to worry. I'm beginning to realize that Special Branch detectives have a knack of disappearing. Keep searching through McKenna's records. Find out if there are any secrets or shadows hiding there. If I'm right, there has to be a point where his path crossed with Detective Hunter.'

He hoped that McKenna would not turn out to be as big a mystery as Hunter. At least he had a photograph of him, a police record and, most importantly, a brother. Enough clues to find a path through the labyrinth.

'Keep searching,' he told O'Neill. 'If you find anything else let me know immediately. I'm going to pay a visit to our sergeant in Dreesh. It's time he told us the truth about his brother.'

A look of unease came over O'Neill's face. 'Before you go, Inspector Fealty has been looking for you,' she said. 'He wants to talk to you urgently. There's an emergency meeting scheduled later with Commander Sinclair. I think it's about the *News Letter* story.'

The reminder of his public exposure was swift and painful. However, he could not give in to his feelings right now.

'Tell him I'll call him. Right now, my top priority is to find Jack McKenna.' He did not add that a trip over the border would be a welcome release from his present state of mind.

CHAPTER TWENTY-SIX

Tommy walked past the heavy dark brows of Morgan's guards, and in through the doors of the huge shed, past the dark eyes of the lorry drivers as they waited by their tankers, past the dark hole of Morgan's mouth as he shouted orders at his men running with slick hoses. Oblivious to the roar of diesel engines and the thud of boots on the dank floor, he made his way to the back stairwell and the door to Morgan's office. His pulse was drumming in his veins, but he moved as if he had known the shed all his life. If he looked nervous, that would count as evidence against him. He had to show no fear, no trace of a guilty conscience. He waited for the sound of Morgan's boots or one of his men following him up the stairs, but none came.

He shut the door on the thunderous blast, the smoke and confusion, and waited, his heart still hammering. The past few days had felt like a daydream, and now he was jolted awake. The agonies of betrayal, the uncertainties of whom to trust and whom not to trust were over. He had phoned Morgan the day before and pleaded for his old job back. He felt he had crawled through a long tunnel on his hands and knees to make it back to this lair. In spite of his dread and the grovelling to Morgan, he was determined not be deterred in his mission.

He waited in the office, and still the boss did not appear. He was glad of a few moments of peace. From the shed floor below, he could hear the roar of lorries resolutely swallowing gallons of fuel, and Morgan's blasting voice shouting commands. It was the last place on earth an informer would choose to collect his thoughts.

As time ticked by his resolve grew. He flicked through the files on Morgan's desk, but nothing caught his eye. He loped around the room, listening for Morgan's familiar heavy tread on the stairs, attuning his ears to the noises below, the smuggling boss's roar like a great wind gusting through the shed, the voice of the man who would soon decide his fate. *As long as he keeps up the shouting,* thought Tommy, *as long as he does not confront me with silence and God knows what diabolical thoughts running through his mind.*

At the other end of the office, a door had opened just a crack. He knocked on it lightly. When there was no response, he stepped into the darkened room. In the corner of the room was a young man in some sort of trance, his head moving in slow motion, his face lit up by the glow of several computer screens. Piled around him were hard drives, untidily arranged file boxes, cases of software and manuals and, half-hidden, an Xbox, which Tommy reckoned the youth was secretly playing.

On one of the screens, Tommy caught a glimpse of charts

and graphs, market updates and numbers gliding horizon-tally, money moving, large amounts of money. He smiled to himself. He had found Morgan's secret illegal bank. The screens suddenly went dark and the youth turned to stare at Tommy. He had prematurely thinning hair and a bluish cast to his face. There was a crouched aspect to his demeanour as he studied his visitor suspiciously.

'Have you worked here long?' asked Tommy.

'About two months.'

'What do you do, apart from playing the Xbox?'

'Whatever Mr Morgan orders.' The youth looked sullen, nervous.

The curtains were drawn but a window was open, the whiff of diesel contending with a stale body odour from the young man, who looked as though he had not ventured out for days. The youth went back to typing at a keyboard. A decade ago, men like Morgan communicated by acts of violence; nowadays they used hackers and computer geeks to take advantage of the dark corners of the internet, cloning cards, transferring cash, encoding conversations, adding young men like Tommy to the staff list of accountants, lawyers, bankers and muscle men.

'When was the last time you changed the passwords?' asked Tommy.

'The passwords?'

The boy's face was a blank. Had he flinched as he turned to one of the screens, or was Tommy just imagining it?

'Don't you know you're not meant to ask about the pass-words?' said the youth.

Tommy sat down on an empty chair. The young man tilted

his screens away from Tommy, his fingers playing on the keyboard.

'A year ago I was sitting where you are now,' said Tommy. 'I had access to all the directories. Tell me, when were the passwords last changed?'

'They change automatically every week. I have no control over them.'

'Why the new security measures?'

The fingers stopped typing and fumbled for the mouse. 'Mr Morgan told me to be on the lookout for someone asking questions like that.'

The acrid smell of his body, the dusty workbench, and unwashed cups reached into Tommy's nostrils like an odorous defence mechanism. He suspected that the young man also used it against Morgan and his cronies. The boy had stopped typing and was staring at Tommy. He could feel the rays of the youth's suspicions, but there was also a hungry, vulnerable look about his face. He seemed in desperate need of a friend or an ally.

The youth spoke. 'Morgan knows that someone copied files from his finance directories. He hasn't found the culprit yet.' A split second of a shared glance was all it took to communicate the warning to Tommy. A message transmitted faster than the numbers on the flickering screen. 'I won't say anything about this conversation,' he said.

'We didn't even talk,' replied Tommy. Amid the huddle of computers, they had made a secret pact. They were both anxious now.

The floor quaked with the thud of approaching footsteps and Morgan burst into the room, swinging his fat belly around to take in the computers and Tommy's presence. He ignored the youth completely.

'What are you doing in here, Tommy?' he asked, rolling his eyes with impatience. 'Sitting with all these computers like an old hen on eggs. Come with me, I've a job for you.'

Morgan strode back through the main office and took the stairs below. Tommy followed him into the shed and its cauldron of noise.

'I need you to do a little fuel run for me, Tommy,' said Morgan, showing him to an empty lorry. He dangled the keys before him but did not hand them over. 'You look like a new man. Have you been on holiday?'

Tommy said he had been in Spain.

'Good,' said Morgan, patting his shoulder.

Up close, the smuggling boss looked older and gloomier since Tommy had last seen him. On impulse, he decided to take advantage of Morgan's relaxed mood. 'Where are we crossing the border?' he asked.

He could have kicked himself when he saw Morgan's surprised reaction. None of the lorry drivers were allowed to query travel arrangements.

'Why do you want to know?' asked Morgan. 'Is it important?'

It was important that the boss knew the details but he could think of no adequate explanation for his own interest. He felt a sudden gust of fear, a taste of the awful gloom in Morgan's eyes. 'Just a question that popped into my head.'

'Do you know how often a driver has asked me that question?' asked Morgan. He placed his hand on Tommy's shoulder and made him look into his eyes.

'I don't know.'

'Well then, do you remember ever asking me that question before?'

'I'm not sure.'

Morgan frowned. 'You're teasing me now, Tommy.'

'I don't remember. I don't think about stupid details like that.'

'And I presumably do?'

Morgan's drivers moved about in the gloom of the yard, pressed for time, oblivious to the rising tension in the air. Tommy sensed their anxiety to get on with the smuggling run, their indifference to his fate. He was barely able to breathe, waiting for Morgan to relax, to cast him a word of encouragement, a casual remark, a signal that the operation could go ahead.

'So you've been in Spain all this time?' asked Morgan.

Tommy nodded.

'Anyone make contact with you over there?'

'No.'

'What about you? Did you make contact with anyone?'

'No one, not even my mother.'

'Not even your poor mother? Why not?'

'I was tormented. I needed a break.'

'You didn't tell me you were tormented.'

'I had to leave in a hurry. The police kept stopping me, asking questions about what I was up to. My head was tortured.'

'Why didn't you tell me where you were?'

'I told no one where I was going.'

'What in God's name would make you disappear like that without telling me or your mother?'

'I've already told you. The police were hassling me. Putting pressure on my mother.'

'Hassling you? Are you serious? You should have told me and I'd have sorted it out.'

At that moment, a horn blew loudly and a thundering roar filled the yard. A new convoy of lorries arrived.

'You look nervous, Tommy. What's frightened you?'

'I don't think I'm frightened.'

'I think you are. I think you're afraid of me.' He reached down to Tommy's leg and felt the inside of his trousers. When he saw that they were dry, he smiled and adopted a friendly tone. 'Why would you be frightened of me, Tommy? Nobody here would harm you. It's our enemies we should be worrying about. The police and the intelligence agencies. Unless of course you're working for those bastards.'

Tommy struggled for an answer but his brain had given up.

'I asked you a question. Did you not hear? Are you working for the police?' When Morgan saw Tommy's hand in his jacket fumbling at something, he stiffened. 'Hand me your mobile phone.'

Tommy took a step backwards.

'Give it to me.' Morgan lunged forward and grabbed the phone. He checked the screen. 'You're hoping your friends will come and rescue you, aren't you?' he said, tossing the phone into the path of one of the advancing lorries.

Tommy's face went white with fear.

'Don't move,' said Morgan, pulling a gun from his pocket, but Tommy had already leaped after the phone, his figure rising against the approaching trucks, legs and arms bicycling for a moment, before he was whipped away like a shadow into the roaring air.

CHAPTER TWENTY-SEVEN

Time stuttered for Tommy in Morgan's howling shed. Moments passed by, and he was no longer sure where he was. He felt winded and bruised. He thought one of the lorries must have knocked him over. Then Morgan grabbed him by his collar and hauled him to his feet.

'Speak to me, Tommy. I'm very easy to speak to. Everyone in the village knows that.' It was the same twisted smile as before, his eyes glittering with the hysteria of a man hemmed in by secrets and shadows. 'Who are you really working for?'

Tommy felt like spitting out the truth, which was that no one in the village had spoken directly to Morgan for years. People hid from the truth, dealing in deceptions because that was the language of the village, the only way it could talk.

'If you answer my questions honestly, no harm will come to you. But you have to tell me the truth. I know you're working for someone. The police in the North. The Gardai.

MI5. Once you've told me, I can let you go.' The look in his eyes had switched from violence to gloom.

Tommy said nothing, and the gloom in Morgan's eyes deepened.

He leaned into Tommy's ear and whispered, 'I've been hunting you for a long time now. I know you slipped the police information about my finances. Everywhere I looked, I kept imagining your silly informer's face, but you had disappeared completely. We spoke to everyone else. It all pointed at you, Tommy.'

Tommy could feel the bristle of Morgan's moustache, a dense mat of hair, caressing his cheek like a rat about to bite.

'I know it's you, Tommy. It's time to spill your guts.'

Morgan had dug with words like that before, burrowing into the dark, retracting souls of informers who knew they were going to die. A gun nestled in his right hand. The yard grew noisier as more lorries arrived, their glaring lights reflecting off the pools of spilled oil and rainwater, mixing the colours madly, throwing shadows across the face of Morgan. Something struck the side of Tommy's head with a resounding blow, and he was on the ground again. He saw one of his shoes lying in a pool of oily water. He got up on his knees and rested, feeling light-headed with the pain.

Morgan pushed him past the drivers, who stood still and watched, propped against their dirty lorry cabs. Another blow struck him on the side of his face. He heard someone giggle obscenely. Time stopped again. He was crouching now in the shadows. Where was he? In a corner of the yard, near the exit. Had he been dealt with? A minor nuisance, now free to go? The blast of lorry engines washed over him.

He was hit again. This time on both sides of his head by a pair of fists. His ears were ringing, and Morgan was shouting at him, but the words made no sense, garbled with echoes. Far away, he heard the sound of someone panting as though they had been running hard.

He crawled to his feet, taking comfort in the shadows, their emptiness, but then he saw a gun raised in front of his face. He braced himself for the shot.

'Get into the van,' said Morgan, pressing the gun to his temple.

So the interrogation would happen somewhere else, Tommy realized. The business of smuggling would continue unhindered and he would be robbed of eyewitnesses to his final torture.

CHAPTER TWENTY-EIGHT

A sign on the door said the police station was closed to the public. Daly looked for a buzzer or intercom but could not find one, even under the heavy fronds of ivy and clematis. When he pushed the door open, it swung inwards. Sergeant McKenna was alone in his office, sitting at a little desk. There were heavy lines on his face.

'I tried ringing in advance but no one answered,' said Daly.

'Things are inconvenient, right now,' replied McKenna. 'If you were anyone else I would say come back another time.' With a sigh, he bent down and produced a fat A4 envelope from a bottom drawer. 'As it happens your arrival couldn't be better timed.' He handed Daly the envelope, his eyes darting nervously at the detective. 'I found this stuck through the letterbox this morning. Your name was on it.'

Daly opened the letter and found a USB drive and a bundle of photocopies. Across the top of the first page were the printed words 'I am no one. Just a concerned whistle-blower.

You need to read these files.' He could tell immediately that the photocopies were from an investigating detective's case notes. However, there was no other communication or guidance from the sender.

'What are we looking at?' asked Daly. 'Do we know who wrote them, for a start?'

McKenna briefly examined the files. 'It's Carey's hand-writing. Looks like someone got hold of his case notes about Morgan.'

'But why give them to me?'

'Maybe they think you're the only one who would be interested.' McKenna appeared edgy, as though the files were contaminated, and their contamination might leap across to him.

'This is important evidence,' said Daly. 'The details of Carey's confidential investigations. These computer files will have to be forensically analysed.'

'From our end of things, we're keen for Carey's investigations to be closed.'

Daly stared at him. Was it his imagination or did he detect a frostiness in the sergeant's manner? He would not wish to be marooned with McKenna in this claustrophobic station in a dead-end village, and he certainly would not wish to be a colleague of his. A heavy, withdrawn personality. He wondered what tales the villagers might have to tell about him.

'Any idea who the informant is?' asked Daly.

'Whistle-blowers aren't well protected in the Gardai,' said McKenna. 'They're better off hiding in the shadows. If I knew the sender I'd have to report him or her, especially if they were a ranking officer.'

Daly was beginning to understand why the envelope had been addressed anonymously to him.

'Tea or something stronger, Inspector?' said McKenna. 'You've come all the way over the border and I haven't even offered you anything to drink.'

Daly asked for tea and watched the sergeant disappear into the kitchen. A suspicious thought took hold. The sergeant had said he was keen to close Carey's investigations. He began to see the role that McKenna might have created for him. Was McKenna the whistle-blower, passing on this dangerous evidence to someone not connected to the village? Certainly, Daly did not object to the role. The sergeant had to keep the peace in the village, and live alongside Morgan and his cronies. How much easier it would be for all involved if a detective from a different jurisdiction were the one who brought the smuggling gang to justice.

McKenna returned with a cup of tea and busied himself while Daly read the file. The pages were dog-eared and smudged as though the whistle-blower's fingers had pored anxiously over them. He tried to glean the importance of the files by scanning through them. Scrawled across the pages were names and addresses, followed by details of property investments, apartments and holiday homes, business premises, import-export companies, farmland and building sites. A well-known accountant's name sprang out at him, and then some solicitors and several local politicians, members of that segment of Irish society which had remained financially afloat in spite of the collapse of the housing market. Daly read on. The scale of their business interests seemed to have grown impressively wide since the recession.

On another sheet, he came across the details of local people, residents and shopkeepers in Dreesh, taxi drivers and tradespeople, farmers in the hinterland. What were they doing on such a high-flying list of the county's wealthy elite? Names and numbers were all muddled up together in Carey's handwriting. Daly realized it would take a team of forensic accountants to impose some sort of order upon the chaos.

McKenna stood in the middle of the room, eyes downcast, apparently studying the pattern of the carpet, but Daly could feel his eyes drift every now and again to the pages on the table, the list of local names and the rich elite, all so far removed from this humdrum police station, another world entirely.

The minutes passed, Daly reading the notes and McKenna surreptitiously glancing at him. Daly was not used to the presence of a police officer from another jurisdiction watching over him in such a way. As the minutes went by, McKenna's hovering silhouette began to get on his nerves. Eventually, Daly cast a bundle of the pages aside, in a gesture intended to signal weary resignation.

'Find what you're looking for?' asked McKenna. Daly's movement had brought the sergeant to his side.

'I think I need a guiding hand,' said Daly.

'I fear it's God's hand you need.'

'Or the man below,' said Daly, manoeuvring some of the pages into McKenna's view.

McKenna glanced over the notes and concentrated. 'There's a pattern to some of the names. They read like a who's who of the local property market, but I can't understand what the names of people like Alice McKinney are doing here. She's a widow from outside Dreesh who sold her farm years before the price of land took off. She wouldn't have more than a couple of thousand euros to her name.' He moved around Daly, peering at the notes, searching through the file. 'And here's a string of bachelor farmers. Old fellas stuck out in their cottages with nothing but boxes of empty stout bottles under their beds.' His fingers skipped through the pages. 'Would you credit that now? Mick Devine, Patrick Ramsey, and Tom Jardine listed with these rich accountants and solicitors. These are men who hid all their lives in the bog or the local pub.' He glanced at Daly and then went back to the file. He stabbed his finger at one of the pages. 'The late Sheila O'Hare. My old housekeeper. She's buried in the graveyard at St Patrick's. Retired with nothing more than a measly pension.'

Beside the names were lists of bank accounts and property portfolios. Staring at their sizable assets, Daly realized something he had not fully grasped before. Property speculation must have been far more widespread than anyone had expected, at least as far as the village of Dreesh was concerned. Behind the colourful failed tycoons, there had been a grey mass of anonymous people – teachers, farmers, taxi drivers, hairdressers – who had gambled their future and that of their children on rising house prices. Low interest rates and an unregulated debt industry had been crucial in satisfying this democratic demand for property portfolios. Unfortunately, the economic conditions had created a mass of people with all their eggs in one basket.

Daly did some rough calculations. The amount of money loaned out to the residents of Dreesh was astonishing, but that heady world of property speculation must be in pieces by now. Daly imagined these anonymous pensioners and farmers sweating and praying through nights of mortgage anxieties, the very walls of their homes menacing them, pressing in with the threat of financial ruin. He envisaged them hovering between Carey's lines of numbers and property transactions. Small people swallowed up by the debt industry. He kept counting the figures, and it knocked him back – the loss of scale to the money they had borrowed. He kept his attention focused on the teeming numbers but what he saw in his imagination was a doomed landscape of empty housing estates, festering building sites, children playing beside unfinished sewer systems.

But what had driven Carey to delve into the finances of the village residents? Their investments and inflated bank accounts did not appear at first glance to be connected to the darker world of criminals like Morgan, at least not on paper. Daly was clear about the difference between the two worlds, the ill-gotten gains and secret financial dealings of flamboyant smugglers, and the grey people of Dreesh at the periphery of the housing-market collapse. Then it struck him that their property portfolios and investments might have been set up as cover for more sinister operations. Daly delved further. He noticed that each of the village residents appeared to be associated with a particular offshore company. There were certificates in their names, lists of shareholders and trustees, invoices and bank transactions. Companies in tax havens all around the world, hidden behind reams of paper.

Daly spoke. 'What troubles me most is there's no sign of the bank accounts of Dreesh's most notorious resident.'

McKenna nodded. 'And just about everyone else's. Morgan's neighbours don't run high-finance businesses and they don't have millions hidden away.'

'Then either Carey's notes are wrong or it isn't their money.'

'Whose money is it then?' asked McKenna, but they both knew the answer to that question.

'It's not so easy to hide money these days,' said Daly. 'To find a nice little resting place away from the prying eyes of tax inspectors and the Criminal Assets Bureau. Criminals like Morgan have to work hard to hide their finances.'

'So he enrolled the residents of Dreesh as legal fronts?'

'That looks to be the line of investigation Carey was working on,' said Daly. 'We need to hand these files over to the Criminal Assets Bureau. Someone with expertise in the area.'

'It'll take years to get a successful prosecution. They've had some high-profile failures in the past.'

Daly kept flicking through the pages. 'You know, it can't just be Morgan behind all these financial fronts,' he said eventually.

'What do you mean?'

'All this paperwork. It suggests a labyrinthine system. He must have lawyers and accountants working for him, banks, and institutions willing to turn a blind eye.' Daly peered out of the window at the front garden full of blooms and beyond at the main street of the village. 'You know, when I first walked through Dreesh, I had the impression that something didn't add up.'

'About what?'

'The finances of its residents. Their wealth.'

'What wealth?' McKenna almost snorted.

'The wealth hidden away from prying eyes. It mightn't be

222

their money resting in their accounts, but your neighbours can still afford to drive top-of-the-range cars.' He held up the file of documents. 'These pages reveal the truth about their links with Morgan.'

'What kind of links are you talking about?'

'I think Carey was trying to work that out. The problem is he never found out.'

They both stared at the pages in silence.

'We need to find out where Carey got all this financial information from,' said Daly.

'He had an informer, someone who worked for Morgan,' replied McKenna. 'Someone with access to his computers.'

'We haven't even looked at the USB stick.' Daly asked to borrow McKenna's computer. However, rather than open the files on the stick, he attached them to several emails and sent them to Detective O'Neill, asking her to share the data immediately with the Criminal Assets Bureau.

'There's something I need to ask you,' said Daly, waiting for the files to upload. 'Have your superiors ordered you to drop Carey's investigation?'

'I cannot comment,' replied McKenna.

'Of course you can. We're both police officers. What are you holding back?'

'I'm not holding back anything.'

Daly shook his head. 'Then tell me why you don't want to investigate Carey's final case? What does it mean for your police force and the people of Dreesh?'

McKenna did not reply, and Daly did not press him for the moment. He clicked the mouse, opening another message to O'Neill and attaching a file.

'All I can say is that Carey's death rattled us all,' said McKenna. 'When a detective dies suddenly there are always loose ends to tidy up.' He hesitated. 'Some milk spilled along the way. Especially when he died on the job.'

Daly stared at the whirring hourglass on the computer screen as the files took their time transferring. 'You mean killed in the line of duty.'

McKenna froze at the directness of Daly's words.

Daly posed another question. 'Do you still think Carey committed suicide?'

McKenna turned to the window. 'Just between us, Inspector?'

'Yes. Of course.'

'When I met you for the first time, you reminded me of Carey. I wasn't sure why, but I think I understand now.' He stared at Daly, waiting for some reaction, but Daly's expression was a blank. 'In the police force, there are those who run with the pack, and those who stay at the margins. When Brian first came to Dreesh, I was something of a veteran. I'd saved my career in this village by hiding with the pack. But Brian was an outsider right from the start. I don't know how he survived as long as he did. I think he was an outsider who kept away from his colleagues to save himself.'

'But you haven't answered my question.'

'Which question?'

'Was Carey murdered?'

'You didn't ask me that.'

'I'm asking you now.'

McKenna made an evasive gesture. 'The week before he died, I could see he was going through a very bad stretch. He looked unhappy.'

'What did you see?'

'I kept seeing him standing at the bridge over the border, staring at the river, dressed in his work suit and holding a briefcase. He stood there during the school run in the mornings and then in the evenings, when the road was full of people driving home from work.'

Daly thought of those stark moments on bridges or wooden piers when desperate people stared at their reflections in the water. Puppets of dread, not in their right minds, brought to the brink by the terrible secrets they carried in their hearts. Something about the image of Carey on the bridge nagged at him, stirring his inner anxieties about Donaldson's death, but he could not quite put his finger on it. Had Carey suspected that something might happen to him? Did he know his life was in grave danger?

McKenna went on to talk about how Carey had been overworked and distracted from the humdrum duties of policing a village like Dreesh. His work with Detective Hunter and his network of informers had been all-consuming.

Daly listened to him, but his thoughts were still fixated upon the sergeant's description of Carey standing at the border. Something important had been said. Some crucial link with the way Donaldson had died had touched a raw nerve in his psyche. The way Carey seemed to have been waiting at the bridge, staring at the water.

When the computer files had been sent to O'Neill's email account, he got up and stood at the window. He wanted to hunt down the vague link he had registered. He felt the tension inside him build. It was the openness of Carey's desperation on the bridge, as though he had wanted everyone to notice it.

A spectacle of sadness as the world went about its daily business. The drowned detective had wanted to hold the gaze of the entire village, thought Daly, to bring them to account in the same way that Donaldson had tried to bring him to account by leaving behind a suicide note. He thought of the names on Carey's list. Had his lonely, stationary figure on the bridge provoked the collective dread of an entire village?

Daly's mind slipped back to Donaldson's letter and its mangled accusations, the intrinsic horror of suicide. His thoughts tumbled towards the threshold of a dark and terrible place. He saw Donaldson and Carey's bodies, dredged from a watery abyss, rise up with the one face, the same pair of relentlessly staring eyes. He came to the paranoid conclusion that Special Branch's release of Donaldson's note represented something subtle and sinister. It was an attempt to shift on to him, the unsuspecting son of a woman murdered by paramilitaries, the burden of guilt, thus depriving him of the single comfort left to any victim: the consolation of their innocence. He grimaced and tried to close his mind to his rising suspicions.

'Inspector Daly,' said McKenna, appearing beside him. The sergeant's voice snapped him back to reality.

'Excuse me,' said Daly, 'I was somewhere else.' He stood very still.

'Not a place I'd like to be, judging from the look on your face.'

'Carey's death made me think of another case, another drowning on the lough.'

'You must have seen some bad things, working as a detective in the North.' McKenna looked at Daly in a strange

226

way, as if he could read things on his face that the detective could not see himself.

'I've been sidetracked by the whistle-blower's letter,' said Daly. 'I came here today to ask you a different question altogether.'

'Fire away.' The tension between the two of them seemed to have evaporated.

'I want the names of the other PSNI detectives Carey worked with.'

'I need to think about that for a few minutes,' replied McKenna. He grimaced a little – or was it an attempt at a smile? 'For a long while Hunter was the only one.'

Daly nodded and waited. When nothing was forthcoming, he prompted the sergeant. 'The last time we met, you told me about a select group of detectives from both sides of the border called the Green and Blue Fishing Club. Carey and Hunter were members.' Daly paused, prolonging the silence for as long as possible. McKenna did not offer any further comment, but Daly waited. There were times when it was a hundred times better to say less rather than more, to hand control over to the interviewee and watch them rack their brains for a more palatable version of the truth. Framed against the window, McKenna's silhouette subtly froze, his hands hanging limply by his side. The Green and Blue Fishing Club was a subject he appeared reluctant to broach.

Eventually Daly spoke. 'I believe your brother, Detective Jack McKenna, was a member of the club. I'm sure you'd remember seeing or hearing about him.'

McKenna's face carried the pain of an apology. 'I've had some trouble with my brother down through the years.'

It sounded to Daly like the truth, but what lie might the truth be concealing?

McKenna spoke again. 'Carey found him hard to work with. He preferred to deal with Detective Hunter.'

'Anyone else, or did Carey find the other members of the group objectionable as well?'

'Probably. There was a swarm of detectives from the North at one point. There was Clive Delargy based in Aughnacloy; then there was Elliott. I think his first name was William. I don't remember the names of the others.'

'All retired, I suppose?'

'Most likely. Delargy died of cancer. I don't know what happened to Elliott. As you probably know, my brother left the force. He's retired now. When he's not in his house in Belfast he's at his holiday cottage in Lisnaskea. He spends most of his time fishing down there.'

Daly asked for the directions to the cottage. 'Good,' he said, when he had taken them down. 'That's some progress.'

'Progress towards what?' asked McKenna. 'What precisely are you after?'

'I can't let go of this Detective Hunter. If I can track down anyone who worked with him it might help shine a light on the mystery. I want to ask your brother what he remembers of him.'

'If you're in a rush there, I know a shortcut,' said McKenna with a sly smile. 'There's an old road that will take you directly from here to his cottage over the border in Lisnaskea. It's straight as an arrow but full of humps and potholes. Most people prefer the new roads, but they go the long way round the border.'

It occurred to Daly that McKenna might be telling him something important. The border parishes were full of shadowy old roads hidden in plain view, sharing the landscape with new roads full of busy commuters, families doing the school run, and farmers puttering about on their tractors. The old roads were the haunts of smugglers, the ever-present ghosts of the past, and police officers on urgent missions.

McKenna gave him the directions of the old road, and shook his hand firmly. 'Good luck with my brother,' he said.

The sergeant's hands were cold, and the affable-sounding words, though they were meant to wish him well, were troubling. McKenna was intimating some sort of warning. How else could Daly explain why the light in his eyes was suddenly snuffed out and replaced by a haunted expression, a look of worried pity, whether for Daly or McKenna's brother, he did not know.

Daly climbed into his car and followed the directions that would take him straight as an arrow to Jack McKenna's house. He had the address and the elusive files belonging to Detective Carey, but somehow he felt he had been ejected from the sergeant's station with more doubts and greater anxiety of mind than before. How had his tactic to get the truth from McKenna foundered, assuming he had a tactic in the first place and wasn't just being misled by the whistleblower's files and the machinations of McKenna and his superiors? He saw in McKenna something he had not seen before: a talent for manoeuvring, a form of tact, a skill that so far in the investigation had been hidden from him.

CHAPTER TWENTY-NINE

When Tommy tore away from his captors, he had no plan. He stumbled up the village main street, hearing Morgan's shouts catching up, unsure of which direction he was headed. The street seemed narrower and gloomier than he remembered, more like a trench leading him deeper into Morgan's lair and everything he had hoped to escape. He could hear the slouching thud of the smuggler's gait behind him, the slow march of terror, hemming him in like a hounded animal. He staggered towards the only lit-up building in the evening light, the welcoming front of the Railway Bar.

He flung open the doors and almost fell upon the group of men standing at the bar. Surprised, they turned to look at him, their round faces and shiny foreheads encircling him. He recognized the bank manager but could not remember his name, a genial, fair man who had lived all his life in the village. Alongside him were a solicitor, an estate agent and a few building contractors, assembled like a reunion of old business partners reminiscing about more optimistic times. A moment ago, they had been shaking with laughter, but now their faces were solemn and stern.

'Jesus, what happened to you?' said the bank manager.

Tommy knew he did not look good in his ruined clothes. The amount of blood and dirt would have frightened most people away. 'Someone please ring the police,' he said. 'I've been in a terrible accident.'

The group of men and the bartender stared at Tommy. They made no move to reassure or assist him. He could hear Morgan's footsteps approaching, his massive shadow looming upon the windows of the doors.

'If you don't help me, I'll take action,' he threatened.

'What action?' asked the bartender, returning to wash empty glasses in a sink.

'I'll give you hell.'

'Will you?' said the barman, glasses clinking as he rustled behind the bar. 'What do you call hell?'

Morgan was standing at the door now, staring venomously at the customers and the bartender. Sweat ran in trickles down Tommy's brow. The ceiling of the room seemed to lower, its corners looming towards him. Surely this was still a safe place. All he needed was for someone to make the phone call that would rescue him. The men at the bar met his imploring gaze, and then bowed their heads. For a moment, he thought they were going to answer his plea and take out their mobile phones, but when they looked up at him again, he saw that their eyes had changed. This time, he was confronted by a single pair of black pupils. He saw the eyes of the same monster staring from each of their pale, glistening faces, the predator who controlled the village through his flow of money. He saw the depths of their greed, as, one by one, they shifted in their seats, put on their coats and left the bar without uttering a further word.

Like the devil himself, Morgan hopped across the room and was on top of Tommy in an instant. The accident happened all over again. A blow struck his face, and then another. Time stopped. He saw Morgan's face, grinning widely, surrounded by his henchmen. More blows followed. There was nothing he could do to stop the violence, Morgan's grinning mouth gaping above him, his eyes bulging with excitement.

Suddenly, inexplicably, the beating stopped. Morgan took several deep breaths, and ordered his men and the barman to leave the room. He hauled Tommy to a booth, pushed him on to a seat, and got a large whiskey from the bar. He downed the contents of the glass as though quenching a deep thirst, and looked Tommy straight in the eye.

'I've lived for years with a secret even bigger than yours, Tommy,' he said. 'You know what I'm talking about, don't you?'

'I've no idea.'

'I'm talking about the way things are along the border, every man spying on their neighbour, everybody double-crossing each other. It's how the security forces keep us down.'

'What are you talking about?'

'I'm going to trade with you, Tommy. I'm going to tell you who I work for in exchange for you telling me who you work for.'

'I don't spy for anyone.'

Morgan's eyes were as still as those of a fox. 'You're lying to me, Tommy,' he said. 'I know because I'm a spy, just like you. There you go, you've heard it from my very own lips.' His face contorted into an expression of sincerity, a moment of play-acting to hide rather than reveal the secrets of his past. 'I've spoken honestly to you, Tommy. Now it's time to tell me your secret. Who sent you back to me?' A hint of impatience – or was it desperation? – had crept into his voice. Tommy felt a new sensation. Was it that Morgan was secretly afraid of him, of who had sent him, afraid of the forces that had decided to penetrate his secrets?

'A secret like that might be my death sentence,' said Tommy.

Morgan's figure stiffened. He seemed to hesitate. He looked around the empty room and then his hands went into his pockets. 'It's a pity you didn't go through my accounts with a sharper eye,' he said. 'Otherwise you'd have never come back from Spain.' He quietly removed a folded page from one of his pockets. He opened it and pointed his thick finger at a line of numbers.

Still dizzy with the blows he had endured, Tommy stared at the page and tried to focus. It was one of the bank statements belonging to Morgan's shell companies. He felt the hairs on his neck bristle. Morgan was pointing to one of the smallest transfers on the page. Five figures only. Deposited into the secret account of a Dreesh resident, an account number sickeningly familiar to him. Unlike the other transactions, this one had been withdrawn and spent by the account holder immediately. He knew this because the account belonged to him. The one his handlers had used to deposit regular payments for information. But how on earth had Morgan known about it, never mind been able to pay into it?

'I understand the money was taken out and used to buy a new motorbike,' said Morgan.

'How do you know that?'

'The same motorbike that's gathering dust in the shed outside your mother's house.' Morgan nodded with glee at Tommy's look of confusion. His eyes glittered with the secret that even he, with all his years of experience in the world of criminality and terrorism, could no longer hide. 'I know all about your bank account, Tommy. The one set up by Detective Hunter to pay for your little tales. Didn't anyone tell you it's my money you've been spending all along?'

Tommy did not believe what he was hearing. He stared at Morgan's bulging eyes, the sinister amusement shining there, and for a second he felt like unburdening himself of all his informer's woes, but then he saw the curl on Morgan's lips, the tip of his tongue flashing, savouring Tommy's ignorance, his humiliation. 'How come?' he asked.

'Too late to ask that question now, Tommy. You should have never come back, that's how come.' Morgan guffawed with laughter and leaned closer to Tommy. 'Can you see it now? I run Detective Hunter, you complete jackass. I run his entire fucking network, the spider's web of informers woven by him and his friends in the Gardai. Are you getting this into your thick head? Are there any brain cells in there? Anywhere?'

Morgan was splitting his sides with laughter. Tommy felt double-crossed and humiliated, and could not bear the derision. His mind in turmoil, he pushed past him and charged into the street, only to run into a set of powerful arms, and before he knew it, Morgan's henchmen had lifted him into the air and deposited him in the back of a van.

'Time for a little spin into the old country, Tommy,' said Morgan, perching himself in the front passenger seat. 'Driver, you know the way.'

Tommy stared through the windscreen at the main street of Dreesh as though it were a deep pit of darkness, the reflection of Morgan's grinning face hanging over it, taunting him with his secrets.

CHAPTER THIRTY

Daly drove through a series of border villages in the dwindling light. He passed through miles of rough, boggy, ungoverned country, unsure of whether he was in the North or South. Had the terrain always felt so empty and bleak? he wondered. He passed by the ruin of a border police station that looked oddly familiar. He realized he had visited the building not so long ago. It had been intact then, sprawling and self-important-looking in the landscape, a buttressed refuge where the sons of defenceless Protestant farmers and shopkeepers could turn into heavily armed police officers, where a fluttering Union flag flew permanently and the IRA's bloody bombing and shooting campaign was a test of Unionist nerve and mettle.

Now the station was a wilderness of concrete stumps, as though the base had sustained heavy shelling and the officers evacuated in a hurry. Even the cement foundations looked wrecked, heaved out of the earth. The one part of the station left untouched, and this looked sinister to Daly, was a wire-fenced plantation of tall antennae and radio masts on raised ground. A lonely chunk of intelligence hardware rising out of the ruins, keep-out signs emblazoning the padlocked gates. Listening posts, thought Daly, but who were they eavesdropping upon?

He drove through more villages with abandoned police stations. Every time he passed under their empty watch-towers, he thought of the new border that was approaching with Brexit, the one that had been in progress for nearly a year, but was still shrouded in mystery. He felt as though the ruined stations were trying to tell him something, some sort of message or signal hidden in the rubble, the whiskers of rusting barbed wire, and the radio antennae that suggested a constant listening presence. These stations and their checkpoints once mapped the border, stamping it with their military authority. He had no idea what the clue or warning might be, but he knew that the border would bring him close to answering the question that troubled him most of all. Who or what had driven Carey to his death? He was sure that Morgan was at least indirectly responsible for the detective's demise. Had Carey through his persistence set in motion forces over which he had no control? Perhaps he had stumbled upon a conspiracy he knew little about, or was ill equipped to overcome. Looking at the empty police stations, Daly understood that somehow the relationship between the police forces, North and South, was the key, a disjointed, precarious relationship of informal meetings and shadowy contacts that had been quietly erased from the official record.

He drove in a distracted state, following McKenna's directions, veering between the extremes of certainty and confusion, trying to work out what role Hunter played in the puzzle. His exhaustion from the night before, the fading light in the sky, the travelling corner of the border road that seemed to keep unwinding before him, and the silence and empty miles piling behind, all combined to make his eyelids as heavy as lead. *I should pull over,* he thought, *park in a lay-by and sleep, but then I'll probably wake up feeling more uncertain.* He accelerated, shifting through the gears, staring at the road, feeling that the figure of Hunter hovered close by, that at times it was just a few metres away from the windscreen, hanging there like his ghostly reflection, leading him deeper into the labyrinth of his suspicions. *I still don't know what Hunter looks like*, he thought. *I should know that by now.*

Hence the uneasiness he felt as his car finally rocked down a potholed lane that felt like the dead end of a wrong direction. He pulled into an untidy farmyard, filled with puddles of water and rusting farm machinery. Jack McKenna's cottage lay before him, hidden in the gloom of an overgrown black-thorn thicket.

It began to rain heavily as Daly walked from the car to the front porch. He tried knocking on the door, but it gave way at his touch. He stepped inside and stood silently, trying to discern what might be human amid the soft creaking noises of the cottage and the drumming of the rain. He took in the dank walls, the water pouring down the cramped windows, and the slovenly darkness within. Part of him thought he might feel safe here in this run-down cottage surrounded by mud and thorns.

'Can I help you?' said a voice. An elderly man slowly

advanced out of the gloom, a blanket gathered around his shoulders. He stared at the detective with such a look of tense curiosity that Daly was forced to take a step backwards.

'I'm looking for Jack McKenna,' said Daly.

'Oh, you have a voice then?'

When Daly introduced himself, the old man seemed relieved. 'I thought you might be someone else,' he said, looking the detective up and down. 'I don't like strangers creeping around my house like burglars.'

'I'm not a burglar.'

'Are you sure? Why didn't you knock and wait?'

'The door was open. I apologize if I caused you concern.'

'Well, you're here now.' He gave a sigh. 'My name is Jack McKenna. I take it you're in on it, too?'

Daly raised an eyebrow. 'In on what?'

Outside, the rain poured piteously down the gutters.

'All these shadows of suspicion.' With a tired gesture, he beckoned Daly to follow him into a room barely lit by a turf fire. The low flames flickered and hissed with drops of rain falling down the chimney. Against the sides of the room lay the blackened carcasses of ancient furniture. The old man waved Daly to a seat. Now that he had time to examine his host closely, Daly began to doubt if he was the same person as the driver in the grainy CCTV images from the airport. For a start, he looked older and much too frail.

'By the way, I've no tea, Inspector,' said McKenna, poking at the fire until the dark red embers lit up the room. 'You'll have to do with this little friend of mine.' McKenna produced a bottle containing a clear liquid and two dirty glasses. 'You know, as soon as you told me your name, I thought maybe

239

my day has come. Here at last is a man who can raise the ghosts of the past and drive them into the light.' He flashed Daly a grin and poured him a large measure of what smelled like illicit booze.

He's trying to win me over, thought Daly, sniffing the poteen. He looked at McKenna's face, wrinkled into senility, a face full of hidden fears, and saw a version of Sergeant McKenna, a more decrepit one, a version of him in hell.

'You're one of those new detectives, aren't you?' said McKenna. 'A man of the future? You understand what I'm saying?'

Daly said he was not so sure.

'No, how could you understand? You don't belong to the past. Let me explain, Inspector. You are the man to rescue me from the mistakes of my career.' He raised his glass to Daly, tipped his head back, and took a greedy gulp. When he'd finished he stared at Daly expectantly.

Daly raised his glass and took a sip. He felt the poteen burn a track down his throat.

'Your colleagues in Special Branch warned me you were coming,' said McKenna.

'When was this?'

'They rang me this morning. They had a pile of questions for me.'

'What did they want to know?'

'They wanted me to reveal a secret.'

'What secret?'

'The secret Carey took with him to the grave.'

'And what did you tell them?'

He spat into the fire. 'Carey knew nothing. Let me

clear that up once and for all. He was stuck in a dead-end investigation, trying to gather evidence to incriminate a thug like Morgan. Working on his own in that back-end of a place with only my brother for company, when he should have pursued his career elsewhere.'

'Was your brother a help or a hindrance?' asked Daly.

McKenna grinned. Again, in the fading light, Daly saw the ghostly form of his Garda brother. 'Sergeant Peter only ever knew half of what there was to know.'

'What do you mean by that?'

'He might not sleep if he knew the other half.'

'What other half?'

'Everything Peter told you is a lie, that's the half I know.'

Daly pushed the old man with more questions but his words felt like stones dropped into a very deep well. He was convinced that Jack McKenna was holding back something important about his brother. He wanted to find out more about their relationship as family kin operating on opposite sides of the border.

'In the early days, Peter was happy to work with me,' said McKenna. 'In an unofficial capacity, that is.'

'What do you mean?'

'As an informer, you might say. And I returned the favour. It wouldn't be the first time two brothers helped each other out in their careers.' The old man admitted that they had operated along blurred boundaries, spying on their own police forces and slipping information to each other, Peter passing on details of Garda officers sympathetic to the IRA, and Jack pinpointing colleagues who had links to Loyalist paramilitaries, and could not be trusted.

'Were there other informers among the Gardai?'

McKenna explained how the net of information-gathering had expanded to include Carey and other Garda detectives. His brother, however, had stopped sharing secrets with him years ago.

'When was the last time you saw Carey?'

'A few weeks ago.'

'What state of mind was he in?'

'It saddened me to see he was still talking about the same plots, the same plans to recruit informers. In reality, he was just as far from arresting Morgan as he ever was.'

'Detective Robert Hunter, who is he?' asked Daly.

'A colleague,' replied McKenna, and hesitated. Somehow, the turf smoke had sneaked back down the chimney and wreathed his face in threads of grey. 'He had cold eyes and a superior attitude. I never warmed to him.'

'Where was he based?'

'What's he got to do with you coming here? Is he suspected of some crime?'

'His name keeps popping up in relation to Carey's death yet I can't find a trace of him anywhere. He's like a ghost created by the border. No one else has met him except Carey.'

'He was here earlier today.' McKenna lifted a finger and pointed at the seat next to Daly. 'Sitting right there.'

'Where is he now?'

'He must have gone. He does that a lot. He comes and goes without warning.'

'What kind of visitor comes and goes just like that?'

'I've lots of visitors like that. People like you, Inspector. How did you get in?'

'What other visitors come and go?'

'Old colleagues. Men from the past. I recognize them as soon as they cross the door, even though they never introduce themselves. I make do with their company because I've no one else.' He filled his glass of poteen and knocked it back. 'You can't shut the past out. That door can never be closed.'

Daly began to doubt if McKenna was in his right mind. A flock of crows cawed menacingly down the chimney, and McKenna adjusted the blanket around his shoulders, his face settling into a sour mask.

Before Daly could ask any more questions about Hunter, his phone buzzed in his pocket, startling him. He saw that it was Detective Irwin. He excused himself and slipped outside, but McKenna did not seem to notice or care about his departure.

CHAPTER THIRTY-ONE

'Where are you?' said Irwin. 'We were expecting you at a meeting this afternoon.'

Daly stood in the porch, the rain hammering on the roof above him. 'I took a wrong turning at the border. These roads are a labyrinth.'

'Where are you now? I can hear the rain.'

'Interviewing someone who knows Detective Hunter.'

'Do you really think you're going to find him?'

'I believe I'm getting close.'

Daly could hear Irwin whispering to someone in the background. Then the mobile phone signal deteriorated. He was about to end the call when Irwin's voice returned.

'Inspector Fealty's orders are that you're not to cross the border. It's a security risk. You're not allowed to pursue an investigation in a foreign jurisdiction without official permission.'

'Is Fealty there? I need to ask him some questions.'

'No you can't.'

'Why not?'

'He's busy.'

'But you haven't asked him.'

'When are you coming back to the office?'

'When you have some fresh leads on Morgan. I emailed Detective O'Neill a set of his accounts.'

'Yeah, we're going through them right now.' Irwin's voice sounded distracted, as though he was communicating to someone else at the same time.

'What have you found?'

'Don't expect any developments too soon. It'll take weeks to unravel the links between all the companies. But we can safely say it's not a family business that Morgan is operating. It's clear he's been using the residents of Dreesh and their reputations to hide his money.'

'It's what I suspected.' Daly turned and glanced into the cottage. Silence and darkness greeted him.

'What's really interesting is that Morgan's umbrella company has links with an account run by Portman Holdings,' said Irwin.

'Why's that interesting?' asked Daly. He didn't feel like dawdling at the cottage front door, but he sensed a change of emphasis in Irwin's voice.

'The account appears to be a payment system for contracted services. The transfers go back more than ten years. Typically a payee receives large cash deposits for a year or so, the money is withdrawn, and then the contract appears to terminate.'

Daly listened closely, wondering what had drawn Irwin's attention to the account.

'We've checked the beneficiaries,' said Irwin. 'Twelve in total. They were typically unemployed, unskilled young men living along the border.'

'Let's get back to Morgan, please,' said Daly. 'At this moment, I couldn't care less who he has on his payroll.'

'Perhaps you should. You see, the last payment to the men usually coincided with a dramatic change to their personal circumstances.'

'What sort of change?'

'Take the case of Declan Murray, an out-of-work brickie from Clones. His payments ended in June 2005. A few weeks later his body was found wrapped in a bin bag near Lisnaskea. A local priest was directed to his body by dissident Republicans, who claimed Murray had been an informer, working for the intelligence services.' Irwin rattled through the names of several more men, all of whom had been murdered amid claims they worked for the security forces.

'Why would a company run by Morgan organize payments to a gang of informers?' asked Daly.

'There are more links between Morgan and these men in the files. We'll have to get specialist help to go through the accounts. I don't know where this is going to end myself.'

'This suggests that Morgan is in some way involved in the recruitment of informers,' said Daly. 'He may even have had control over these men. That's what the links are telling us. Somehow, Morgan is helping to run a spying agency.'

'That wouldn't be as odd as some of the rumours flying around about Morgan. Organized crime infiltrates every aspect of life along the border. Why not counter-terrorism?'

'I think it's time we sent a message to Morgan,' said Daly.

'Let him know we're investigating his companies, how he cleans his dirty cash, and the flow of money to these dead informers. Get the financial experts at the Criminal Assets Bureau to draw up a chart showing the true extent of his business empire. In the meantime, concentrate on Portman Holdings and the owners of the bank accounts. Try to establish the exact links Morgan had with these men. Some of them might have gone on the run, and still be in hiding. They'll have an interesting story to tell.'

Irwin was silent for several moments. 'What about Hunter? What role do you think he plays in all of this?'

Daly was reluctant to share his suspicions with Irwin, especially with Fealty hovering in the background. He was afraid that his latest line of inquiry would cause the Special Branch inspector to apply the brakes and restrict his investigation for security reasons. Of all the vague and obscure facts of the case, Hunter's role was the most nebulous.

Daly chose his words carefully. 'I believe that Carey was cold-bloodedly murdered because he had discovered the truth about Morgan's relationship with Hunter.'

'That Morgan was his mole?'

'Or vice versa. Hunter might have been on Morgan's payroll all along. I'm visiting someone I hope will fathom the mystery.'

'Be careful. If Hunter knows you're on his trail, he could be waiting for you.'

'I hope so.' Daly stared at the pools of rainwater gathering in the yard. 'I haven't been able to find him, so he has to find me. I believe Carey had the same problem in the weeks before he died. He had to draw Hunter out of the shadows.'

'In that case, I think Inspector Fealty and I should join you with some proper back-up.'

'That would be silly, Irwin. I don't want to scare him away.' And with that Daly hung up. He slipped the phone into his pocket and peered into the cottage. He was close to the border, a place for settling old scores, where allegiances and politics could be easily erased if the price was right. Morgan's links with the dead informers had unsettled him. It reminded him of his own unstable contingency as a police detective in Northern Ireland, his entanglement in the troubled order of things, a country where ex-paramilitaries and comrades of Morgan now ruled in government with their former enemies, while the security services ran in the darkness, searching this way and that for criminals like Morgan, who roared and laughed in their gruesome sheds.

CHAPTER THIRTY-TWO

The moonlit road was empty and long, a wave of dips and rises through patches of forest and boggy little fields. Shut off in the grimy interior of the van as in a hearse, Tommy knew his life and death were no longer his own. He stared at the hunched figures of Morgan and the driver, the van speeding on in silence. The time had seemed interminable from the moment he'd first entered Morgan's yard and shivered in the blast of his voice and thundering lorries.

'Take me back to Dreesh,' said Tommy. 'My mother's waiting for me.'

Morgan turned round and stared at Tommy. 'You still have to tell me the truth, you little bastard.'

'Which country are we in? Where are we going?'

Morgan shrugged his shoulders and said nothing. His eyes were alight with some strange inner enjoyment. It was clear he had some distance still to go, worse things to say and do, and there seemed no point in hurrying to the end. The van came to a crossroads and Morgan directed the driver to take a right, and then another immediate turn. The van followed a sunken lane almost completely hidden by bent-over bushes, eventually emerging on to a tract of bogland.

Seeing the track meander through a sea of heather and clumps of thorns, Tommy felt such an anxiety that he had to wipe the sweat from his hands. No matter how much he willed his imagination to work out Morgan's next move, the same loosely connected images kept running through his mind. He saw a ghostly hare struck by fear in the middle of the road, and a fox waiting in the hanging mist with a huge grin.

'Keep driving,' ordered Morgan as the van swayed dangerously. 'If we stop now, we'll not get started again.'

Whatever happened, it seemed, they had to keep going. Morgan turned and flashed him a look of contempt, as though his fate had long ago been decided and there was nothing anyone could do about it. The smuggling boss seemed to be in no rush to get a confession from him. In fact, he appeared to be restraining himself. With his eyes fixed on the dwindling road ahead, Morgan began telling Tommy about how he had kept tabs on Carey's investigation all along. The Garda detective had made a grievous mistake in assuming Hunter was on his side, setting out on a personal vendetta to bring down the entire village, threatening the financial well-being of everyone. But Morgan had been waiting for him.

'The truth is my men and I killed him,' said Morgan. 'We got him to meet us at Lough Neagh so he would drown there. And he drowned. We knew he was on our case and wouldn't quit, so we had to finish him off. And that's what we did.'

The van pulled to an abrupt halt, and Tommy knocked his

head against the seats in front. The driver switched off the ignition and got out.

'Why have we stopped here?' asked Tommy.

'Your shadow.' Morgan produced a gun and rested it on his lap.

'What do you mean?'

'The car that's been following us since we left Dreesh. It's about a mile behind. If you take off now they'll be with you in a minute.'

What car were they talking about? He glanced again at Morgan's gun. 'If I set off now you'll shoot me in the back.'

Morgan waved the gun at him. 'I'll fucking shoot you right now if you don't get out.' He clambered out of the van and opened the back doors so that he could confront the frightened informer in the back. 'Why shouldn't I kill you right now?'

Tommy huddled where he was, waiting for whatever would happen next.

'You're still one of us, Tommy,' said Morgan as he hauled the young man on to the road. 'A Dreesh man. You might have betrayed me but you'll always be one of us. I don't forget that.' He gave him a push down the road. 'Take off, now. I don't want to see your silly informer's face again.' With that, he raised the gun and fired a warning shot into the air.

Tommy made a lunge along the road, and then veered off into the bogland. He still had his wits about him, whatever Morgan might think, and he knew he had a chance of freedom if he could find a hiding place in the darkness. He heard the roar of Morgan's voice behind him and another gunshot. He stumbled forward, splashing through bog pools and jagged trenches of rotting turf. A rifle fired again, and this time he felt a searing pain in his left thigh. He had been hit. He floundered, the pain barely registering. He used all his strength to throw his body to the left and then to the right, seeking a refuge, waiting for the next shot to knock him off his feet, hearing the murderous shouting of Morgan steadily gaining ground.

CHAPTER THIRTY-THREE

When Daly returned the room had grown darker and McKenna had fallen asleep, his hunched figure flickering by the fire, the rattle of his heavy breathing filling the room. The old man looked exhausted and miserable, and Daly felt weary at the thought of enduring his hospitality any further. When he cleared his throat and sat down, McKenna looked across at him, his face frightened.

'Who are you?' asked the old man.

Daly repeated his name.

'Oh yes, I remember you now. Inspector Daly, the man they said would rescue me.'

'Who told you that?'

'Detective Hunter.'

'Why did he say that?'

'You can ask him yourself.' McKenna grinned and poured two fresh glasses of poteen. 'He'll be here shortly.' He handed one of the glasses to Daly and raised the other in a toast before knocking it back. 'To you and me, Inspector. Long-suffering Catholics trapped in the North. The greatest losers in Irish history.'

Daly sipped his glass, and said nothing. The old man was probably right, at least as far as his father's generation was concerned, if not his own. They had been the stigmatized losers on the wrong side of partition and the border, suffering protracted decades of discrimination and bigotry, Loyalist violence, and then the IRA running amok with their murder campaign. It had all been a grievous burden, with Catholic police officers like McKenna having to bear the brunt, enduring distrust within police ranks and threats of violence from their own communities. Still, the experiences of working-class Catholic families during the bad days of rampant sectarianism could not fully explain the rot along the border. Daly's father had survived those years with his dignity intact. No, the decline had really set in afterwards, post ceasefire.

Daly listened to McKenna mumble about smuggling gangs, agricultural-subsidy fraud, inflated land transactions, dubious property deals with the National Asset Management Agency, contaminated meat processed at illegal abattoirs, illegal landfill sites, and the rapacious behaviour of banks who threw money at poor stooges hoping to realize their wildest dreams by buying apartments in Bulgaria and building sites in Spain. McKenna kept up his rant. It sounded like the moralizing discharge of a failed detective drenched in cynicism. Inwardly, Daly agreed with him. The country had become hysterically obsessed with property, trying to make up for the lost decades of the Troubles, believing the country was immune to financial failure. However, no one was immune to a property crash, not even the wealthiest men and women along the border, and few of them had foreseen the humiliating disgrace of bankruptcy and the grinding effects of debt. The rot, the lawlessness slithering about the border might have sprung from the Troubles, but it was magnified by the desire of so many people living beyond their theoretical means.

'I warned you there'd never be an end to your greed,' said McKenna, addressing the darkness.

'Who are you talking to?' asked Daly. 'Me or your ghosts?' It struck him that McKenna would much rather entertain the shadows of the past than broach the subject of Hunter. 'I came here looking for Hunter. I'm not interested in your ghosts.'

'Then tell me what you want to know.'

'Who else worked with Hunter?'

'There were dozens. First, let's drink another glass, the lot of us.' McKenna flashed a hallucinatory stare around the room.

Daly sighed in annoyance. He suspected that McKenna was luring him into a deliberate derangement of the senses in order to hide the truth. He had no alternative but to continue with the game the confounded old man was playing, and hope that he would learn more about Hunter. McKenna was the only guide he had to the tortuous path taken by Hunter, and he had to keep following him even if that meant abandoning the dictates of reason and sobriety. *Of all the interrogations I've done in my life, this is the most pointless*, he thought with desperation. How could his colleagues in

Special Branch regard him with any measure of respect? Here he was, a prisoner to the ghosts of a demented drunk, drawing closer to the final border of sanity. McKenna's eyes narrowed and his head nodded towards his chest. He seemed incapable of more than a few moments of conversation before drowsiness overcame him.

The door banged, startling McKenna from his sleep. 'Who's there?' he cried.

'It was the wind,' said Daly.

'You're wrong, Inspector.' McKenna threw a shovel full of slack on to the fire, snuffing out the light. Again, the door banged. 'My visitors have come back.'

'It's nothing,' said Daly, but his words did not appease McKenna.

'They're doing this on purpose, you know.'

'Who?' asked Daly.

'The shadows. They roam the rooms at night, plotting ways to kill me.' He looked up from under his heavy brows, his eyes flickering at a room full of ghosts. 'Who did you say you were again?' he asked Daly, his voice suspicious, his eyes puzzled. 'Are you that fellow Hunter sends to keep an eye on me?'

'Who are you talking about?' Daly tried to rein in his impatience.

The old man gave Daly a blank look, and poured out more poteen. They both fell silent, captive to the cottage's decomposition and its encroaching darkness. McKenna's drunken eyes watched Daly, repelling him. The minutes passed by. The door behind Daly tugged open slightly, letting in a draught of cold air, and then slid shut again. Daly grew aware of the quietness outside. The rain had ceased and the birds had abandoned their restless fidgeting on the roof. It occurred to him that McKenna might be right, and someone else was hiding in the house, monitoring their conversation, eavesdropping on their thoughts. He caught another whiff of fresh air. His suspicions alerted, he heard a small sound echoing back from the kitchen that might have been a door handle clicking or a revolver setting. He listened intently, but the house sank back into silence.

McKenna leaned forward and drank with the exaggerated care of a man whose movements were no longer under his own jurisdiction. He used his left hand, while his right arm hung by his side, lifeless. Daly was reminded of the way his brother, the Garda sergeant from Dreesh, had drunk a similar glass. Only he had used his right hand. It was as if the two men were mirror images of each other, or the one police officer divided and refracted by the border.

McKenna poured more drink. When the glasses were full, he tipped back the empty bottle and held it in the air. He sat for several long moments without moving, as if he had fallen into a trance. Daly's eyes grew heavy with the effects of the poteen. In the absolute darkness of his ignorance and the old man's confusion, he felt as if he had fallen into a trance too, his mind suspended at the edge of a precipice.

McKenna collected himself and raised his glass to Daly. He struggled to think of a toast, but no words came out. He downed the glass in a single gulp. He retrieved a fresh bottle from a cupboard and brandished it before Daly. 'Try this, Inspector, it's the best of the batch.'

With diminishing reluctance, Daly accepted the alcohol.

Flames crept across the slack in the fireplace and lit up the room with a dull glow. Daly glanced at the clock on the mantelpiece. 'It's getting late,' he said, hearing the slur in his voice. 'I have a feeling Hunter isn't going to show tonight.'

'God, if only that were true,' muttered McKenna. 'Don't get impatient. He'll come when he's good and ready. Stay awake, Inspector, any lapse in concentration, even the blink of an eye, and he'll slip away again.'

The minutes ticked by.

'Not long now, you'll see.'

Daly grew resigned to a sense of helplessness, slipping with his host down into bottomless drunkenness, the clock growing more blurred, until time itself lost its urgency. The glow of the fire drew his eyes in, and his thoughts grew numb. *This is madness. I should be hunting down Morgan, rather than getting drunk with this old fool.* But he knew he couldn't leave now. The prospect of meeting Hunter, no matter how faint, was too tantalizing. He wanted to see his face, find out whom he worked for, and where exactly his allegiances lay.

'Hunter will stir things up, good and proper,' promised McKenna. 'You'll see. He'll give you all the ammunition you need against Morgan.'

In the weak light, there was something about McKenna's hunched figure that began to disturb Daly, the way the fire-light flickered in his dull eyes. Something he did not quite understand. Was this a hallucination presenting itself before him, or the ghost of his dead father?

'Listen,' said Daly in his drunkenness, his voice heavily slurred. 'I never meant to stay in the old place. I wanted to leave but I never had the strength.' He looked at McKenna's troubled face and saw it set in the frown of another old man, one who had been dead for years, a vision of his father sitting in a dark corner. McKenna did not speak.

'I had to knock the old place down,' Daly went on. 'It's been my home all my life, even though it's never been mine. I hope you understand that.'

McKenna lifted an eyebrow. He removed the bottle of poteen and placed it under his chair. 'Have you forgotten why you're here, Inspector? This investigation of yours?'

'What investigation?'

'This.' McKenna gestured at the darkness. 'Me. Detective Hunter. My brother. The fishing club.'

But Daly kept staring at the other face floating by the fire. He shook his head. 'This isn't an investigation any more. It's my search for the past. For home. When I first saw this cottage, I thought I might see you inside. I knew you would be waiting for me. An old man wearing my father's frown.'

McKenna stared back at the fire with downcast eyes, in the same way Daly's father used to do.

'I never felt able to live the life I wanted to in your cottage,' explained Daly. 'For Chrissakes, I couldn't even buy furniture and arrange it the way I liked. I never had any guests stay the night. I could never bring a woman into my own bedroom.' He drained his glass and handed it over to the double of his father, who reached under his chair for the poteen and filled it.

'You see, I always felt as though you were watching and listening, even when you were gone. I've carried the cross of your judgment since childhood. It's defined my entire life. It and that hungry cottage, that ruined bit of property you saddled me with.' Daly stared at the old man by the fire, the

259

same man with the same heavy emotions he had known all his life. 'I had to knock it down, don't you see? I didn't want to rot away in it like you. And now I've destroyed it. I've torn myself away from its wreckage.'

McKenna held his glass aloft. 'A toast to you,' he announced. 'Inspector Daly's ghost.'

In silence, the other old man stared back at Daly.

'Well,' said Daly, his voice eager and anxious. 'What do you say?'

But the ghost of Daly's past did not answer. Daly grew aware of McKenna's awful curiosity, his glinting eyes watching him. McKenna sniggered, and the image of the old man silently disappeared. Daly fell back into his chair. He raised his shaking hands to his head, his mind reeling with the strong alcohol. He fought to regain rationality, to untangle his past from the chaos of the investigation.

'Didn't I warn you, Inspector?' said McKenna. 'This place is crowded with ghosts.'

The room grew dark again. Completely drunk now, Daly watched McKenna as through a narrowing tunnel. The old man twisted and turned with an agitated look on his face. He had heard something Daly had not. His eyes lifted towards the door, full of anxious enquiry. Daly turned unsteadily to look behind. A tower of shadows had gathered there while they had been drinking, hidden shapes watching them from a dreadful height, leaning in from all sides, listening to their thoughts.

'Who's there?' shouted McKenna. His voice had an elated old man's whine.

Daly thought of negotiating his way through the cluttered room and switching on all the lights in the house. He imagined finding the switches and flicking them on to reveal a house full of intruders. However, he knew he was dreaming – he could not open his eyes. Or was that because of his intoxication? Nothing had changed. He was still in his seat, staring at McKenna, the old man hiding at the end of his drunkenness – or was it madness? He strained forward and fell on to the flagged floor. When he looked up, he saw McKenna peering down at him.

'Easy now, steady there, Inspector,' he murmured.

Daly clambered to his feet, and the dimly lit room spun around him. It was the darkness that added to his vertigo, McKenna's condemned black corner emptying into an infinite blackness. He realized with a rush of exhilaration that he was drunk to the core of his being, and could say or do anything he wished. He luxuriated in this strange and powerful loss of inhibition, trying to hold on to its precariousness as he steadied himself before the old man. It was time to clear a path, to fling light into darkness. He lunged towards the door. He was master of the house now. He grunted, swinging it open, ignoring McKenna's feeble protestations. He knew he could solve the mystery by sweeping away the shadows, ask the questions he wanted to ask, discover the link between Hunter and Carey's death, all those enigmas that had stretched before him.

McKenna cursed at him, his frail hands trying to shove him back into his seat. With a cry of victory, Daly sidled along the walls and began flicking on the light switches, flooding the place with light. He picked up the empty poteen bottle and waved it in the air, swinging it dangerously close to McKenna's face. He lumbered through the house, tracking down the silent listeners, the unknown intruders, from room to room. He was ruthless in his pursuit, blocking off their paths of escape, one by one, and then he froze. A stranger had stepped through the front door and was standing in front of him. Daly felt a pang of fear, noting the hard and determined look on the man's face, and the black crowbar swinging in his hands.

'My name is Inspect—' said Daly but he never got the chance to finish his introduction.

CHAPTER THIRTY-FOUR

The moonlit bogland was full of wriggling paths, some wide enough for the zigzag run of a turf barrow, others large enough to accommodate a tractor or a small car, tracks now sinking from view, buried in heather and scrub, disappearing one by one because the old men who knew them like the back of their hands and cleared them regularly, the turf cutters, the bachelor farmers, and the poteen brewers, were also disappearing one by one.

Tommy lurched across the terrain, his eyes scanning the myriad of tracks. For a while, he had been aware of Morgan's figure teetering after him, his ogre-like panting in the dark, but he had not heard anything for the last mile or so. The only sounds had been his laboured breathing, and the trickling of hidden rivers and pools, treacherous in the dim light. In his shock, he mistook the dripping sounds for blood pouring from his leg wound. He felt dizzy, almost ghost-like, stumbling over the rough ground, waiting for the blood to thicken and stop its horrible trickling. His footfalls were so quiet, absorbed by the quaking layers of prehistoric vegetation piled beneath, that for long moments he almost felt weightless.

Deep trenches shimmered into view, reflecting the weak moonlight. His feet squelched through wet ground, the mud and slime creeping inside his shoes and coating his trouser bottoms. The ground beneath gave way, and he plunged up to his waist in a sucking bog hole. He gulped for air and strength, waded through the muddy depths, and hauled himself on to the bank, clutching fistfuls of heather, the ground as soft as a cadaver beneath his squirming body. He tried to get to his feet but his legs folded beneath him with the shock of the pain in his leg and the wound seeping blood. He crawled through the slime, pulling upon ancient roots, his injured leg feeling cold and heavy as though it had filled with bog water. It sagged strangely as he struggled to his feet, and the pain left him slightly deranged. 'You're coming with me,' he said through clenched teeth, dragging his leg behind him. He stumbled and lurched in a zigzag direction, one hand groping his leg, squeezing it close.

He came across the skull and ribcage of a dead sheep, the bones phosphorescent in the moonlight. He suspected his pursuers were close by, waiting for him to tire. Perhaps this was how they wanted him to die, chased to exhaustion like a dumb animal. The blood from his wound started to coagulate, spreading like a chill down his leg, and the bog grew eerie, full of shadows. Everywhere he looked he saw gaps in the ground that might open up into his grave.

Shots rang out from a pair of rifles close by, their echoes

reverberating in his ears, followed by a roar and shouts. He had thought the distance between his pursuers and him had widened, but somehow they had found a shortcut. He crouched down, at a loss over which direction to take. Flashlights moved in jumping circles across the low cover. A light flashed in his face, and he was running again.

Ahead, two halos of light, the headlamps of an approaching car, blazed towards him. Somehow, he had stumbled on to a road. He waved his arms in the air and brought the vehicle to a stop. He leaned against the bonnet, dragging his bloody leg behind him, and tried to peer through the windscreen, but the headlights had blinded him. The surrounding bogland grew quiet and dark. If there were shadows watching, they were careful enough to keep their presence hidden.

He grasped and fumbled at the passenger door handle but his hands were trembling too much. The driver leaned over and opened the door. There was a voice singing on the radio; for a while the driver did not speak, and the wailing sounds of the radio enmeshed Tommy, weaving his desperation and the night's emptiness into the song. Tommy hesitated at the driver's silence. Nausea washed over him and his good leg began to shake.

'Get in, Tommy, your running is over,' said the man behind the wheel as he raised a gun. 'Don't even think of taking another step.'

The voice had betrayed his hopes of rescue, just as it had betrayed him before. He had found Detective Robert Hunter.

CHAPTER THIRTY-FIVE

Daly woke to the sound of loud voices and a throbbing band of pain across his forehead. He sat up and tried to get his eyes to focus, opening them just wide enough to see what lay before him in the dim light. With his fingers, he could feel a sticky mess of blood on the back of his head. Slowly he turned his head, searching for the voices in the mistiness, seeing them come clear, the other figures in the room. He was still in McKenna's sitting room, only now it was early morning. He watched as a police officer carrying a gun dragged the moaning McKenna to his feet and bundled him out of the door. They hung there, framed in the perspective of the bright hallway and his hangover, and he was not sure that it was actually happening.

'McKenna,' he called, getting up and moving towards the hallway. He stooped in the porch, massaging his eyes, trying to rub away the pain. He watched as the policeman helped McKenna into a car. The old man spoke in a whimpering voice, his face dark and bruised, and the car door slammed shut on him.

'What's going on?' shouted Daly.

The policeman turned round, and began explaining something. Meanwhile, the car had taken off, accelerating up the lane, with McKenna in the back, his injured face staring out at Daly. Oddly, the car had a Southern registration, but the policeman walking towards him wore the uniform of the Northern Ireland police service.

'What the hell are you doing?' snapped Daly. 'Where are you taking McKenna?'

'He's away with it, Inspector,' said the officer. 'We had to hide the poteen on him, or he'd have polished off another bottle. The ones you drank last night were just an appetizer for him.'

Daly blinked, remembering with a new wave of nausea the amount of alcohol he had put away.

'He needs to sleep it off. Perhaps you should try to do the same, sir.' The officer gave him a wink, as if to suggest the entire situation was entertaining. 'You're in no fit shape to go anywhere.' The officer kept on talking, apologizing, guiding Daly back to the cottage. There was something exaggerated and careful about his movements. 'For your own safety, sir,' he said.

'I was in the process of interviewing Mr McKenna,' said Daly, his voice sounding stiffly formal and a little ridiculous, given the state he was in. 'What happened to me?'

'All in good time, sir.' The officer smiled and led him into a back room with a narrow bed.

Daly cleared his throat. 'Where are my car keys and phone?'

'The boss will be with you shortly. He'll explain everything. In the meantime, I'm here to watch over you.'

'Why? Am I under arrest?'

'It's purely for your own protection, sir. While they debrief you.'

'Someone knocked me out last night. Was it you?'

The police officer did not answer. His tall figure blocked the doorway.

'What's to stop me walking out right now?'

'I'm not your jailer, sir. This is just a security measure.'

'What do you mean "a security measure"?' demanded Daly.

'Like I said, I'm here to guard you,' replied the officer and left the room.

Weary, his thoughts on edge from the poteen he had drunk, his hands shaking slightly, Daly sat down on the bed. He lay down, and for a while he listened to the light rain pecking the windowpane. Later, he thought he heard creatures with clawed feet creeping in the roof-space. He thought about his latest haul of mistakes, his confused conversation with the ghost of his father, and the stupidity of his drunkenness; reproach after reproach; the lack of clues and connections and his endless back and forth in the labyrinth of the investigation.

Finally, on the edge of sleep, about to let his tired mind give up, with his eyes fixed emptily on the curtained window, he heard a new sound, the crunch of light footsteps on the stones outside. He sat up in bed. He heard someone enter the cottage and converse in a hushed voice with the police officer, before advancing along the corridor. Expectant, he sat on the edge of the bed facing the door. The footsteps stopped outside the door and, suddenly wary, Daly crouched, his fists tightening.

It was in this odd defensive position, his eyes glowering, that Daly met the young man with pale blue eyes as he stepped lightly into the room, his overcoat speckled with raindrops.

'Did you get some sleep, Inspector?' was the first thing the visitor said, before introducing himself as Detective Robert Hunter.

'No, I had too much on my mind,' said Daly. Hunter's youth surprised him. He had expected a much older detective. 'You're not an easy man to find.'

Hunter turned to take off his coat, placing it on a chair, which he pulled towards Daly with a pleasant but determined gaze. 'What's been on your mind?'

'The fact that I'm being detained here. There's also the small matter of being knocked unconscious last night.'

'Ah,' said Hunter. 'An over-zealous protection officer, I'm afraid. He thought you were an assailant come to torture some old secrets out of McKenna.' He spoke in a light-hearted way. 'I gather the two of you were completely crocked. Knocked back several bottles of poteen between you. My men had to tidy up the mess. Furniture upended and broken glass everywhere.' He smiled at Daly with the amused disapproval of a younger brother, his face devoid of the darkness and anxiety that had plagued McKenna. 'They also found quite a lot of blood. Seems someone smashed a bottle over poor McKenna's head. Don't know anything about that, do you?'

When Daly did not reply, Hunter waved Daly's detective ID at him and flipped it open with a flick of his fingers. 'Inspector Celcius Daly. Where have I read that name before?' He leaned closer. It wasn't just youth that dominated his features, but arrogance also. 'Wait, wasn't there... yes. A report in the *News Letter* accusing you of unprofessional conduct. Remind me, what were the claims?'

Daly felt himself recoil. Hunter clearly knew the answer in advance. 'That was a story based upon false accusations.'

'Made by your former commander before he committed suicide. I find it very interesting that he accused you of hounding him to death.' Hunter dropped the ID and drummed his fingers on the table. 'Isn't that a coincidence? A report on how you persecuted a fellow officer appears in the newspaper, and then you turn up here, like an old bloodhound sniffing out its latest quarry. What do you think, Inspector, interesting or not?'

'What I find interesting is that I was told this was going to be a debriefing, yet you've no pen or paper to take notes. Is our conversation being recorded by a hidden device? Who else is listening in?'

'Now you're just being paranoid, Inspector. Consider this as just a little chat between colleagues.'

Hunter was not going to tell him the truth, that much was clear to Daly. In spite of his smile and calm eyes, a line of perspiration had formed on the younger detective's forehead. Daly suspected that the stakes were much higher than Hunter dared let on. He felt under intense scrutiny. Why else would they detain him in this godforsaken place? He braced himself for more questions, more personal attacks.

Hunter smiled again, his youthful confidence returning. 'Apologies for bringing up your past; I was curious, that's all. Inspector Fealty has vouched for you. I'm satisfied your credentials are bona fide.'

'You got through to Fealty?'

'You seem surprised.'

'I didn't know he answered his calls,' said Daly.

'He has a special number for emergencies.'

'Tell him I need to speak to him urgently. I have important information for him.'

'What sort of information?'

'About the murder of Detective Brian Carey.'

'What has McKenna told you?'

'Which McKenna are you talking about?'

'You tell me.'

Hunter stared intently at Daly, and then leaned back in his seat, clasping his hands behind his head, waiting for Daly to speak. The young man's eyes were bright and friendly, almost innocent-looking. Daly had the eerie sense that in spite of his own maturity and years of police work, Hunter with his boyish blue eyes considered himself the master detective. A silence developed.

'So,' said Hunter.

Daly repeated the word and returned the young man's stare.

'Does anyone else know you're here?'

'No.'

'You're off the radar, then?'

'Off the radar.'

'Just you and me, and the police guard?'

'Just the three of us.'

There was a silence, and then Hunter spoke. 'Tell me what you know about the Green and Blue Fishing Club.'

'Funny, that's the first question I wanted to ask you.'

'You start.'

'No, you start.' When Hunter did not reply, Daly said, 'I'm tired of being the one who always has to start.'

Hunter laughed. 'I'm glad you've a sense of humour. Otherwise you might not enjoy this little game of ours.'

'Why don't we stop playing games?' said Daly, leaning forward. 'Why don't you come through that door again, and tell me the truth about you and the Green and Blue Fishing Club?'

Hunter did not flinch. 'My name is Robert Hunter. I'm a PSNI detective. Before he retired, Detective Jack McKenna took me on fishing trips with his Garda friends.'

'What happened on these fishing trips?'

'I learned how to fish. Or rather tried. Fly-fishing is an art, and salmon are so mysterious and elusive.'

'The night Detective Carey drowned, was that another fishing trip for you and your detective pals?'

'If Carey was fishing, he went on his own.'

'Sounds as mysterious as your elusive salmon.' Daly sat very still, assessing his interrogator. 'Why are you detaining me?'

'The only way to guarantee your safety is to keep you here.'

'If you want to keep me safe why don't you make me invisible?' said Daly.

'Invisible?'

'Like you. How do you manage that trick? I've spent long days and nights trying to track you down, and so did Detective Carey. No paperwork exists describing what you do for the security services. Nor is there any trace of your joint operations with the Gardai. It's as if you and the fishing club never existed. I don't know exactly who you are, but I know you're more than a PSNI detective.'

'Such as?'

'You're connected to secret intelligence work, the military, undercover work of some sort.'

'What makes you think that?'

'I haven't been able to dig up any information on you. You're an agent.'

A glint appeared in Hunter's eye. 'I'm glad you're here, Inspector. It means you have an opportunity to join my little club. Turns out we're not that much interested in cold rivers or mysterious salmon.'

'What is the purpose of the fishing club?'

'To prevent anarchy along the border. As long as there is political confusion, there will always be a weakness that criminals can exploit. Over the years, we've established connections between the two police forces. North and South. Important lifelines, a foundation for joint investigations, shared intelligence.'

Outside, a shadow moved along the window, a figure carrying a rifle. Daly stood up in alarm.

'Don't worry,' said Hunter. 'It's your guard.'

The shadow moved out of sight.

'My role in this club, what do you propose?' said Daly.

'Whatever you want. You know the border. Surely you understand the need for better co-operation with our colleagues in the South? Think of how many times you've chafed against the political constraints.'

'And if I decline the invitation?'

'You're going to miss out on a lot of interesting fishing trips.'

'First I need my own questions answered.'

'Fire away.'

'I'm still wondering who you are. Until I find an answer there is no basis for our conversation.'

'Is there pressure from Fealty to find out about me and the club?' Hunter's tone was pointedly casual.

'The opposite really.'

'You're sure?'

Daly nodded. He wished there *was* more pressure from Fealty, the pressure of uncovering the truth about intelligence work, but he doubted it was very high on Fealty's list of priorities.

'Fealty's right. My role and the fishing club are not that important.'

'You and Fealty are both wrong. They are the most important things in this investigation.' Daly looked at Hunter and saw something dark and undetective-like in his expression, some complexity that suggested he had betrayed men like Carey in the past. 'I want you to tell me about Carey's links to the club and why he was killed.'

'The activities of the club are bound by the Official Secrets Act. All I can divulge is that Carey was a trusted member who took risks to supply us with valuable information.'

'Which you failed to act upon.'

'Security services the world over miss out on results because information is wrongly assessed.'

'Carey suspected that Tom Morgan was being protected.

Is that because he's a secret agent? If that's the case, it's hard to see justice ever being done in this part of the world.'

Before Daly could see his words register on Hunter, the young detective turned his face away, and hunched his shoulders, his gaze concentrating on the window. Watching him in his slightly bent posture, Daly wondered what mask was he going to whirl around wearing, what façade he would assume to regain control of the conversation. So far, all Daly had been able to discern in his expression was the energy and optimism of youth. Hunter got up and pretended to take an interest in the view from the window. Outside the trees were whirling on the hill above the cottage, their flickering glare filling the horizon, a shadowy world brimming with light and leaves.

With his back to Daly, Hunter said, 'When it comes to this little country of ours, it's sometimes better to know less rather than more.'

'I've read books and newspaper reports about underhand intelligence agents and their meddling in this country. Part of me suspected it was propaganda. Now that I've met you, I'm not so sure.'

'Are you accusing me of being underhand?'

'Yes.'

'And why do you believe that?'

'Because you will put on any mask to stay in control, commit any subterfuge to advance your goals.'

'These masks and subterfuges are your preoccupation, Daly, not your commanders'.'

'You don't want to admit the truth about Morgan because that would be to admit the underhand way you work. Which is why there is no trace of you or your operations in the official record.'

Hunter sighed and turned to Daly. 'Discretion is the name of the game, Inspector. The club's network of informers is not the business of the rest of the force. There is no reason to tell my commanders about every secret meeting, every whispered word. That always was the case with the club. We keep our investigations secret.' He returned to his seat and pulled it closer to Daly. He tried to keep his voice coldly professional. 'Detectives like you and me must be allowed an occasional breathing space. Our commanders need to close an eye every now and again, indulge us in our little notions. Otherwise, we'd rust and fall apart.'

'But you deceived yourself,' said Daly. 'You convinced your-self and Carey that you could keep Morgan under control. You were wrong, and Carey paid the price for your mistake.'

Hunter rose from his seat again. He appeared to have come to a decision. 'You will have to stay here for a while longer,' he said. 'I'm going to talk to my commander, and then I'll let you know if we need more information from you. In the meantime, you'll have to wait.'

'Where are my car keys and phone?'

'We're going to hold on to them for safekeeping. I wouldn't try to leave or talk to anyone on the road. You can't be too careful along this part of the border, especially when it comes to police business. Use your common sense. You're already in a dangerous mess.'

'What do you mean, a dangerous mess?'

'McKenna is considering filing assault charges against you. He claims you mistook him for your father and went on a drunken rampage. He says you attacked him with a poteen bottle. Given your recent publicity, the press would have a field day with his story.'

Daly absorbed the ramifications of this new development. He was hung-over and tired, and there were things he did not want to think about right now, let alone discuss with Hunter.

'Hopefully, my department and Fealty will allow me to draw a line under this whole sorry business,' said Hunter. 'I aim to put an end to this investigation of yours before it brings out things you and your superiors would rather not know about you.'

'McKenna's exaggerating,' said Daly.

'Exaggerating?'

'Yes. Stretching the truth. I don't remember hitting him at all. You can't use his claims to stop me from finding out the truth about you and the fishing club.'

Hunter's blue eyes widened. 'Let me be clear, Daly. You are under no obligation to go searching for me again. I operate in secrecy and you have never heard of me. You are a respected detective. You never assaulted a defenceless old RUC detective, and you never hounded your former commander to his death. We never had this conversation. If we ever do meet again, the two of us will look the other way as if we know nothing about the other. If you have a single grain of common sense you will follow these instructions, and avoid a humiliating end to your career.'

'What a strange coincidence that would be, our paths crossing again. It would make me very suspicious of the circumstances.'

'We don't know each other, Daly. We might work for the same police force but we're complete strangers.'

'Most days I think everyone in the police force is a complete stranger,' said Daly. A wave of tiredness and reproach, the effects of his hangover, overcame him. 'Which is my fault, I suppose.' Or the fault of his childhood, he thought. His upbringing must have taught him this estranged view of law and order, that everyone in an official uniform was hiding something, and carried a secret guilt. He blamed the little boy inside him, the little boy who still believed he was roaming through the Troubles, the worst murders still to come, the little boy who'd been robbed of every ounce of innocence by his mother's murder.

'You're wrong, Daly. It's the fault of this difficult little island, where detectives and police officers are forced to work in parallel, operating on different levels of intelligence information. The distance between us is so great that usually we never hear or see each other.'

'Until a detective from another jurisdiction is murdered. That brings us all out of the shadows.'

'What do you intend to do? Keep stepping on everyone's toes?'

'I'll do what I have to do to bring Carey's killers to justice. Nothing more or less.'

'Since you are intent on ignoring my advice this interview is concluded. I will have to pass the details of last night's assault to my superiors, and let them decide your fate.' He stood up to go. 'You should feel quite at home here until you've worked out the effects of last night's drinking.' He waved his arm around the shabby room in a show of hospitality.

'A crumbling cottage must feel like a real home from home. A meal will be arranged for you later. In the meantime, *ensconce* yourself.'

So they knew about him, his domestic situation, where he lived. Someone must have been following him.

'Goodbye, Inspector,' said Hunter.

'Goodbye, Detective Hunter,' said Daly. 'See you at the next dead body.'

Hunter opened the door and slipped out, saying nothing in reply.

CHAPTER THIRTY-SIX

Daly wondered what he was doing in McKenna's cottage. Why was he wandering through its warren of dimly lit rooms, staring at the cracked walls, the doors forced out of their frames by subsidence, the skewed pictures hanging from the crumbling plaster, the cracked black mirror in the hall? The entire shambles of the cottage looked as though it might collapse at any moment and slide into the mud.

In the back corridor, he came across a door that reminded him of his father's bedroom. Seeing a faint light seeping beneath the door, he eased it open and was disappointed not to find a ghost waiting on the other side. The room was another mess of old furniture and empty bottles. At least an hour had passed since Hunter had left the cottage and Daly was beginning to realize that he could not just wait for his hangover and the air of ill omen to clear by themselves.

A soft rain began to fall outside, thickening into a downpour. He did not want to stay, but Hunter had taken his car keys and phone, and the thought of wandering through the dark rain disquieted him. He stared at the low-roofed ceiling and sighed. Was it his fate to be confined to a series of smaller and more primitive dwellings? First his father's cottage, then the cramped caravan and now this squalid hiding hole along the border. How much farther did he have to fall? He called out for the police guard but there was no answer. The stillness of the cottage grew in direct relation to his agitation.

He shouted hello several times in an uncertain voice. Still no sign or sound of the guard. His anxiety increased. Had Hunter gone back into hiding, leaving him to his fate? Intelligence officers needed to hide from time to time, but Hunter seemed to make it his permanent habit. He listened more intently. Outside the rain was drumming upon the eaves, gurgling in hidden channels, playing upon the broken guttering. He opened the small window and listened again. Amongst the trees and blackthorns, the rain made a looser sound, dripping in free-flowing rivulets down through the leaves and branches. This was the opposite of hiding, he realized. This was sitting out in the open in border country, badly exposed to invisible enemies. He should leave this empty shell of a cottage, and seek out a proper refuge.

He found an old raincoat in the hall, and ducked his head through the front door in the furtive manner of an escaping prisoner. There was no one in the yard, and just one vehicle, his own car. Again, he shouted, and listened to the sound of the rain. He had a sense of being on the edge, the farm sloping away and fading into the downpour. He felt on the brink of vanishing himself. The mud surged around his shoes, and he hopped towards firmer ground.

Before him, a small lane forked off the main entrance to the farm. It led into a hollow surrounded by ragged thorns. Daly took shelter there, surveying the cottage and its surrounding fields of thistles and nettles. Decay had gutted the farm as effectively as a fire, the stone outhouses sunk in shadows, their tin roofs collapsed, rusting farm machinery strewn through the mud, and puddles of dirty water everywhere. McKenna's smallholding resembled the ideal safe house, with just the right amount of neglect to deflect the attention of passers-by. He wondered how many agents had been sequestered and questioned there, and how many had quietly slipped from view afterwards. The worry he had felt before increased. Why had Hunter been so anxious to find out if Fealty was interested in the Green and Blue Fishing Club? He had seemed as ignorant as Daly about the Special Branch inspector's machinations.

He followed a path that ran up to the brow of a hill, giving him a clear view of the road that ran by the farm. As he approached, he saw a car whip over the brow of the road. He was about to run back down the field and flag it down but at the last minute he saw that it had a Southern registration number. The car turned down the lane towards McKenna's cottage. On the final stretch, the driver turned off the engine and let the car roll silently along the side lane that skirted the property, steering as if he knew exactly the width of the overgrown lane, and just how far he could take the car up to the point where a thicket of thorns concealed it from the cottage. Daly saw a dark, overcoated figure slip out of the driver seat with a rifle.

He dropped out of sight and loped along the hedge.

He found an old lane that ran parallel to the road, infused with gloom and sinking beneath the surrounding landscape. He set off, head hunched under the onslaught of the rain, hurrying through the shadows of previous generations, the marshy ground gulping at his feet.

After a while, he came across a set of fresh-looking car tracks in the mud. He examined them with an uneasy feeling that he was being watched. He looked all around. Ahead were the crumbling outhouses of a farm that looked even more decrepit than McKenna's. The rain stopped. The silence filling the air felt like an ache, amplified by the ancient trees and empty outhouses. It was the final short hour of daylight. He crept towards the buildings, following the recent tracks, feeling that the place held a secret, and it was his duty to uncover it. He drew closer and heard rainwater from the gutters gushing into an old slurry pit, which was loosely covered by a sheet of tarpaulin. He moved towards the sheds. The instinct that he was drawing closer to something mysterious sharpened. He stopped. He had spotted something out of place. A flicker of metallic blue, easy to miss, in the corner of his vision. Something hidden under the tarpaulin covering the slurry pit.

Someone had left a tap running, creating an additional stream of water that mixed with the rainwater and turned the pit into a churning pool. The rising water level slowly pushed the tarpaulin aside. Daly saw that the metallic blue belonged to a half-submerged car.

He waded into the pit, thinking the car might be McKenna's, all the rot and stink of the farm swilling around him. He slipped, and was almost pulled down by the ripe dregs. A circle formed in the scummy water like the dimple of a creature coming up for air. He rushed towards it and felt something smooth and flaccid slide in front of him. A head bobbed out of the water. A pair of pink-rimmed eyes and a snout grazing the surface. The head of a dead pig, followed by its trotters, rolled over in front of Daly's face, and then its hairless belly. Suddenly, the pit bloomed with more unmentionables, lumps of dung, curds of animal waste, half-rotten carcasses rearing up from the depths, disturbed by the flooding water and Daly's stumbling progress. The neck stump of a calf sprouted into view and drew alarmingly close. Daly was frozen with disgust for several moments, incapable of wading any further. He thought of the spring-fed bog pool by his cottage, the water that had run so cleanly for generations he imagined he was soiling it every time he dipped beneath its surface. Another carcass rose from its appointed resting place, a hungry-looking dog with a squashed face and a patched coat of fur and gristle. The corpse sauntered stiffly alongside Daly, carried by the flow of water. He braced himself and pushed forward, steering carefully through the flotilla of carcasses, the heavier ones seemingly drawn in his wake.

He was all over the place now, breathing in shallow gasps, wobbling off course, his arms thrashing until his body knocked against something hard. It was the half-submerged car. He clambered on to its bonnet, glad of firmer footing in this miserable pit of death. The windows of the vehicle were smeared with mud and slime. He thought he heard someone knocking inside, the frail thump of fists from a weakening body. He pulled at the driver's door, but the handle clicked uselessly against the pressure of the rising water. Pushing his feet against the side of the car, and using all his strength, he managed to open the door just a crack.

The water changed sides, now in favour of Daly's efforts, funnelling through the narrow gap, flooding the car with its brown current. The door swung open and the flow strengthened. A body shot from the back of the car, arms outstretched towards Daly. He groped towards it, his eyes blurred by the splashing water. He blinked and the blur resolved into comprehension. The features aligned themselves into old Jack McKenna's face. He blinked again. There was another body in the car. Another pale, slack face, this time a much younger man, barely out of his teens. Even in that filthy mire, Daly would have given mouth-to-mouth resuscitation, but then he saw the bullet holes in their foreheads. He sank back from the car. The turbulence and disorder of the rising water, the sad grimaces of McKenna and his companion condemned to this bestial burial pit, combined to create an intolerable vision of chaos in his mind.

The ricochet of a bullet brought him back to his senses. McKenna's body convulsed against the car as though he had taken one last desperate gasp of air. A fresh wound had opened in his chest. Daly heard a curse behind, and realized he was not alone. He turned round and saw Hunter standing at the edge of the pit, raising a gun and taking aim. The first shot had narrowly missed Daly, but the next one struck him in his arm. Ignoring the searing pain, he made a mad scramble for cover on the other side of the car.

'You saved me the effort of dragging your body up here, Daly,' shouted Hunter. 'I gave you the opportunity to drop the investigation but you turned it down. Stubborn, aren't you?'

Daly calculated that it would take too long to wade to safety on the other side of the pit. Instead, he dived blindly into the putrid water. When he came up for air, Hunter had walked to the other side of the pit and was waiting for him.

'You walked straight into a trap,' said Hunter, gloating at Daly's pathetic state.

Daly stayed in a crouch, keeping only his head above the water, and tried to inch his way back towards the sunken car. Hunter positioned himself at the edge of the pit, ready to shoot again.

'Why did Carey have to die?' said Daly in an effort to keep Hunter talking.

Hunter looked down at him, weighing up the rising water and its coldness, the desperate nature of Daly's situation. 'Carey rattled me,' he said. 'I couldn't risk having him sniffing around Morgan's yard. I had no way of keeping an eye on him or check who he was talking to. I couldn't let him have that hold over me and my network.'

Daly's thinking was hampered by the coldness of the water and exhaustion. Hunter's voice seemed to slip farther and farther away, but his figure loomed closer, the gun pointing directly at Daly's head.

'All Carey wanted to do was haul Morgan to justice,' said Daly. 'Why did that make you lose your nerve?'

Hunter shrugged his shoulders. 'Morgan is important to this country's future. In the end, that's all that matters.'

'But he's a criminal. There's no limit to his brutality, and his manipulation of the intelligence services.'

Daly was convinced Hunter had been in conspiracy with Morgan, but he could no longer distinguish between instinct and rational thought. The water rose higher, pitching and rolling around him. It was getting harder to stand upright. 'But you're doing Morgan's dirty work for him,' he said, 'eliminating police officers that get too close to the truth. What's to stop him getting someone to eliminate you, too? Think about it. It's the only way he can ensure his secrets will never come out.'

'You're trying to buy yourself time, Daly. It's to be expected. In the circumstances I'd do the same.' Hunter raised his gun and took aim, but then he hesitated. 'What secrets are you talking about?'

'Carey had all the details of Morgan's bank accounts. He'd traced money that went from a company called Portman Holdings into the accounts of dead informers.'

'Those files were destroyed.'

'I've seen them with my own eyes. Right now, they're being sent to the Criminal Assets Bureau.'

'I'm getting tired of this conversation, Daly,' said Hunter with a look of exasperation. 'My only mistake was to drown Carey north of the border. If it had been in the river at Dreesh, it's very likely no one else would have had to die.' He pressed the trigger and fired.

Daly ducked his head underwater, but it was too late. He heard the shot ring out, a little more distant than he expected, its echoes lingering among the empty outhouses. He waited for the impact but none came. Another shot went off. This one closer than the last. He looked up at the side of the pit and saw that Hunter's body had fallen to the ground.

By the time Daly had waded to the side of the pit, the figure of Sergeant Peter McKenna was standing over Hunter's dead body.

'I was beginning to think we would never find Hunter,' said McKenna, pushing the elusive detective's body over with his boot and inspecting his face. 'My first real criminal in forty years and I shoot him dead before I can make an arrest.' The sergeant's face looked bewildered and weary. He glanced back down at the overgrown lane that led to his brother's cottage.

Daly watched McKenna and wondered if he could trust him. The border was playing tricks with his detective's imagination. He had exposed the restless interplay between criminals, informers, and intelligence agencies, in which protagonists swapped places, and sudden mysterious deaths and disappearances abounded. A never-ending game of shadows.

McKenna must have sensed Daly's questioning gaze. 'I tried ringing your mobile this morning, but there was no answer,' he said. 'Then I thought I should pay Jack a visit.' He told Daly that when he arrived at the pit, he had seen Hunter standing over the detective with a gun. He had listened as Hunter answered Daly's questions and when the moment came, he did not hesitate. He shot Hunter in the chest and head, two bullets in rapid succession.

'Why did you wait?' asked Daly.

'I wanted to hear what Hunter had to say for himself.' There was a mixture of anger and relief in his eyes.

'If you'd waited any longer you could have charged him with another murder.'

Daly felt too weary to ask any more questions. He took the sergeant's hand and pulled himself out of the pit. McKenna tightened his grip on him, and urged him to his feet. Once again, Daly felt he was a prisoner to a shadow. He remembered the gun wound in his arm. His eyes glanced at the mud and blood covering his clothes, feeling the pain shooting up his shoulder. His eyes locked on to McKenna's. Was that a blind spot he saw forming where McKenna's face should be? He puzzled over the growing darkness. McKenna grew quiet and still, joining Daly, it seemed, in his anxious preoccupation. Doubtful now of who exactly had rescued him or why, Daly struggled to stay standing, and then he passed out.

CHAPTER THIRTY-SEVEN

Daly came round in a hospital room with the figure of Fealty watching him from the bottom of his bed. His arm was bandaged and the pain gone. A nurse had just finished checking his blood pressure and was leaving the room. Fealty regarded him with a hard, cool look that might have been displeasure – or was it feigned concern?

'Feel any better?' asked Fealty. 'Your arm was not a pretty sight but the X-rays are clear. No broken bones.'

Daly sat up and instantly felt nauseated.

'You're lucky it's not much worse,' said Fealty. 'The man who tried to kill you wasn't Detective Robert Hunter after all.'

Daly's thoughts grew troubled. 'What did you say?'

'The man who died: his name wasn't Robert Hunter, and he certainly wasn't a serving detective. He was using the name as an alias.'

'Who was he then?'

'Our records show his real name was Charles Gordon.

A former colleague of Jack McKenna's. He was dismissed from the police force under suspicion of taking bribes from criminal gangs.'

'Who was he working for?' Daly searched Fealty's features, but try as he might, he detected no signs of strain, no ominous shadows or anxiety haunting his eyes. If anything, the Special Branch inspector looked self-satisfied.

'We now believe Gordon's identity as Hunter was a fiction designed to extract information from Carey. The body found beside Jack McKenna in the car was that of Tommy Higgins, a young informer recruited by Carey but taken over by Hunter when he began to threaten Morgan's criminal empire.'

'But who was he working for?' asked Daly again.

'Certainly not Special Branch or any of the intelligence agencies. As I told you when you first brought his activities to our attention. We knew nothing about this so-called Detective Hunter or his operations. Our main concern was that it would reflect badly on the work of Special Branch and intelligence-gathering in general along the border. This informal network of border detectives sharing information. The last thing this country needs is a scandal involving a serving police officer.'

The pieces of the puzzle began to form a pattern in Daly's mind, as though a mirror had been held up to them. Clues took on a new meaning. He saw the symmetry and the monstrous extent of the deception. Hunter had been an illusion, the murky criminal double of Carey, operating on the other side of the border, mirroring his movements, his lines of investigation, pursuing the same suspects and recruiting the same informers. The border had been central to the deception. The lack of communication between the two police forces, the absence of a proper working relationship had allowed Charles Gordon to maintain his false identity as Hunter. No other border in Western Europe presented the same possibilities for criminals to exploit. But whom had Gordon been working for? The question kept ringing in Daly's mind.

'Do you still think an intelligence agency was behind Carey's death?' asked Fealty. 'Or are you satisfied he was killed by Gordon acting on his own?'

'I'm not sure if I know what's true and what isn't. Why did Gordon have to kill Jack McKenna and the young informer? How do their deaths fit into the puzzle? Are you saying that the Green and Blue Fishing Club was run by Gordon for his own criminal ends?'

'Unfortunately, Gordon isn't alive to tell us. You and your Garda friend Sergeant McKenna have landed us with a lot of confusion. Not to mention dead bodies. Special Branch will be kept busy for quite a while.'

Daly saw the professional mask slip slightly from Fealty's face. He stood straighter, stiffening slightly. Naturally, his department would never reveal exactly what they did or did not know.

'Something tells me we're still on the wrong track,' said Daly. 'The pieces aren't fitting together. For a start, what about Morgan's secret accounts and his links to these dead informers? What about the residents of Dreesh? What part did they play in the conspiracy? Hunter told me something before he was shot. If Carey's body had been found in Dreesh and not over the border, it's likely no one else would have had to die. What did he mean by that?'

'For God's sake, Daly, he was talking about you. He meant he would have been well clear of you and your dogged obsession with the border.' He stared intently at the injured detective. 'Who exactly are you planning to pursue now?'

'I don't know. I still have to work out the exact role of the Green and Blue Fishing Club.'

Fealty sighed. There was a look of suspended disapproval on his face. 'I'm beginning to think that the border is your way of getting away from your colleagues and your commanders,' he said, shaking his head. 'You've found a place where suspicion does not fall upon you, but radiates from you on to all the figures of this country's troubled past, the ex-paramilitaries turned smugglers, the informers, and their handlers. You've turned them into your own gallery of rogues and ghosts.' He took a step back. 'If you insist on pursuing this investigation, I hope you know your way back.'

Daly tried to get up, but, overcome by a sudden swooning sense of being deceived, fell back into his bed. He felt sick in his stomach.

Fealty began talking about Irwin's investigation into Morgan's secret companies. The Criminal Assets Bureau and HMRC were launching their own investigations. He would update Daly soon with their findings. He tapped Daly on the knee. 'You should recover from your injury first. Take a couple of weeks off. Rest up in that little caravan you call home. And if you're still plagued by doubts, you can pick up the investigation when you return to work. Is that fair?'

'More than fair. But I can't ignore my doubts.'

'I'm asking you to take things easy. Let Irwin handle things while you rest.'

Daly said nothing.

'Look after yourself,' muttered Fealty as he left the room. 'The doctors say you can go home any time you want.'

Daly stared at the closing door. Hunter's true identity left him with nothing but more questions. Fealty had been correct. He was making himself tired thinking of everything. He might as well face it: he was doomed to keep chasing shadows.

CHAPTER THIRTY-EIGHT

No one in Dreesh witnessed Daly's arrival later that evening. Weariness hung over the village as though its occupants had already slipped into darkened bedrooms, unaware of their visitor's urgency. Daly crossed the bridge and pulled up at Morgan's sheds, their doors wide open and their empty interiors lit up with a fluorescent mist that gave them an aquarium-like quality. The fatigue had settled even here. Gone were the blustery roar of Morgan's lorries and the haze of diesel fumes, the shed entrances no longer hive mouths of illegal activity. Pipes and hoses sat idle on the cement floor stained with oil and diesel spills. A chill filled the air.

Daly entered the main shed, wondering why all the lights were still blazing. Was he walking into a trap? Someone had left a metal door open on the other side of the building. It banged without a regular rhythm, according to the gusts of wind. He strained his hearing for any sounds of life above the wind, but there were none. Cautiously he advanced across the vast concrete floor, his hand gripping the gun in his pocket.

In the centre of the shed, the lifeless figure of Tom Morgan was sitting at a card table upon which several hands of cards had been hastily scattered and a bottle of poteen knocked over. A few chairs sat upended on the floor, as though Morgan's card-playing companions had left in a hurry. Morgan's right hand lay on his belly, his neck resting against the back of the chair, his legs stretched under the table as though he had just enjoyed a gluttonous meal. Though his face was turned towards Daly, Morgan's expression was empty and far away. Whatever the card game, Morgan had been unaware to his final moment of how high the stakes had risen.

Daly approached the table, watching Morgan's stillness, noting the wound in his left temple where a bullet had been driven like a nail flush with the back of the chair. He had been killed quickly and efficiently. A single, well-aimed shot at point-blank range. In spite of its lifelessness, there was still something oddly menacing about Morgan's corpse. It was the eyes. The glint in his dead eyes. Was it the reflection of the unreal fluorescent lighting above or something intrinsic to the corpse? Just enough evil left in his body to keep his eyes sinister and moist, his pupils floating in the spark of light? A wash of blood seeped down from the bullet wound, rimming the eyes, bathing them in the blood that had pumped so fiercely in his veins.

After checking the body and getting no vital signs, Daly left the shed. He still had to find answers to the questions that tantalized him, and were now compounded by Morgan's murder. He made his way up the street, through the village that darkness and fatigue had made unfamiliar. There was no longer any reason to postpone the moment of confrontation. It was time to face up finally to the sergeant with the odd propensity for solitude and humility. Could a police officer be any better than his surroundings? If you lived and worked in the company of people who ignored the presence of evil in their midst, you too became a shadow. Or worse, a shadow that despised itself.

The houses in the village lay in their self-imposed darkness, blind and hearing nothing. What kind of criminals were they hiding? A murderer and a traitor? But these were ordinary decent shopkeepers, tradespeople and professionals. Morgan had not been killed in a moment of anger or fear. He had been executed and the order must have come from someone very powerful, someone eager to protect his or her anonymity.

As the residents of Dreesh slept snugly, Daly thought of the secret bank accounts in their names, the money sloshing from one tax haven to another. Were they victims or willing participants in this chain of greed? He couldn't help thinking that if culpability were a rambling plant, he could watch it sprout from Morgan's gruesome, infernal sheds, its creepers twining their way around the window frames and doors of the silent houses and shops, climbing the mounds of rubble and scaffolding of the deserted building sites, smothering even the fanciest houses with clumps of dense foliage. In his imagination, he was no longer walking through a subdued village, but through a jungle, one in which a single grotesque life-form had taken hold, knotting together every building with its thick stems, welding the inhabitants together in a grip tighter than death.

When he had reached his destination, he paused, and decided not to do anything rash. He stood in the shadows outside the police station and waited. Eventually, from his vantage position, he saw a figure move quickly from the building. In the oblique light of the streetlamps, the moving shadow resolved itself into the shape of Peter McKenna. For a moment, the sergeant stopped and reached into his pocket, hand fumbling as though worried he had left without his key. Daly saw the gleam of a gun revealed in his hand, and a look of grim relief passing over the sergeant's features.

CHAPTER THIRTY-NINE

Driving in his car, McKenna stared straight ahead. He crossed the serpentine River Blackwater and miles of bogland wedged between barren-looking hills and pine forests, a natural frontier, a good place for a border if you had to put one somewhere. Except that in the world of organized criminal gangs, there were no borders any more, just gathering points for smuggling operations and predators, a hunting ground full of death and violence. He was on his own hunt for the man who had secretly pulled the strings and orchestrated the killing of Detective Carey, and his brother, Jack, as well as Red Tom Morgan and countless informers.

He was tired but now he had a focus point for his suspicions. He saw it all clearly. The true border ran between the two forces of law and order, the Garda Síochána and the Police Service of Northern Ireland, the two police forces sliding darkly past each other like blips on a radar, separated by the whim of politicians, detectives passing each other in the night, their murmurs breaking the static on their radios, their car lights strobing the hills at night.

What could he have done differently? He could have warned Carey of his suspicions, urged him not to travel north of the border. But what would that have accomplished? Carey would have carried on regardless, dragging the forces of law and order into open warfare with Morgan and his gang. For some detectives, the desire to see justice done overrode self-preservation and common sense. He had never allowed himself to feel that burning conviction for the truth, a conviction that drove police officers like Carey and Inspector Daly. He had cut it off at the roots long ago. He had hidden from the truth, like his neighbours in the village, because it was such a painful reminder of the qualities he lacked.

He had decided long ago that Morgan and his smuggling operations were none of his business, in the same way that he and many of his compatriots had ignored the paramilitaries and their bombing campaigns. What was his business? Dog licences, livestock rustling, petty vandalism. His entire career he had lived blindly in Dreesh, enjoying it as a parochial little village, a backwater with an eerie atmosphere of peace, the surface of its life unblemished by the currents of violence that ran deeply below.

The accumulation of overlooked crimes created an unbearable trembling inside him, and he felt as though he was going to collapse with their weight. The face and voice of Detective Carey haunted him, upbraiding him for his forty years of solitude and negligence, warning him of the lonely nights that lay ahead, the nights that belonged to smugglers and criminals, the filthy haze of diesel fumes pouring from their mud-spattered lorries, their roaring voices blasting through the border villages in gusts, their ogre-like fingers tightening the knots of greed.

Tonight, deep in border country, everything was black. He drove for miles, feeling as though he were heading towards the meeting place of countless shadows. For a while, his determination faltered. He wondered was it safe travelling to his destination and pursuing his new line of inquiry? His suspect was an important man with powerful political connections. To justify questioning him, he would need more than vague suspicions and half-confused thoughts. He would need eyewitnesses who had seen him murder Morgan, courageous eyewitnesses and naïve ones at that, because the safest thing for any sane person to do would be to swear they had seen nothing, and forget the entire incident. No, he would have to obtain the conclusive evidence himself.

It was the middle of the night when he reached his journey's end. A large moonlit lake swung into view, a breeze wrinkling its surface. The road skirted the water, leading McKenna to a strip of lights and a plush-looking marina. He switched off the engine and headlights, and ghosted the car down to the harbour. He swung the vehicle behind a row of bushes and parked it in darkness. Without making a noise, he slipped out and followed the lights and the wash of waves to the far corner of the jetty, imagining he was weaving his own dangerous walkway over the waters, like a spider scuttling across the most tentative of webs. Eventually he came to a large yacht, shimmering in its own lights and swaying in the water. He almost did not recognize the figure dressed in a thick woollen sweater leaning out from the bow of the boat.

Commander Halligan was pulling in the fenders that protected the boat's hull from the jetty when he noticed McKenna's presence. Halligan seemed more in charge than he had ever done before, standing and staring at the sergeant with a glint in his eye, the undulation of the water lifting him up and down slightly. 'Sergeant McKenna, you've come to see me off,' he said.

'Boating along the border in the middle of the night?' replied McKenna, feeling for the gun in his pocket and seeking its cold comfort. 'Any law-abiding person might think you were a smuggler.'

Halligan laughed and waved with his hand, inviting McKenna on board. 'I told you about my little boat, didn't I? Just perfect for a fishing trip, I said. What do you think?'

McKenna climbed the stainless-steel ladder and stepped on to the deck. He felt light-stomached and unsteady on his feet, and reached out to get his balance.

'I'd almost forgotten about your boat until tonight,' said McKenna. 'I thought you were talking about some little motor boat, not a luxurious yacht like this.' He stared at the hardwood deck, the saloon with its own bar, the expensive-looking technology in the cabin. It was impossible to guess how much a boat like this would cost. Even a conservative estimate put it far beyond the reach of a police chief like Halligan.

'She's very comfortable,' said Halligan with false modesty. 'Like I said, just perfect for two retired policemen on a little fishing trip.' He strolled into the saloon and emerged with a bottle of wine and two glasses. 'I know it's pretentious of me, but I even had a wine cellar installed below.'

'I didn't realize indulgence was your weak point.'

Halligan kept grinning, impervious to the sergeant's barbed comment. 'There's salmon and cheese in the fridge,' he said. He seemed keen to make his guest feel comfortable and cared for, spoiled even, watching with interest as McKenna surveyed the boat. 'You know, Peter, I don't let any ordinary guests on board. If I give you the full tour you must swear yourself to secrecy.'

McKenna nodded and accepted the glass of wine.

Halligan raised his glass in the gesture of a toast. 'Well done, by the way, in rescuing our inspector from the North. Just a little unfortunate that your timely actions happened over the border.' His gaze hardened a little. 'Needless to say, the paperwork's going to be a nightmare. If you and Daly had hauled the dead bodies back to our side, things would be much easier to sort out.' He grinned and watched McKenna carefully. 'It didn't occur to you to notify me first before you took your little excursion into a foreign jurisdiction?'

'If I'd known how things were going to work out, I would have. My suspicions were vague.'

'And you were keen to eliminate your brother from your suspicions. Understood.'

McKenna flinched at the mention of his brother.

'Condolences for your loss, by the way.' Halligan smiled falsely. 'I should have called earlier but I had more pressing matters to deal with.' He sipped from his glass and then drained it. 'Think nothing more of it. The incident is closed. I've already put you forward for a commendation. As long as I have your assurance you'll take no more trips over the border with your gun without consulting me first. The politics are very delicate – surely you know that?'

'The moment was critical.'

'Just be careful of exceeding your remit, Sergeant.' Halligan's voice was conciliatory.

McKenna gathered his courage, sensing that this was the point to voice his suspicions. 'Is this where the Green and Blue Fishing Club met?'

'Sometimes.'

'I noticed how the murder of informers coincided with your little fishing trips. The identities of those men were known only to the members of the club.' McKenna let the tone of his voice carry the full weight of his suspicions.

There was a shift inside Halligan, as though a buoyant inner tide had changed direction. He turned away and glanced at McKenna's darkened reflection in the cabin window. It seemed to puzzle him: a grey disembodied head and a rounded neck emerging from the depths like a lough monster.

'Why did you send those young men to their deaths?' asked McKenna. 'What did you get out of the fishing club?'

Halligan pulled himself together, adjusting to the changed weight of suspicion. 'Money. Lots of money. Nothing wrong with that, is there?'

McKenna eased his gun an inch or two from his pocket.

Halligan continued speaking. 'Morgan and his IRA cronies were willing to pay for the intelligence we gathered. And the disinformation we fed back into the police force in the North.'

But there was more to the fishing club than money, thought McKenna. It was the twisted desire for power and control. The fishing club's existence was based on calculation and manipulation, an attempt to pull secret strings and deceive honest, hard-working police officers like Carey. 'Why drag my brother into it?' he asked. 'You knew he was just a drunk.'

'We needed him to convince Carey that Hunter was a serving police officer. Unfortunately, Hunter thought your brother was expendable and decided it was necessary to kill him to tidy up any loose ends. That was a mistake and I'm sorry it had to happen that way.'

'But you've made mistakes, too. Big mistakes. You've left a trail of evidence that will point in the direction of the fishing club.'

'True, which is why I've decided to wind up the club and cancel its membership. Intelligence-gathering and smuggling are risky businesses, at the best of times. Brexit is looming and the authorities are going to beef up security on both sides of the border.' Halligan paced the deck, while McKenna felt unsure of himself, wrong-footed. 'I knew the days of the club were numbered after the UK referendum. I decided to put my money on the safest bet in town, and, in this case, that happens to be our police friends in the North.' He spoke with the air of a man of the world explaining his business plans to another. 'You see, when Hunter and Morgan decided that Detective Carey had to die, I didn't want the murder covered up or left unsolved, which is surely what would have happened if Carey had been killed on your turf in Dreesh. I never wanted Hunter to get away with it. Which was why I instructed him to leave the body in Lough Neagh.' He jabbed a finger at McKenna. 'Suppose I'd left the investigation to you and your colleagues? What do you think would have happened?'

'Nothing.'

'Precisely, and I as your commander would have been implicated by your negligence. No, it was time to call in the battle-worn professionals. I wanted detectives who would do everything by the rule-book, sparing no reputation, including your own, Sergeant.'

'So you set Hunter and Morgan up?'

'Hunter was already a dead duck. Carey came to me and told me his misgivings about Hunter's true identity. He was threatening to go to the police service in the North and demand answers.'

It explained a lot, thought McKenna. The strange sense that Halligan had been waiting with excitement for the arrival of Daly, the way he'd called him the seeker of truth, the stubborn detective from the North. 'But what if Morgan and Hunter had lifted the lid on the fishing club? Revealed your true role?'

'They could have made wild allegations, but who would believe a criminal and a disgraced ex-cop posing as an intelligence agent. Besides, no proof exists. There are no records of the club anywhere.'

'The police in the North, they very nearly screwed it up.'

'True, but Special Branch now has Carey's file on Morgan's secret bank accounts. They're as happy as pigs in shit, wallowing in all that financial subterfuge. It's only a matter of time before they wind up Morgan's business empire.'

'How do you know Special Branch has Carey's file?'

'Because I sent the envelope to your friend Inspector Daly. I was the nameless whistle-blower.' Halligan began edging towards the side of the yacht. 'Morgan had big plans for Brexit. He told me all about his grand dreams. He thought he had me at his beck and call, keeping him in the clear, serving him up informers, protecting him from any investigations.'

The right pieces of the jigsaw began to fall into place for McKenna, events and actions over the preceding months, the shadowy meetings of the fishing club, his brother and Halligan's evasive answers. He saw how Hunter had pulled off an exquisite feat of disguise, passing himself off as the Special Branch detective Carey had needed to arrest Morgan, mirroring his movements, shadowing his investigations, haunting him like a ghost.

McKenna pulled out his gun, intending to arrest Halligan, but before he could do so, the police chief stepped nimbly to the aft of the boat and released a line. Ropes sliced through the air so smoothly McKenna barely noticed them. A beam swung forward and knocked him heavily in the chest. He fell to the ground, his gun clattering across the deck to Halligan's feet.

'You're finished, Sergeant,' said Halligan, picking up the gun and looming over him. 'Not because of me or Morgan or Carey and his meddling. You're finished because your only ambition in life was to live in a dead-end village. And now you think that you can finish me, too, a lazy bastard like you.' Halligan took aim. 'Hanging on all these years for your retirement and a fat pension. A time-waster who sat at the same desk for forty years, indifferent to all the smuggling and criminality under your nose.'

McKenna spoke back with anger. 'It's true I've carried the cross of Morgan for decades. I've paid the price for not stopping him at the start.'

'And now, after I've finally killed Morgan, you're spurred into action, like a slave who's finally been handed his freedom.'

Halligan pressed the trigger, and McKenna flinched, closing his eyes. However, when the gun retort came, he felt no pain. He opened his eyes and saw that Halligan had fallen to his right. The police chief picked himself up and staggered towards McKenna, his jacket smeared in blood. He peered at the darkness of the marina and shouted, 'What?' his call echoing across the empty lake. He pointed his trembling gun at McKenna's face, gritting his teeth into a grin of ultimate bitterness. His eyes closed with the effort of firing, and then another crack sounded. The second bullet struck Halligan in the jaw, ruining his grin. His head sank forward on to McKenna's chest, blotting the sergeant's vision in bright red.

McKenna pushed aside Halligan's body and listened as cars pulled up at the jetty, doors opening and slamming shut. The boat shifted as figures boarded. For a moment, he thought they were going to start the engine and take off.

A man with his right arm bandaged stepped out of the darkness. 'Are you hit?' asked Inspector Celcius Daly.

'I'm not sure. What happened?'

'Can you sit up? We need to get you off the boat.'

'Yes.'

Daly assisted McKenna to his feet and they made their way across a deck filled with Halligan's blood. Other figures had surrounded the boat, members of An Garda Síochána in uniform and with guns at the ready.

'We followed you to the marina,' said Daly. 'We waited in the darkness and heard Halligan's entire confession.'

'What took you so long to intervene?'

Daly smiled. 'I wanted to hear what Halligan had to say for himself.'

The words mirrored McKenna's own when he had rescued Daly, and for a moment, the sergeant stared oddly at Daly, as though he had been saved by a reflection of himself.

The scene of Halligan's death lay on the border, necessitating the involvement of both police forces, and by the time the two sets of ambulances and forensic teams had arrived the blue shadows of dawn were stretching across the lough. McKenna and Daly stood on the jetty at the edge of the water, staring at the shimmering view. Their minds were exhausted, but their thoughts searched for symmetry, a sense of order from the chaos that had stranded them in a world of criminals and betrayal. They felt as though they were floating as the morning sunlight tilted across the lough surface of ripples and reflections. There was no border any more, no lines to step over, no barriers to breach, just their thoughts groping in the void and this strange alchemy hanging in the air, as if the border had been transformed into a perpetual looking glass through which they peered with all their concentration, haunted by reflections of themselves rather than what really lay on the other side.

A letter from the publisher

We hope you enjoyed this book. We are an independent publisher dedicated to discovering brilliant books, new authors and great storytelling. If you want to hear more, why not join our community of book-lovers at:

www.headofzeus.com

We'll keep you up-to-date with our latest books, author blogs, tempting offers, chances to win signed editions, events across the UK and much more.

If you have any questions, feedback or just want to say hi, drop us a line on hello@headofzeus.com
or find us on social media:

@HoZ_Books

HeadofZeus